THE LIGHTHOUSE INN

A WOMEN'S FICTION MYSTERY, NANTUCKET POINT BOOK 2

JESSIE NEWTON

JEN PUBLISHING

COPYRIGHT

ISBN-13: 978-1638760221

CHAPTER ONE

Julia Harper faced the building where she'd be living soon, the pit in her stomach the kind that could swallow a woman whole. She'd tried filling it with chocolate-covered raisins, but that had only left her a few pounds heavier and somewhat sick to her stomach.

Outside the car she'd ferried over from the mainland, the wind tugged at the American flag flying high from the deck of the front part of the building.

The Lighthouse Inn.

Julia had spent years living in Nantucket with her family, both as a single woman, a married one, and a teenager. Sometimes she swore she had the white sand from the beaches out here on Nantucket Point in her blood, and something about this patch of land in the middle of so much water called to her soul.

She'd been planning to leave Manhattan anyway—at least she'd told everyone that so often that she'd started to believe it might have been true at some point. Whether it was or not didn't matter anymore.

She'd left.

She was here now.

"Go inside," she whispered to herself, and Julia took a deep breath, her pulse suddenly throbbing in the vein in her neck. She'd carefully applied her makeup that morning—her last in the hotel where she'd been staying in downtown Nantucket while she waited for her car and the clock to do what it was about to do.

Tick to ten o'clock on September first.

The first day of the rest of her life.

The first day of true freedom from the life she'd been encased inside for the past twenty-five years. A life where someone else knew when to change the furnace filter. A life where someone else paid the mortgage and replaced broken doorknobs and helped the children learn how to drive.

Alan had taken very good care of Julia, and while she'd known it at the time, she'd still had quite the rude awakening when he'd walked out, and she'd been faced with the enormity of taking care of their historic brownstone.

Five stories to take care of, with all of the children gone, and Julia found she didn't want to make the trips up the steps anymore. Not to empty bedrooms. Not to a master suite with a king-sized bed that only she slept in.

Not back downstairs every morning for coffee in the breakfast nook that overlooked the garden—which she now had to take care of by herself.

Her mother said she'd lived a sheltered and pampered life, and Julia hadn't argued with her. Mother also had no room to talk, as she lived in a gorgeous, sprawling house in Southampton, sipping lemonade next to the pool while Dad took care of the house, the land, the cars, and the bills.

Julia stood from her sedan, hitched her purse higher onto her shoulder, and faced the inn. The bottom portion of the building had a flat roof and could only be described as a two-story cube. The double-wide front doors sat smack-dab in the middle of the square structure, a deep, rich mahogany frame filled with glass that actually settled her nerves slightly.

She'd been to The Lighthouse Inn first as a teenager, delivering groceries to the caretakers. Now, she was going to be the caretaker.

Along with someone else, she reminded herself as she took the first step toward the entrance. The Nantucket Historical Society had originally wanted a couple to live in the inn and run it, the way the previous caretakers had done. Phil and Margo Michaels had taken care of The Lighthouse Inn for over thirty years, and they'd retired at the beginning of the summer.

The Historical Society had had a terribly hard time finding a replacement couple, and the inn had been closed when suitable caretakers hadn't been found. They'd then changed the job listing, and since Julia couldn't seem to stay away from Nantucket, when she'd seen she didn't need to be one-half of a couple to apply for the job, she'd taken the bold step and done it.

Shock coursed through her even now that she'd gotten the job.

Ironically, working in and managing Alan's real estate office had been the deciding factor in her application. She was very used to a lot of moving pieces, and she'd once managed a diner as well. As The Lighthouse Inn operated as a bed and breakfast, the job required cooking skills. The inn traditionally had offered activities for its occupants as well, and Julia's old, unused marine biology degree had come in handy too.

She had not met the other person who would be living in The Lighthouse Inn with her. She didn't even know the other woman's name. She'd been told to be at the inn today, at ten o'clock to sign her contract, and then she'd be able to move into the tiny private suite where she'd be living for the foreseeable future.

A sense of giddiness and the urge to throw up hit her simultaneously, and she wobbled slightly in her heels. No one who came to Nantucket Point wore heels, but Julia had wanted to appear sophisticated and professional. Heels also firmed up her legs and gave her a sense of confidence, despite the extra pounds she enjoyed due to the chocolate-covered stress eating she did.

The breeze pulled at her dark hair, which she tucked

behind her ear as the thwapping, rippling sound of the flag met her ears. She loved that sound, and she calmed further.

She reached the door and pulled it open. All the signs she'd seen when she'd come for her interviews were now gone, but the door still squealed on its hinges. That would be one of the very first things she'd fix, because why endure such a sound when a couple of spritzes of WD-40 would make this door open silently?

Pride filled her as she first tasted the air conditioning inside the building. The weather had started to cool slightly at night, and come Tuesday next week, the tourists would be mostly gone from the beaches of Nantucket.

"Julia," a woman said, and Julia turned toward the familiar tone.

"Vivian." Julia smiled and changed direction. "Good morning."

"It's good to see you again." She stood in the doorway leading into the small office where Julia would work with her partner to run the inn. The lobby of the inn sat right in the middle of the building, with staircases moving up and down from behind the ten-foot counter that served as the check-in desk.

The Lighthouse Inn only had five rooms available per evening. Both she and her partner would have a private suite located on the basement floor, and while Julia hadn't lived in a basement in a very long time, she was actually ready to get her things moved in, roll up her sleeves, and get The Lighthouse Inn back open.

The Historical Society had said there would be a budget for renovations and cleaning, and that they'd like the inn open in time for the holidays. Julia couldn't imagine a scenario where she couldn't get a five-bedroom house operational in two months, because when she'd toured the inn, it wasn't in that bad of shape.

Yes, all of the carpet needed to be replaced. The walls required a fresh coat of paint. The deck off the back of the inn needed to be reinforced and re-stained. It connected via a narrow walkway to the fishing dock that extended right out into the water.

The main level housed the lobby, a public restroom, the small office, the kitchen, and the dining room. All five guest rooms were located on the second floor, and the third floor became the lighthouse tower that extended another seventy-four feet above the main building.

The lighthouse itself was no longer operational, though it had once been responsible to help guide seafarers at night. Another lighthouse down the beach and out on the isthmus of the Point did work, but no one stayed there as part of their magical visit to Nantucket Island.

Julia reached Vivian and shook her hand, her smile cemented in place now. She wasn't going to let it slip, not even for a moment, until she had all of her boxes moved in and her car parked in the single employee slot.

She'd been told that the other woman didn't have a

car, and she'd readily agreed to share hers so the two of them could get to the downtown area or anywhere else on the island where they needed to go.

"Maddy isn't here yet," Vivian said, turning back to the office. "Come on in, and we'll get your contract signed. She signed hers last night, and she's all moved in already too." Vivian sighed with a measure of exhaustion in the sound as she sank into the chair behind the desk. "I caught sight of her leaving for a morning walk when I got here."

She flashed a professional smile and picked up a pen. "I'm sure she'll be back soon enough, and the two of you will finally get to meet."

"Mm." Julia sat in the single chair opposite the desk, perching right on the edge of it and letting her purse fall to the ground. She just needed to get her name inked on this. Then she'd be ready to take the first step into the next phase of her life.

Almost fifty. Single. Trying to figure out how to parent adult sons.

And now, instead of reading her favorite novels while Alan went to work, checking in with the progress of her children as they went to college, and going to lunch with her friends, Julia was about to become co-caretaker of The Lighthouse Inn.

"So this is a year-long contract," Vivian said, as if Julia hadn't paid attention the first time they'd gone over the requirements of the job. "You must give us three months' notice, so we can avoid shutting down the inn as we've had to do this summer." Vivian looked at Julia over the rims of her black glasses.

"I understand," Julia said.

"After the first twelve months, there is no contract in place holding you here. We simply ask for the long notice at that point." She passed Julia the pen. "You've had a chance to read over it?"

"Yes," Julia said, though she hadn't paid much attention to the contract Vivian had sent earlier that week. She wasn't going to back out of this now. She didn't have anything left in Manhattan, and that chilling thought ran through her as she signed her name on the lines Vivian indicated.

The blonde woman scooped up the papers the moment Julia finished and tucked them neatly into a folder. Her smile seemed more relaxed now, and Julia looked between it and the woman's name tag, pinned neatly to her red blazer.

She worked for the Historical Society, and she was the contact should Julia and her partner need anything at The Lighthouse Inn.

"All right." Another sigh leaked from between her lips as she stood. "You're in. Done. I've put hard copies of the guest guide, policies, and anything else you need in your room. You've got the digital copies. I'll let you get moved in and settled. You and Maddy will be able to sit down and meet at your earliest convenience, and I trust that when I see you both again, you'll have a plan for the restoration and clean up that will get us open by November first."

"Yes," Julia said, standing too. "Thank you."

Vivian looked past Julia's outstretched hand, her smile widening and relaxing. She clearly saw someone she liked much more than Julia. "Oh, here's Maddy now."

With one painful thump of her heart, Julia turned toward the doorway. She took in the elegant, beautiful woman standing there, and her mind whirred as she placed once-familiar features.

Those eyes...so bright and so blue.

That heart-shaped face...could wear such a look of disgust and disdain, Julia remembered.

The blonde hair that held more gray than it once had... but still looked perfectly styled and sophisticated.

"Maddy, this is your partner," Vivian said, her voice warbling like a doorbell that needed a new battery. It had high tones and low tones in Julia's mind as a wail started somewhere inside her brain.

Vivian made it to a spot between the two women, which put the unsuspecting woman in a precarious position. She didn't even know it, if her smile was any indication.

But Julia had placed the identity of the woman in front of her, and she literally could not be any worse.

Madelynne Lancaster.

She obviously recognized Julia too, because she cocked

one hip and folded her arms, as if the two of them had been transported thirty-five years into the past.

Maddy scanned Julia from the top of her head to the high heels, and just like she'd always been dismissed as insignificant, Julia could see the scoff forming in Maddy's mouth before it even came out.

Vivian didn't seem to notice, because she simply said, "This is Julia Harper." She looked at Julia, her smile almost blinding—if Julia could look at anyone but the woman who'd once made her life a living nightmare.

"Julia, this is Madelynne Lancaster. You two are going to be co-caretakers of The Lighthouse Inn."

Madelynne Lancaster. The woman whose boyfriend Julia had stolen and then made her husband. At the time, she'd felt nothing but vindicated. She'd gotten the last laugh. After a long string of losses, she'd finally *won*.

There was no way she could live with and work with Maddy for the next twelve months. Absolutely no way.

The silence stretching between the two women held a charge that could've called lightning from the sky, and it only increased with every passing second while each woman waited for the other to break and say hello first.

CHAPTER TWO

Madelynne Lancaster adjusted the designer purse on her arm, almost arranging it as if she could so easily order all the things in her life that had gone askew. At least she'd gotten to keep the bag in the divorce.

Disgust made her upper lip curl, though it wasn't for the woman in front of her. Julia Harper. Once, Julia Brunner, as that had been Alan's last name. She wondered why Julia had given up the name she'd fought so hard to get.

Maddy had often thought about what her life would be like had she managed to hold onto Alan, and it had never ended up like this. She blinked, and the past twenty-five years vanished into dust—the kind that made her throat stiffen and narrow until she began to cough.

"Hello, Julia," she said at the tail end of the noise,

almost like she was trying to disguise the words into something else.

Julia visibly flinched, as if Maddy had flicked ice water in those milk chocolate eyes. Maddy knew the color well, for she'd made white milk into brown with chocolate syrup hundreds of times. Her son and daughter knew how to wheedle her to get what they wanted, and she automatically raised her chin as if she needed to defy them in this moment.

"Maddy." Julia blinked so furiously that Maddy wondered if she had an eye condition. She flicked a glance at Vivian, the woman she'd interviewed with. Tension rode in her face as an unwanted passenger, but she smoothed it away easily.

She reached up to touch the black glasses that gave her face some personality. "We're all ready for Julia here to move in." She spoke with the radiance of the sun, as if moving into a tiny, hundred-square-foot room should be the stuff middle aged women should dream of.

Vivian half-turned toward Julia. "We'll help you get that done, and then I'm sure you and Maddy will need to get some groceries. You both have the checklist, and I'll leave you two to get to work."

"Are we to begin today?" Julia asked, getting to her feet. She wore a darling blouse the color of vanilla bean ice cream, complete with the dark specks of real vanilla bean. A black pencil skirt. The perfect heels in a hue of white that Maddy could only label as freshly churned butter.

The kind one might find at a posh farmer's market here on the island, perhaps over on the Wainscott side, where the filthy rich lived.

Maddy worked hard not to curl her lip now. She'd just returned from that wealthy strip of Nantucket, because her father lived there. She'd borrowed his car to return to The Lighthouse Inn, but she kept her mouth buttoned about it right now. She couldn't fathom a situation where she'd willingly get in a vehicle with Julia Harper. To have to sit so close—almost shoulder-to-shoulder—argue about the radio station, and...talk.

No, no. She did not want to talk to Julia. Not about anything of consequence, at least.

Julia also reached for a bag that had cost near four-digits, and she too looped hers over her forearm. Another blink, and Maddy saw that her life with Alan wouldn't have been any different than the one she'd shared with Christopher Lancaster for so long.

Twenty-four years long. More than half of her years on this planet had been dedicated to that man.

Familiar bitterness coated her tongue and seeped down her throat. She would not attempt to clear it away, for she'd done that in the past, and it hadn't worked. Nothing had worked.

"Your official start date is Tuesday, as agreed," Vivian said, tugging at her crimson blazer. "Maddy took the blue room. That puts you in the garden room, Julia. It's this way." She went around the check-in desk, and Maddy tried very hard not to notice the stacks of folders there—what were in those?—or get too close to Julia.

The scent of the other woman's perfume lingered in the air behind her, and it smelled like roses, fresh air, and money.

Maddy frowned, feeling all the lines in her face she didn't like deepen and groove through her skin. By the time the trio of women had reached the bottom of the stairs the led down from the lobby area of the inn, she'd smoothed the wrinkles away as much as possible. Her bedroom sat down the hall and around the corner to the left. She'd chosen it, because Vivian had told her she could have either of the rooms down here, and the door to the blue room couldn't be seen from this vantage point.

To her right, however, the door to the garden room stood in plain sight. For some reason, she hadn't liked that. In her mind, if a guest came looking for one of the caretakers, they'd go to the first door they saw—and that was now Julia's room.

The blue room wasn't nearly as cobalt as the name made it sound. A pair of frilly curtains Maddy had already removed and a lot of paint she would soon had given the room its name. She'd inspected the garden room too, and it actually had a great window she'd been hesitant to give up.

Vivian moved to the right seamlessly, and she already had the door open by the time Maddy realized she'd fallen behind. Both she and Julia watched her take the five strides from the bottom of the steps to the now-gaping door, and heat crept into Maddy's face for some reason. She was dressed far more casually than Julia, and the other woman's eyes scanned down to her sandals and back to her scalp as quickly as a price-reader at the market.

Maddy wasn't sure if she was the one out of place, or if Julia was. Vivian also wore a skirt, and that made Maddy's navy cotton shorts seem downright criminal.

"We think you two are the perfect pair," Vivian said, her tone bordering on gushing now. "Maddy has experience in the kitchen, but so does Julia. The two of you can work out the responsibilities however you'd like. Of course, only Maddy will be able to operate any sea vessels, and it's obvious that Julia will do the marine life classes. But the budgeting, the food, the day-to-day scheduling, you two can work those things out among yourselves."

She beamed at Julia, the brightness of it bouncing all around the garden room. The walls here boasted flowery wallpaper in a shade of pink that hadn't been used in thirty years. Perhaps longer. It also looked like it had once been white behind those blooms but had seen so much in the past several decades that it simply couldn't hold onto the innocence of that color.

The same blond wood as in the blue room stared up from the floor, and Julia got a billowing, gauzy set of curtains covering the window that was twice as big as the one in Maddy's room.

A single door led into the bedroom, and a single door stood open to reveal the tiny closet where Julia would have to make her clothes fit. Another door right next to that one led into the bathroom, and again, Julia had gotten the better of the two rooms.

Maddy had paid a lot to have a door that wasn't visible from the bottom of the steps, and she wondered if she'd made the right choice. She'd been doing that a lot lately—constantly going over and over the decisions she made. Were they right? How could she know? Why couldn't someone see into the future and let her know the outcome of each step she chose?

Julia said something that didn't make it through the shouting in Maddy's head, and she turned to leave the small bedroom. She couldn't breathe in here, and she once again thought she'd chosen a terrible first job for herself post-divorce. Every room in the lighthouse was tiny. All the walls crowded close. None of the windows were big enough, and she'd had to brush her hips against the walls as she climbed through the narrow passageway to get to the upper deck of the inn. If it were up to her, she'd close that off and not allow guests up there. The last thing she needed to deal with was an elderly man or woman breaking their hip coming down those steps.

Her father's face flashed through her mind, and she shoved against it.

You're going to end up like him.

Alone. Old. Forgotten.

No, Maddy wasn't going to be like him. She wasn't.

You are, the sinister voice in her head whispered. *You're already alone and forgotten.*

"Maddy?"

She turned toward Vivian's voice, not truly seeing the woman. "Yes," she said, not phrasing it as a question though she had no idea what the woman had said.

"Wonderful." Vivian smiled again, this one only rivaling the brightness of the moon. Perhaps just a star. She must be ready to bolt from this place too. "I'll leave you two to it then." Her footsteps went crisply up the steps, leaving Maddy and Julia in the narrow hallway on the basement level.

Maddy didn't even look at Julia. She simply hitched her purse higher onto her arm and marched toward the blue room. Once around the corner and out of sight, relief rammed into her with the strength of a charging rhinoceros. A sigh spilled from her lips as she fitted her key into the doorknob, and satisfaction buoyed her up as she entered her living quarters. Nothing had ever sounded as safe and as wonderful as the clicking of the lock on the door, effectively sealing everyone out and Maddy inside the room.

Only then did she allow her purse to drop to the floor and the tension in her shoulders to release its great hold on her. She sagged onto the tiny couch beside the door, leaned her head back, and closed her eyes.

Her breathing into the silence seemed to penetrate the walls of The Lighthouse Inn, until the building itself was slowing inhaling, pausing for a moment, and then letting the air out of its ducts and vents.

She wouldn't be able to avoid her responsibilities for much longer. She had to call her sister and give a report on their father's health. She needed to logon to her bank and make sure Chris had made his monthly deposit. She'd have to talk to Julia and make a plan for how they could survive the next twelve months together.

Deep down, she had the naughty idea that she could quit this job this afternoon. She didn't need the money; she only needed purpose in her life. Perhaps taking care of her father would fill that well.

Maddy wasn't a quitter though. She'd only conceded on one thing in her life, and that had been Alan Brunner. She'd only done that because he'd asked her to. She wondered if Julia knew about that visit, the last time she'd seen Alan, all those years ago. Maddy could still remember it as if he'd shown up on her doorstep yesterday.

She'd fought for her marriage with Chris, but in the end, it took two to make a marriage work, and Chris had decided she wasn't worth working for. Tears pressed against her closed eyelids, and she didn't fight them. Sometimes, she just needed to let them come, and they'd disappear faster than when she caged them, held them in, and then finally relinquished control to them.

She'd fought for her children, but Kyle and Chelsea had chosen their father. The sting in her chest felt like the scorpion kind, with poison rushing through her bloodstream and staining every part of her.

She'd fought for the right to be the one of her siblings that came to take care of their father. Brittany, her younger sister, had volunteered since Maddy "was going through so much," but Maddy had refused to let her sister get her way. She did so often, in so many other things, and Maddy had claimed the sea air would be good for her and the constant needs of her father would give her something to focus on besides herself. They had done that this summer, but she wasn't sure how she'd balance her new workload at the inn with the needs of her dad.

No matter what, she wasn't going to call Brittany for help. Not again.

She opened her eyes, the sight of that navy ceiling nearly ripping a scream from her throat. That definitely had to go. After getting to her feet, she moved over to the bed—a feat that only took two steps—and began unpacking the box there. Yes, all of her boxes were inside the inn, but that didn't mean she'd put everything away.

This one held clothes, and Maddy reached for her purse, where she'd stowed the plastic hangers she'd bought on the way back to the inn that morning. She'd only inspected the closet with a cursory glance before choosing this room, and she had never stayed here overnight. She would tonight, and she needed to clear the bed so she could sleep in it.

The door on the closet opened without a sound, and

the blue paint extended inside the small space. Another sigh slipped from Maddy, but it sounded like a groan more than anything else.

She hung the T-shirts and blouses in the closet, broke down the box, and opened another one. Jeans, shorts, and socks. Maddy pulled them out and moved back to the closet. The room wasn't large enough for a dresser, but the closet had two shelves.

She filled them with her clothes and shoes, getting nearly everything unpacked in under a half-hour. The last box contained three photo albums Maddy hadn't been able to part with, and as she held the leather-bound volumes in her hands, she had the distinct thought that they represented the past three decades of her life. She could easily put a match to one of them and watch all that time, all those memories, everything she'd once thought was so important, turn to smoke, ash, and flame.

Matter moving from one state to another. It would be so easy.

Instead, she returned to the closet and stepped up onto the little stool she'd found folded against the inside wall. She stood the photo albums up and pushed them to the right, intending to store them out of sight, out of the way.

They didn't go far enough, and she frowned as she leaned further into the closet to see what had obstructed them. A box sat there—stashed out of sight, out of the way.

Maddy let the photo albums fall to the left as she reached for the box on the right. It wasn't heavy, and it wasn't marked. Perhaps the last person to use this room hadn't seen it and left it behind accidentally. As far as she knew, the previous caretakers of The Lighthouse Inn had been a married couple, and they'd used the garden room because of its slightly bigger size, better bathroom, and more attractive window. Vivian had mentioned how the blue room had often been used as a guest room during busy months, and an office or storage room for the caretakers during the slow season.

She took the box to the couch and sat down with it, something rattling inside as she moved. For some reason, Maddy paused, the leaping of her heart akin to when Chris had proposed to her. They weren't the same situation at all, but her nerves didn't seem to be able to categorize the two events differently.

The flaps on the box lifted easily, as if they'd been worn down over time from frequent opening and closing. They were soft, pliable, and Maddy peered past them and into the box to find another box sitting there. Beside it, a cup of pens had toppled over, and the writing utensils had been making the rattling sounds.

She righted the cup and scooped all the pens and pencils into it. They looked ancient, some of them sharp as needles and others worn down from use. The scent of dust and must and rust emanated from the box, as if no one had touched it in many long years.

The box inside reminded her of her grandmother's recipe card holder, and Maddy gingerly lifted it out. The orange lid had paled from Father Time's touch, and the yellow, flowered bottom of the box seemed as equally as worse for the wear.

It didn't disintegrate at her touch, and Maddy lifted the lid, her heartbeat acting like it had taken on the role of drum major, flapping and waving through her whole body in perfect time.

Instead of recipes or cards inside the box, Maddy found folded, lined papers. Letters. Where the dividers would be, with the neat tabs along the top, colored cardstock marked the different sections, all in various shades of blue.

The front one glared at her in a bright, almost circusy, blue, and someone had scrawled READ FIRST on the top of it. She pushed the crudely cut divider forward, but nothing rested behind it.

She exhaled and shook her hair over her shoulders. "Calm down," she told herself as she realized how tightly wound she was. If someone let her go, she'd spring all over the place from the release in her coiled muscles.

After removing her fingers from the box, the cards settled back into place. She noticed the writing further down on the circus-blue card and plucked it from the box.

Welcome to the blue room. There's only one rule here: Don't try to change the paint color. She doesn't like it.

That was it.

"Who doesn't like it?" Maddy asked, looking around

the room as if someone would appear and provide further details. No one did.

Beside her, someone rapped on the door, sending her pulse into overdrive and causing her to yelp and throw the recipe box all at the same time.

The cards spilled out everywhere, and Maddy saw the same blocky, half-cursive handwriting on several of them. She left them where they'd fallen as she jumped to her feet and pulled open the door.

Julia stood on the other side, one hand on her cocked hip.

CHAPTER THREE

Julia noticed the smell coming from Maddy's room. It matched hers in the garden room—stale air, decades of dust, and the scent of the elderly. The whole place needed to be aired out and then sprayed with copious amounts of Lysol. Preferably the scent that reminded Julia of fresh laundry drying on a line or lush, waving lavender fields. She was fairly certain the company made both scents. Perhaps she'd spray them simultaneously.

"There's someone here to see us," she said.

"Who?" Maddy asked, glancing past Julia.

Julia turned and started for the corner. No wonder Maddy had wanted this room, though hardly any sunlight had greeted her upon the opening of the door. It couldn't be seen, and no one would even know it was here unless they came looking.

A great weight settled on her shoulders as she rounded the corner and started for the steps. "I don't know. A woman. She said she wanted to meet the new caretakers." Insisted would've been a better word for the brunette who'd shown up five minutes ago.

Julia had been carrying in another load of boxes, and the other dark-haired woman had offered to help. Since Maddy had pulled her famous disappearing act, and Vivian had cited the fact that she needed to get back to the Historical Society, Julia had been moving in herself. She much preferred that, in truth, because then she didn't have to explain why she'd meticulously labeled her boxes or why she'd thought she needed to bring an entire box of Christmas decorations.

Those had been stowed safely under the bed in her room, thankfully, though the foolishness she'd experienced while carrying them in had yet to abate.

Up the steps, Julia found Janey Forsythe right where she'd left her—gazing at the old black and white photographs of the lighthouses here on Nantucket. "Here she is," Julia said, enough snap in her voice to bounce off the walls. She drew in a deep breath and tamed her impatience. She'd raised three teenagers, so she was a professional at pretending like she cared about things she didn't.

Maddy came up the stairs much slower, and Janey had turned completely from the photos by the time they all stood on the same level.

"I'm Janey Forsythe," she said, taking the few strides

around the check-in desk to shake Maddy's hand. "My sister and I have a cottage just across the sand." She nodded as if sight could go through stone and plaster. "To the west. It's the first one you see." She smiled as if this were the best news either of them could hear.

"Wonderful," Maddy said fluidly, like water moving past rough rocks without a care in the world. She'd always been so charming and sophisticated, the perfect politician's wife. "What's your sister's name?"

"Tessa," Janey said. "She's living in the cottage right now. I'm staying with—well, a friend—over in Wainscott."

"My father lives over there," Maddy said, and that drew Julia's attention like a whip to the woman she'd once known. She hadn't grown up on Nantucket, and curiosity pricked at her the way carbonation bubbles in a soft drink. Little bursts and pops of it, all prompting her to ask more questions about him and how he'd come to be here. Was that why she'd applied for this job? Where was her big-shot husband?

Julia kept all of her questions under her tongue. She didn't truly want to know; she only wanted ammunition against Maddy should she need it later. And she would need it later. Maddy was one of the smartest, savviest people Julia had ever known. Her wit was quick and sharp, and she'd been a master debater for a reason. She'd also married a politician, and that meant her tongue could twist anything to paint herself in a better light, and Julia had already determined to say as little as possible to Madelynne Lancaster.

"Who's your friend?" Maddy asked, slicing a look in Julia's direction. It said so many things in less time than it took to inhale, but Julia simply crossed her arms and waited for Janey to answer.

She had the same dark, nearly-black hair as Julia herself. Janey colored hers with streaks of blue too, something Julia would never do. She had jewelry where it didn't belong on a body, but she seemed so perfectly at ease with herself, and Julia did envy that. She didn't feel quite right inside her own skin, as if everything she did and every word she said wouldn't be right.

Alan's last words to her had been such a blow. *I've put up with so much for so long. I just can't keep doing it. I'm sorry.*

She'd asked him to elaborate—she knew she wasn't perfect. She had done her best, if that counted for anything. She made dinner for him and the children. She kept the house up. She attended the dinners and the multitude of events required of her for his hefty job as one of the top real estate agents at a prestigious real estate firm in New York City. She kept the calendar for the family and made sure he attended all the most important events. She'd gone to everything for their three boys. She arranged the window-cleaning because she knew it bothered Alan to have dirty windows.

Julia had started to spiral, and she pulled back on her

thoughts as hard as she could. She wished they acted more like a horse and would respond instantly when she yanked. They didn't, and they continued to stab at her despite Alan's final apology.

"A woman named Viola," Janey said, her words barely breaking through the shouting thoughts in Julia's head. A smile accompanied the statement, almost as if Janey didn't have anything to hide. Julia, however, had gotten a completely different impression when she'd first seen the woman coming toward her.

She wore a ring on almost every finger, and her billowing tank top was definitely a focal point. A piece that would attract conversation. Something that would take the attention off of what Janey didn't want it on.

"I love your tank," Maddy said as if on cue. "Where did you get it?"

"There's a fabulous shop downtown," Janey said, her smile rivaling the brightness of the sixty-watt bulbs in the lobby. "Pier and Piedmont. They have the nicest stuff on the island."

"I'll have to check it out," Maddy said.

"Don't tell me when you go," Janey said with a laugh. "I'll want to tag along, and my pocketbook is already groaning."

Julia put an obligatory smile on her face when Janey looked toward her. She'd seen Pier and Piedmont on the way in, and yes, it did look like her style of boutique. She reminded herself she hadn't come to Nantucket to shop, and everything stayed still on her face.

"So, how do you two know one another?" Janey's gaze played ping-pong between the two of them. "I almost applied for this job, you know." She seemed innocent enough, but Julia sensed something teeming beneath the surface. This woman was like the ocean: Tranquil and beautiful at first sight. Danger lurked below, though. Sharks swam down there. Storms could brew and send waves as tall as skyscrapers toward the shore.

No, there was something not quite right with this woman. Her eyes glinted with happy light, a shade darker than Julia's. So many other things about her were so familiar, and Julia had initially thought her cousin had made the trip to Nantucket to see how Julia's move was going.

Janey had to be close to Julia's age, though it was hard to tell with the dyed hair, the baggy clothes, and the rings in her nose and ears.

Maddy hadn't answered Janey's question, and Julia had honestly forgotten it. She tossed Maddy a blank look and refocused on the other brunette. "Where do you work?" See? She could carry a conversation too, and she almost tossed Maddy a so-there look.

"I'm starting at a law office soon," she said, her tone the kind that dodged heat-seeking missiles. She drew in a deep breath and blew it out. "Anyway, I just wanted to stop by and introduce myself. We came to the Point so often as kids, and I knew Phil and Margo Michaels. They were so great."

Maddy wore a wooden smile now too. "That's wonderful," she said. "We'll do our best to live up to their legacy." She might as well have slung her arm around Julia's shoulder, as if the two of them would really do that.

Smiles for miles, and Janey left through the double-wide glass doors. The silence she left behind felt as sharp as a serrated knife, and Julia had only felt like this one other time—when Alan had returned to the brownstone to finish packing. Thankfully, the boys had not been home. Of course, they'd all been out of the house for over a year now, and Julia had been struggling in her new role as an empty-nester. Perhaps that was what had pushed Alan over the edge.

I've put up with so much for so long. I just can't keep doing it. I'm sorry.

No, it had to be more than just her behavior and anxieties over the past year, since her youngest had left home. *So much for so long* indicated that he'd been unhappy inside their family and marriage for a long time.

Julia simply wanted to know when he'd started feeling that way. Then maybe she'd know what she'd done wrong, and what she should've done instead.

"By the way," Maddy said, turning away from the front doors. "I have my father's car, so I don't need a ride to go get groceries." Her footsteps went down the stairs to the basement before Julia could pull herself from her thoughts and focus on the situation in front of her.

"Okay," she said anyway, the dead air probably appreciating the sound she'd infused into it. She then hurried over to the glass doors and locked them. She still had a few boxes to bring in, but she could while away a couple of hours unpacking the things she'd already brought in.

Plus, then she could hide from Maddy and anyone else whose curiosity prompted them to interrupt her.

CHAPTER FOUR

Janey Forsythe pressed her back into the exterior wall of The Lighthouse Inn and sucked at the air.

I'm Julia Harper.

Julia Harper.

Julia.

Harper.

Janey knew exactly who Julia Harper was, and it had been so hard not to stare at the woman and pick out all of their similar features. The same hair color. The same curl in their eyelashes. The same freckles splashed across their cheeks and nose.

"Lots of people have freckles," she told herself, her voice one that would accompany ghosts.

The sound of the waves coming ashore stole her attention, and she turned her head to the right. She wasn't sure she could hold herself up quite yet, so she didn't move. She'd heard The Lighthouse Inn had hired new caretakers —not a couple. She'd seen the sign, and she *had* considered applying.

She hadn't, though, because, well, she wasn't sure why. It didn't feel right? Janey had no idea. She felt as lonely, lost, and loathsome as the foam on the gentle waves she could see. Everyone pushed that foam away. No one wanted it. It drifted on the water, trying to find a place to belong, until it eventually bonded with other foam pods and made it ashore.

She wondered if her mother had felt that way. Ryan Harper had been her lover, once-upon-a-summer. He'd been married, and he'd chosen to stay with his wife.

Janey gave her head a little shake. She didn't know if Mom had even told Ryan Harper about his baby. She wasn't even sure he knew she existed.

That great unknown had paralyzed Janey, and she still wasn't sure what to do about her biological father. Tessa, the sister she'd grown up with, had said Janey should probably go to Southampton and introduce herself.

She simply couldn't find those words. They existed somewhere out in the vast universe, but Janey couldn't simply pluck them from the sky and get her voice box to say them.

"Are you okay, hon?" an elderly woman asked, and Janey released her grip on the bricks behind her as she turned to face her. She had a kinship with women older than her, something she hadn't known until recently.

"Yes, ma'am," she said, glad the ghosts had fled her throat. "Thank you."

"It's hot today." The white-haired woman turned her face toward the sky.

Janey did the same, soaking in the vitamin D, the warmth, the comfort. "Yes," she said. "It is."

"Are you from around here?" she asked, her bright blue eyes still as vibrant as Janey knew they'd been in her youth. Her body had aged and sagged, just like all bodies did. Her hair had lost all the pigment. But this woman still possessed spunk, and Janey fed off of it and used it to curve her lips into a genuine smile.

"I'm quite familiar with the island, yes," she said. "Are you looking for something?"

"No," the woman said, returning the smile that reached all the way up to crinkle her eyes. "My husband and I used to own a cottage just on the other street there. I do still own the cottage. Dear Kenneth's been gone for a few years now."

"I'm so sorry." Janey closed her eyes and found herself dressed in all black, standing beside her mother's grave, and overcome with grief.

"He lived a very good life," the woman said. "I'm Helen Ivy. You look like you could use some lunch, and I was just on my way to The Glass Dolphin. Would you like to join me?"

"I would love to join you," Janey said, her mind firing at her about her other obligations. "I was just on my way to see my sister." She tipped up onto her toes to see past Helen, but the dunes blocked the view of the blue cottage where Tessa lived. "We have a cottage right there on the end of the first street."

Sudden light filled Janey's heart. "I'm Janey Forsythe. Used to be Janey Clarke. Maybe you knew my mother. She came to Nantucket all the time. The cottage has been in our family for generations."

"I think your mother was Lydia." Helen's voice could've painted pictures full of blooms and butterflies. She linked her arm through Janey's. "Oh, yes, I knew your mother." With a tug, she drew Janey closer. "I was very sorry to hear she'd passed." She patted Janey's forearm with her wrinkled, weathered hand, and Janey had never felt something so soft.

"Thank you," she said, gazing up into the sky again. "It is a beautiful day. That's what my mom would've said."

"She loved the sand and the sun," Helen said, which summed up Lydia Clarke in just a few words. She'd do anything to be on the beach, and Janey had loved that about her.

"Did you know my dad too?" Janey asked, glancing at the entrance to The Lighthouse Inn as she and Helen passed. She had no idea what had possessed her to approach the dark-haired woman getting boxes out of the back of her luxury SUV. Perhaps Janey had seen some of herself—or who she wanted to be—in the tall, beautiful woman.

The fancy car. The shiny hair. The expensive clothes. Julia Harper seemed to be living the life Janey had often fantasized about, and she'd been thrown right back to junior high when it was death not to have the jeans with the designer label on them.

She blinked her way out of the encounter, cataloging it so she could tell it all to Tessa later, and focused on taking the next step off the sidewalk and into the parking lot so she wouldn't twist an ankle. Helen made the step too, somewhat slower than Janey, and they continued toward The Glass Dolphin.

"I met your father several times, yes," Helen said.

Janey wondered if she meant Ryan Harper or Gregory Clarke. She couldn't get her mouth to form the question, and a sliver of darkness slipped back into her mood. She didn't want it there, and she found it hard to believe such a thing could exist among so much sunlight and so much oxygen.

"I should text my sister and ask her if she'd like to come to lunch," Janey said. "Would that be all right?"

Sean moved through her mind, and she added, "And another friend of ours. He's a lawyer here on the island. Sean Masterson?"

"Sean is a wonderful man," Helen said. "I'm sure your sister is lovely too. Invite them."

Janey released Helen's arm and dug her phone out of

her pocket to get the texts sent. Both Tessa and Sean responded quickly, and they said they were on their way.

Did you forget I was bringing lunch to you two? Sean asked, a smiley face at the end of the question.

Janey's breath lodged somewhere south of her tongue. She quickly started tapping out an apology, because yes, the conversation with Julia and Madelynne had thrown everything out of her brain. She'd simply been walking from the shuttle station to the beach house. *Why* had she approached that woman?

It's totally okay, Sean said before Janey could get the apology off. *Tessa and I were just wondering what had grabbed your attention.*

A pinch and a pricking pop swept through Janey's chest. Sean was a wonderful man, just as Helen had said, and Janey had put him and his life on hold. *For what?* she wondered.

She hadn't accepted the job at his law office, but she'd be perfect for it. His current secretary had less than a month before he'd be leaving for a new job in Manhattan. Sean needed someone, and he needed someone good. It would take time to advertise for the job, do interviews, and hire.

Janey needed to let him know if she was going to take the job or not. Again, she simply didn't know how to take the words from wherever they floated and put them in the right place inside her mouth.

She also liked Sean as more than a potential boss and a good friend who'd helped her and Tessa over the summer. She'd kissed him, and they'd been intimate, and she'd enjoyed both of those things quite a lot.

She'd broken up with another boyfriend recently, claiming she needed time to find herself. That much was still true.

She sent her *I'm sorry, Sean,* sighed into the sky, and faced Helen. "How do you find yourself? I mean, if you feel lost, what's the first thing you do?"

Helen looked at her with eyes that had seen things Janey couldn't even fathom. "When Kenneth died, I felt untethered. It was as if someone had cut the string holding me to the earth, and I just..." She waved her hand with long, bony fingers up into the atmosphere. "Floated. Drifted."

"You don't seem drifty to me," Janey said.

"I came back down," Helen said, her smile barely touching her mouth but beaming light from those sapphire eyes. "It took a while, but I came back down. I grew a new string."

"How?" Janey asked, the desperation prevalent in all three letters of that single word. She could feel it dripping from her fingers slowly, as if she'd dipped them in honey and could only stare as the viscous liquid took its sweet time drip, drip, dripping off.

"I didn't let those I love get too far away," Helen said.

"It's easy to feel alone and abandoned after a loved one dies. People don't know how to talk to you. They don't know what to say, and it's easier for them to stay away. It's easier for you too." She groaned as she sat on the bench in front of The Glass Dolphin. In the circle drive leading up to the posh seafood restaurant, indeed a glass dolphin statue raised right up out of a bubbling, chirping fountain. Water spurted from the dolphin's beak, and Janey couldn't help smiling at the cheerful mammal, even in sculpture form.

"After a while of being alone and abandoned and feeling sorry for myself," Helen continued, and Janey sat beside her. Normally, she'd want to go in and put her name on the waiting list, but today felt...different. Helen possessed magic Janey needed, and she didn't dare leave her side for fear the elderly woman would poof away as if she were a figment of Janey's imagination.

"I stopped staying away from the people I knew loved me. I loved them too, you know. They were probably feeling alone and abandoned by me. So I started going to lunch with my sister again. I called Kenneth's brothers and sisters regularly. I kept up with my children and invited them and my grandchildren to the beach." She smiled with enough warmth to rival the sun that day. "And you know what? They came, and we started building new memories. We reconnected, and it was wonderful. They're my string now."

"That's beautiful." Janey needed a new string, and as

her phone buzzed and she saw Sean's name and message—*It's totally okay, Janey. They're sandwiches, and they'll keep*—she knew exactly who she wanted her reconnections to be made with.

Now, to find the words...and then say them out loud.

CHAPTER FIVE

Maddy and Julia did an amazing job of avoiding one another and existing in The Lighthouse Inn with the perfect dance of silence and movement for three days.

Come Tuesday morning, however, and Maddy was tired of standing at her door, listening for Julia's footsteps to first go up the stairs to the main level of the inn, and then come back down once she'd finished breakfast.

She then gave Maddy free rein of the kitchen without intruding on her space. Maddy then usually donned a big, wide-brimmed hat and spent hours on the beach with only her cellphone for company. She wasn't even sure why she needed that. She had no one left to text or call, and she'd played hours of mind-numbing games and scrolled trough asinine social media posts until she wanted to scream, scatter her phone in the ocean, and stomp back to the blue room.

She had no idea what the handmade cards in the recipe box meant, and she'd picked them up from when she'd spilled them and tucked them all back inside without reading or looking at any more of them. The box sat back on the top shelf in her closet, for she also couldn't bring herself to throw them away.

"You have to talk to her today," Maddy told herself as she bent to tie her sneakers. She and Julia had a job to do. She was getting paid to live here, and the work officially started today.

Today.

She stood and straightened, stretching up to release the tension in her neck and shoulders. That done, she moved into the bathroom to tie her hair back into a ponytail. When she did this, she could see the white and gray that had started to creep into her blonde. For a while a few years ago, she'd promptly colored over this imperfection. Chris was a state senator with his eye on a prominent position in the President's cabinet. He couldn't have a wife with even a speck of dust on her sleeve. Gray hair? Nope. Not for the rich, famous, or political. They had to be perfect all the time—say the perfect thing, walk the perfect walk, look the perfect way.

Maddy had borne that burden with gladness for the first couple of decades of her marriage. Chris had swept her off her feet at one of the lowest times of her life. He'd seen her at her worst, and he'd helped her and loved her anyway. She'd felt such a debt of gratitude to him, and her love had been seeded in that ground, where it had grown and bloomed and flourished for a long time.

Losing him hurt worse than anything else in her life, even having Alan choose Julia over her all those years ago.

She turned away from her reflection and twisted the lock on her memories. She couldn't afford to let them run wild today. Drawing on every steely ounce of resolve she had, Maddy left the blue room without pausing at the door to listen. The clock had just ticked past eight, and Julia was nothing if not scheduled and routined. Maddy actually appreciated that about her, because she herself loved a good checklist and the order to getting things done right.

Expecting to find Julia in the kitchen, Maddy made her footsteps heavier and more pronounced than she would have otherwise. Sure enough, Julia perched on a barstool in the kitchen, her cup of coffee frozen halfway to her mouth.

Their eyes met, and thunder rolled through Maddy's chest. It vibrated down her arms and through her torso and up into her sinuses.

"Good morning," she said, turning slightly to move over to the coffee maker. Julia had not yet dumped the coffee, and Maddy's lips turned down as she realized the other woman had been doing that for the past three days. "Is it okay if I have some of this?" She lifted the pot to indicate the coffee, not truly looking at Julia. She still saw enough of the woman's profile in her peripheral vision to get the nod.

"Thank you." Over the years, Maddy had dealt with plenty of people she didn't particularly enjoy. She knew how to deploy her manners and her professionalism, and that was all this job required as well.

After pouring her coffee and stirring in a spoonful of sugar, she turned toward Julia. She'd put her mug down, but her eyes still held the wary quality of a jackrabbit who'd just spotted a wolf. She held just as still as said jackrabbit would as well.

"It's our first day," she finally said. "I suppose we need to sit down and make some plans."

Relief roared through Maddy, though she felt like *she* was the one with every right to carry hurt feelings all these years. It had been Julia who'd started dating Alan when she knew—she *knew*—Maddy liked him and had been dating him for several weeks. Back then, there were no "define the relationship" acronyms or formal events where two people talked about whether they were exclusive or not.

Maddy had assumed she and Alan were dating. He'd asked her out several times. They'd gone one eight dates. She'd kissed him dozens of times.

She blinked, and a much younger version of Julia Harper now sat on the barstool. Her hair was the exact same shade of deep, freshly-dug dirt as it was now. She carried more lines in her face, and more wisdom in her eyes, but so much about her was exactly the same.

She could see Julia sitting with Alan on a stool at a bar very much like the one where she now perched. They'd laughed together, and while Alan threw back his drink, Julia put her hand on his arm. Maddy had watched it all from across the diner. She could still smell the oil where French fries turned crisp and the sickeningly sweet scent of coconut cream pie in the refrigerated case directly in front of her.

Julia had leaned in closer to Maddy's Alan. The man who'd told her he had a study group that night and wouldn't be able to meet for dinner. Maddy had made plans with her roommates—all except one.

Julia. Who'd had "other plans."

Maddy hadn't asked what they were. Neither had either of the other two girls they'd lived with while they went to NYU. That was simply how they lived together. They invited each other, and if someone couldn't come, that was fine. No big deal.

Except for Maddy, on that autumn night, while her other two roommates chit-chatted and followed the hostess to a horrible booth with plastic faux-leather seats, the fact that Julia had "other plans" became a very big deal.

"Maddy?"

Maddy blinked her way out of the past, wishing the brain didn't hold on to such damaging memories in high-definition clarity. She replaced the thoughts with images of puppies and freshly washed white bunnies and slicked a smile onto her face that felt as slippery as the woman now standing in front of her.

"Yes," she said smoothly, as if she'd heard the question and already answered it. "We should sit down and make some plans for what we need to do. How we'll split the duties. Our strengths and weaknesses." She fought the urge to clear her throat. In college, Julia had been brilliant in math and science, and Maddy could admit she'd followed her long enough to know she'd graduated in marine biology.

Alan had finished his business degree and gone on to get a realtor's license. He helped people buy and sell property all over the city and into New Jersey, and since he was charismatic and personable, he was very, very good at his job.

Julia had money—or she had. Maddy had no idea what the fallout from her divorce was, and while curiosity brewed in the back of her throat, she kept the questions silent.

"Do you want to go into the office?" Julia asked.

"Yes." Maddy turned on her heel and marched out of the kitchen the way she'd come in. A second exit sat to the right, beside the huge stovetop, that led into the dining area for guests. Maddy didn't remember being impressed with that room. In fact, she recalled it being one of the spaces in the inn that needed the most work.

The enormity of the task before them—two women

who could barely be in the same room as one another—caused Maddy to feel like she'd stepped into Atlas's shoes. She had no idea how many steps the Greek God had been able to take, but she felt like her next one would bring her to her knees.

It didn't, and she made it into the tiny office where she'd first met Julia four days ago. The shock of that day still ran through her, but she ignored it as she went around the desk to take Vivian's spot. That left the guest chair for Julia, who took it without a word.

"Okay," Maddy said, sighing immediately afterward. She glanced around the desk and reached for the yellow pad of legal paper. Upon opening a drawer, she located a black pen and the bottom drawer held a clipboard. "Perhaps we should go room-to-room and make notes."

Julia looked like Maddy had smacked her with a frying pan. Then her eyelashes fluttered as she blinked rapidly. Once she got that under control, she asked, "Do you really think we can get this place open in two months?"

Maddy tilted her head to the side, a nasty remark shrieking through her mind. *It's two whole months. You stole Alan from me in less time than that.*

Instead, she said, "Honestly? No." She shook her head. "But I think we should pretend like we can, and then talk to Vivian when we've made some progress."

"Smart." Julia actually dared to put a smile on her face, but Maddy simply didn't know how to return it. She couldn't believe the conversation had been as civil as it had been, to be honest.

As a reply, Maddy got to her feet. "I think the office is fantastic." She clipped the pad of paper to the clipboard and wrote OFFICE at the top of it. Without waiting for Julia to corroborate with her opinion, she put a checkmark next to the word.

"The lobby is decent," she said, nodding for Julia to leave first. Maddy didn't want to get that close to her yet. Just because they'd exchanged a few sentences about their job didn't mean they were suddenly best friends forever again.

"It looks like they painted out here at the very least," Julia said, glancing around at the walls and ceiling. The front of the lighthouse housed a lot of windows, so there wasn't much to paint or maintain here.

"Do the windows lock?" Maddy asked, moving to the furthest one across the lobby and checking it. They completed this task for all the windows, and yes, they all locked. Maddy made a note of it.

"Front desk, check. Floor, check, though I do think new rugs and new curtains in this room would make things better." She cocked her eyebrows at Julia, who nodded.

"We'll just have to check the budget. That dining room is disgusting." She hooked her thumb over her shoulder and then led the way past the stairs and past the kitchen to the room in the back corner of the main level of the lighthouse.

The kitchen needed a good scrub from top to bottom, but as Maddy had used it over the weekend, it was functional. The floor came in giant, burned-red titles not to her personal aesthetical liking, but they didn't have cracks or issues with the mortar keeping them together.

She scrawled *Kitchen – professional cleaning?* on her pad and walked into the dining room. Julia had been right, and Maddy had remembered correctly about the woeful state of the dining room.

"Windows need to be cleaned," Julia said, already going around the room. "No dining room should have carpet. It should be ripped out and replaced with something classic and nautical and sensible. We need new tables and chairs." She continued naming items—curtains, paint on the walls, and light fixtures—and Maddy wrote it all down.

"Are you thinking nautical then?" she asked, and Julia turned toward her from the window that faced east. "Whites, blues, deep reds? Almost patriotic?"

"I don't know," Julia said, obviously not wanting to commit to something Maddy wouldn't like.

Maddy didn't want to admit to what she liked. Watching Julia squirm the teensiest bit made her feel...powerful.

It's about power, Maddy. You understand. The words flashed through her mind, and she slammed the door on that memory.

She would not be like Chris, and she shoved against

the feelings of satisfaction and pride that she made Julia nervous. Of course she did. Julia made her nervous too.

"I love the idea of a blond wood on the floor," Maddy said, her voice so low it almost sounded male. "It feels rustic and charming at the same time. Very nautical." She turned toward the nearest wall, which had been painted a brownish-taupe-ish color at someone's most insane moment.

"The walls could be a cool gray-blue," she said. "Not like, bam-in-your-face-Patriotic-blue."

"Something light and cool, yes," Julia said.

"Deep red," Maddy continued. "Not lifeguard-red. Not picnic-blanket-red. Something almost maroon, and as an accent, like in the curtains and napkins."

"Yes." Julia sounded like she'd swallowed a frog. "And since the ceiling is raised slightly in here, and we have all the windows on this level, putting a bright white up there will make the room seem and feel bigger than it is."

Maddy turned and looked at Julia, some of her nerves and fear melting into nothing. "You sounded like Alan right there."

Julia clapped one hand over her mouth, her eyes bulging in her head.

Maddy found that comical, and a smile brushed against her lips. "It's fine, Julia. He was a real estate agent, and I'm sure he talked to you a lot about his job." She did clear her throat then. "Chris never shut up about his."

Maddy studied the floor, surprised she'd let that last sentence come out of her mouth.

Her entire life had been supporting Chris. She should've gotten paid for the past twenty-four years he'd been in politics and she'd been right there at his side. Instead, she'd gotten divorce papers, a speech about power, and all of her calls and texts to her friends and children blocked.

"Let's go upstairs," she said, pain streaming through her. Pain she didn't want to acknowledge. Pain she didn't know how to deal with. Pain she didn't want Julia to see.

Upstairs, they moved through each of the guest rooms, starting with the two above the dining room and office on the main level, noting the cosmetic changes and improvements that needed to be made. Structural items Maddy started to detail on a separate page.

"Do you like the names of the rooms?" Julia asked as they traipsed into the fourth room. "Green room. Blue room. Garden room. It feels like someone was a little obsessed with the White House."

"And we're not going to keep those colors," Maddy said. "Are we? I rather like the idea of ordering simple things in bulk. We can dress up the rooms in various shades of our blues, reds, and creamy-whites. We can make them different with the accent pieces we choose, like rugs, linens, lamps, curtains, and the décor."

She checked over her shoulder as Julia opened the closet door in what was the palace room right now. Pink shouted at Maddy from nearly every surface, and she had no idea what kind of palace the interior decorator had visited to draw inspiration from for this nightmare.

"Good idea," Julia said.

"We can rename the room based on the décor. Like the lobster lair. Or the seascape room."

Julia turned from the closet, those eyes wide and filled with shock again. She scoffed or coughed, her smile growing. Maddy realized then that she was trying—unsuccessfully—to hold back a laugh. She finally failed, and Julia dissolved into giggles. "Lobster lair?"

"Okay, so not that one," Maddy said, allowing a smile to ease onto her face too. When she'd first seen Julia rise from the chair as Vivian introduced her, Maddy thought they wouldn't last a single day here together. Because of their dance, they'd made it four, and this walk-through hadn't been...terrible.

Maddy wouldn't put it at the top of her list of Things To Do Again, but it hadn't been terrible.

"I like seascape room," Julia said, still grinning like a fool. "We could do 'beach retreat' for this one, as it has a great view of the beach, and 'lighthouse view' for the one in the corner where we could see the operational lighthouse out here on the Point." She raised her eyebrows, her want of Maddy's approval obvious.

"Wonderful," Maddy said, jotting down her ideas and hoping she was being kind enough. She'd never given much thought to forgiving Julia, but her mind filled with the idea now.

Julia stepped into the closet while Maddy's pen continued to scratch. "Look at this," Julia said, and the awed tone brought Maddy's head up mid-word from writing "shipwreck island" as an idea for a room name.

"What is it?" She lowered her pen and clipboard and started across the small room. The beds had all been stripped to the bare mattresses, and she hated how abandoned and forlorn it made the rooms look. Like they had no personality without somewhere beautiful and inviting to lay a weary head.

Julia backed out of the closet with a photo album in her hand. "It's an album, and it says *The Lighthouse Inn* on the cover."

"Fun," Maddy said, getting as close to the other woman as she dared. "Open it."

Julia did, sliding the book so that Maddy held the bulk of it on the right while she held the open front flap on the left. "Look. Someone started it in 1931."

"Incredible," Maddy said, her love of old things rearing up and sniffing out the dusty, musty quality of the pages in this book.

Julia delicately turned the page, obviously trying not to touch the plastic sleeve with too much pressure. "Some of the papers are disintegrating."

"A clam bake announcement," Maddy said, scanning

the paper that was indeed nearly in dozens of pieces. "A fish fry. A boating expedition."

"Rowing," Julia said, reaching to turn the page. "Oh, there's people."

The photographs were clearly old, with muted colors that had been washed out by time. Men wore swimming suits that went up over their shoulders, and swim caps that made them look nearly alien-like.

Maddy loved the old-fashioned swimming suits women wore, and she determined from looking at the black-and-white-dotted one on this page that she'd search one out online and buy it. It would be too cold to wear here on Nantucket this year, but she'd be here next summer.

"Wow," Julia said, continuing to flip the pages. They held more pictures of what Maddy could only assume were guests at the inn, and they turned progressively more modern faster than she anticipated they would.

"1965," Julia said, reading the labels at the top. "This can't be all of them."

"Maybe they're VIPs."

"Mm. 1969." Another two flips, and they landed in 1974. The picture closest to Maddy featured a man and a woman, both of them grinning like it was Christmas Day and Kris Kringle had brought them exactly what they wanted—each other. They had their arms around one another, had turned into one another and then twisted back to face the camera, and joy poured from the picture.

Maddy's heart bounced against its own pulse and then dodged up into her throat. She made a noise halfway between surprise and a cough and managed to say, "Look." She couldn't quite get Julia's name out, though she would've liked to.

"What?"

She pointed to the picture, and while she'd only met Julia's dad a few times, many years ago, she said, "Isn't that your dad?" Maddy lifted her eyes to take in Julia's reaction, which flashed across her face in pulses of emotion.

Confusion.

Dis-be-lief-*lief*.

Denial.

That one stayed the longest, but then dissolved into an additional round of confusion.

Shock. *Sh-shock-shock.*

That one practically hummed through Maddy's veins the way her heartbeat filled her ears.

Julia began to peel back the protector, a horrible ripping, squelching sound accompanying it.

"Stop it," Maddy said. "You're going to ruin the other pictures." She put her hand over the page as much as she could, stalling Julia's progress.

Their eyes met, and Maddy felt Julia's *shock-sh-shock-shock* radiate from the other woman and into her own pulse.

"That's my dad, yes," Julia said. "But that's not my mom."

CHAPTER SIX

Julia had to get that picture out of the album. She wished Maddy would move her hand, and she almost batted it away and ripped at the plastic covering. These old photo albums didn't preserve pictures anyway. The colors were already warped and faded, some of the oranges and browns and yellows creating a tie-dye effect that obscured important details.

Like who that woman was with her father in 1974.

Julia had been born in 1974, probably only a few months after this picture. It definitely looked like summer in the photograph, and Julia would celebrate her forty-seventh birthday in just a few weeks, near the end of September.

So who was that woman?

She had dark hair like her mother, but Sandi Harper would've been at least six or seven months pregnant in a picture taken in the summer of 1974. Not only that, but Julia's mother stood almost as tall as her father, and this woman definitely didn't.

She exhaled and stepped away from Maddy and the album, nearly causing the other woman to drop it. Maddy bobbled the book, but she managed to keep it from spilling to the floor. Julia half-wanted it to, because then maybe the picture would fall out and she'd be able to check it.

People from forty-five years ago often wrote on the backs of photographs, detailing where they were, when, and who was in them. Her grandmother had, as had her mother. Julia had a few pictures of herself as a child, smiling like cheese was the best thing she'd ever have in her life, every time she had a new sibling.

She wondered if Eric or Annie knew anything about this woman.

Julia quickly dismissed the thought as she moved over to the huge window in the corner of the room. This one looked west, though she could see the dock which extended off the front of the lighthouse to her right. The beach extended in front of her, with cottages and homes in her view if she looked left.

The sand dunes swelled between The Lighthouse Inn and the first street of cottages, but she could make out the rooftops on them. The one on the end had been painted a bright blue, and it looked so beachy and inviting.

She put one hand on her hip and wiped the other through her hair. "Who do you think she was?"

"Who?" Maddy asked.

Of course, she'd be thinking of something else by now. Julia told herself she could come back later and get the picture out. Maddy couldn't guard it forever.

Changing tactics, she turned back to Maddy. Sure enough, she'd closed the photo album and tucked it beneath her clipboard, where she continued to write. Julia should be glad someone was taking meticulous notes. She'd originally thought it wouldn't be too terribly difficult to get the inn functioning and open, but her initial walk-through hadn't included cobwebs, peeling paint, or stripped beds.

Everything needed to be stripped, and Julia saw days of hard work in front of her. Days she'd move all the furniture out of a room to paint it, then have to reload everything back in. Days where she and Maddy would have to spend hours on the common areas of the inn, as hallways needed new paint and new fixtures too. Days where she wasted time trying to find the just-right lamp for a themed room.

She could online shop with the best of them—she loved online shopping almost more than in-person shopping—but her head ached at the idea of scouring websites to find the perfect piece for their Nantucket Point palace.

Perhaps they should stick with blue room and green room and garden room.

"We should take the pictures out of that album and put them in a proper display case," she said. "Those sleeves aren't acid-free, and they'll just continue to get ruined." She approached Maddy, who looked up from her clipboard with plenty of interested intensity in her expression. She was a smart woman, Julia knew that. She always had been, and she still couldn't believe that she'd somehow won Alan away from her.

At the time, she'd been nothing but vindicated and satisfied. She'd reasoned that Alan was a grown man, and he'd made his own decision.

Now, faced with the other woman—someone she'd hurt—regret filled Julia from top to bottom and came spouting out of her mouth. "I'm so sorry about Chris," she said.

Maddy's face hardened, her emotions getting hidden behind strong gates of iron that snapped closed over her eyes. They shone like marbles, hard as granite. "I'm fine," she said, turning away from Julia. She just-as-quickly turned back and pushed the album toward her. "Do what you want with this."

She walked away, leaving Julia standing there with the prize she'd wanted. "We only have one more room to do. Let's get this done."

Julia let her heartbeat thump in her chest for a couple of seconds, and then she drew her shoulders back and followed Maddy. She wasn't going to feel bad for apologizing. She knew Maddy had been divorced, because her husband was a prominent politician in Boston. News out of Massachusetts reached New York City too.

If it had happened when the media had reported it, Maddy had been enduring a divorce about the same time Julia had been. She could practically feel the irony seething between her and Maddy, as they'd also gotten married within one month of each other.

The moment Alan had chosen Julia over Maddy, she'd started dating someone else. That was what Maddy did. Nothing ever got her down. No one ever got in her head. Nothing ever looked like a failure for her.

She took things, and she moved on. Her romance with a man named Winn had been a whirlwind and hadn't lasted more than a couple of weeks. Then she'd met Christopher Lancaster, and while they'd accelerated things quickly too, Julia had seen the lovestruck look in Maddy's eyes after her dates.

Julia and Alan had endured a proper engagement, with almost a year of planning between the proposal and the I-do. Maddy had not. She'd gone from single to married in less than three months, which still made Julia's head spin a little bit. Back then, her younger self had felt like Maddy was racing her, almost daring her to move up her wedding date just to be first.

After all, everything was a race with Madelynne, and it always had been.

They'd probably get The Lighthouse Inn done on time, because Maddy wouldn't allow Julia to defeat her again. As she followed her into the fifth and final bedroom on the second floor, she knew she'd never win against Maddy again anyway.

She gripped the album and said, "I think we should be able to talk about our lives."

"Nope."

"Alan left me," Julia went on anyway. She had to live here with this woman. She had to run this inn with her for twelve months. "Our youngest had been out of the house for a year, and we'd been distant for a while. He said he just couldn't do it anymore."

Her lungs quaked, especially when Maddy turned toward her, those bright-as-fire eyes burning in Julia's direction.

She shrugged and looked around the last room. "I don't know what he meant. I was a good wife. I thought we were happy enough for most of our marriage. You know how they are. There's ups and downs." If he didn't want her, she hadn't wanted to keep anything of his, and she'd changed her last name back to her maiden name once the divorce was final. She wandered over to a nightstand that looked like it had been made from a shipping crate. "I hate this. It looks...cheap."

The Lighthouse Inn was getting remodeled from floor to ceiling, and that included the prices of the rooms. She saw this place as a luxury inn, for luxurious people to come stay while they vacationed on Nantucket. They had white-sand beaches to go with the experience, and five-star restaurants just down the beach. The inn should match that opulence.

Maddy stayed silent, and Julia looked over to her, then past her to the extra space behind the door. "This is a big room. We could put a loveseat over there and call it a suite. Charge more for it."

Maddy cleared her throat. "I was thinking about naming it the shipwreck room. We could put up art of ships, get some lamps with those poles...you know what I mean?"

Julia offered her a smile, her mind racing through décor possibilities that went with ships. "I think they're called masts."

"Yes," Maddy said, the word bursting from her mouth. When she smiled, she could light up a room, and Julia found she missed that. She hadn't seen her former roommate and best friend smile since she'd been here. She must be hurting so much, and Julia knew exactly what that pain felt like.

She'd caused some of Maddy's pain, and at the risk of getting smacked with the clipboard, she decided to try one more apology. "I'm really sorry about Alan."

"I don't want to talk about it."

"I know, but I need to say it," Julia said, desperation rising up and overflowing. "I'm sorry, Maddy. You were just so amazing, and everyone loved you. Every single man looked only at you. It was thrilling and...somehow I told myself that I was as good as you, because Alan liked me." She couldn't explain, at least not in a way that Maddy would understand. Maddy had never had to deal with being second-best—until Alan. She'd never lost to anyone or anything. She'd always held the planet in the palm of her hand, as her family had been rich, and she'd been smart and knew how to work hard.

"You were everything I wanted to be," Julia continued, though Maddy had turned her back and bent her head. Whatever she was writing on that silly clipboard couldn't make her deaf. "But I shouldn't have gone out with him when he asked."

Maddy turned back to her. "He asked you?"

"Yes," Julia said, shame filling her completely. She'd only felt like this one other time in the past twenty-five years, and that was when Maddy's family had been dragged through the media during Chris's race for the governor. Journalists weren't all that kind, and they always took an angle that painted someone in the worst light.

"I should've said no. I was just...I wanted to be you so badly, and he was so handsome." Alan Brunner had been going places, that was for sure. He'd lived up to that expectation too, becoming one of the top real estate agents in the city. He did deals for millions on a weekly—and sometimes daily—basis, and Julia had never truly wanted for anything in her life.

Perhaps a little more time with her husband. Perhaps more affection. Perhaps to be noticed for her contributions to their family. Raising children and running a household wasn't easy work, and she'd supported Alan through starting the real estate firm—which she'd organized and put many systems in place that he still used.

"I thought you'd come onto him." Maddy lowered her clipboard, and the two women simply looked at one another, the scent of dust mingling with the sunlight coming in the windows.

"Maybe I did," Julia said. "I don't remember that. I was never very good with boys. Surely you remember that."

Something changed on Maddy's face, but she plastered over it so quickly that Julia couldn't tell what she'd been feeling. She lowered her head again and lifted the clipboard. "I think this room should definitely be our shipwreck suite." She crossed something out and wrote something new.

Frustration filled Julia, but she couldn't make Maddy talk to her. She'd apologized, and she'd actually confessed some pretty embarrassing things. The other woman could do what she wanted with them.

When Maddy looked up again, she said, "I'm sorry about Alan too. I wouldn't wish a divorce on anyone." Her unspoken words—*not even you*—streamed through Julia's ears.

She nodded, because she didn't need to drag out the conversation. The entire bridge wasn't rebuilt, and maybe it never would be. But she felt like she'd put the first plank in place, and right now, she couldn't do more than that.

THAT AFTERNOON, JULIA HAD TO GET OUT OF THE INN. She couldn't sit for another moment, and she and Maddy had been over every inch of the place, even the deck off the front of the lighthouse and the upper balcony, which seemed to be newer than the rest of the building. All they could do was climb up to it, though Julia had been sure there should be a way down the center of it, as that was where all of the electrical wiring should be. The trapdoor had been absent though, and the floor had been painted along with the rest of the railing. Less for them to do, in her opinion.

They'd gone over some of the programming they wanted to do. They'd gone over pricing. Maddy had started talking about software and websites, and while Julia acknowledged the need for those things, the to-do list was a looming monster, and she felt like David up against a Goliath.

They'd agreed to take a break, and Julia burst out of the double-glass doors and onto the sidewalk along the entrance to the inn. It was really the back of the lighthouse where guests entered, and Julia sometimes got disoriented with what was the front and what was the back.

She took one look at her car and thought, *Nope. Not sitting down again.*

Her legs got moving, and she went west, her sandaled feet sinking into sand only a few steps later. Relief poured through her, though the sun had been warming the sand all day. She bent down and removed her sandals, and with them lilting lazily from her fingers, she began her trek through the soft, loose sand to the harder packed stuff closer to shore.

The breeze picked up off the water, and Julia took a deep breath that knocked free some of the tight things in her chest.

This was Nantucket Point. A fresh breeze in the face. Softly lapping waves. Sunshine. Gulls calling. Children laughing as they ran and splashed in the water. People lying on the sand, reading or talking. There was joy in Nantucket Point. There was peace here. There was fun.

Those were the things Julia had always associated with Nantucket Point, and her parents had brought their family every summer without fail. They didn't own a home here, but they'd rent from someone else, and she walked all the way to the last street in the neighborhood on the west side of the Point.

She couldn't see the house they usually rented, as it sat down on the corner, the first house everyone saw when they finally arrived on Bakery Avenue.

The bakery still operated at the end of the street, and Julia went that way next, her mouth watering for something chocolatey and sweet. This late in the day proved that bakeries were early-morning establishments, as it was closed.

The hours listed said they'd be there tomorrow, from

seven to three, and Julia determined to come get breakfast. When she'd come here in the past, she'd gotten sausage and egg quiches she could carry in one hand and eat as the birds circled overhead, hoping she'd drop a crumb they could snatch up.

She turned and started back toward The Lighthouse Inn. The beach wasn't nearly as populated as it would've been in the summertime, but a fair few people had come this afternoon. Nantucket Point had year-round residents, though some of the houses and cottages to the immediate south of where she walked were definitely vacation homes.

She wondered where her father had been standing with that mystery woman. Perhaps right here on this stretch of sand, though she hadn't seen any water in the background. There hadn't been any buildings either. Just sun, sky, and sand.

A woman with shoulder-length brown hair walked in front of her, her hand held up to her ear as she spoke on the phone. Julia only caught snatches of what she said, as the wind stole some of the words, and she wasn't following too closely.

She also didn't care what a stranger talked about with the people she knew. But when the woman said what sounded like, "...yes, Harper. That's right. Ryan Harper," Julia stumbled in the sand.

The woman kept walking, but Julia froze.

Ryan Harper.

Her father.

The photograph pulsed in her brain, like it had been made into a home movie on very old film. She could hear the clicking from the machine and everything. The image flashed as the machine gave it light and took it away every half-second.

The woman got further from her, and finally Julia's brain screamed at her to *follow her! Find out who she is and what she knows.*

Perhaps she was the woman in the photo.

"No." She scoffed out loud too, because that woman wasn't anywhere near old enough to be a young twenty-something in a photo from 1974. She looked around to see if anyone had caught her talking to herself. She'd always spoken out loud to herself, something her children liked to tease her about. Her heart squeezed at the thought of her kids and that she'd left their core home in Manhattan, the place she'd once envisioned all of them gathering for holidays with their spouses and kids. None of them had either yet, but Julia couldn't wait to be a mother-in-law and grandmother.

She got her feet moving again, faster this time, to keep pace with the woman. She lowered her arm, her phone call obviously over. Could she approach her right here on the sand? What would she even say?

I heard you say Ryan Harper. How do you know my father?

The woman didn't pause to enjoy the sunshine or the sea breeze. She continued down the beach and then started away from the hard-packed sand and through the looser stuff, her goal obviously that street closest to the inn.

In fact, she went up the steps at the very first house—the bright blue one Julia had seen from the window on the second floor of the inn.

Julia paused down the beach and watched the house, her thoughts in utter turmoil. She looked toward the inn and knew what waited for her there. A building that had been trapped in time, and walls that held their breath around two women who obviously didn't like each other.

She looked toward the blue cottage. She had no idea what waited for her there. It could be a situation far worse than what she'd find at The Lighthouse Inn, and Julia didn't consider herself one who sought out trouble. Perhaps she could learn who that woman was privately.

When she stepped, it was south, not east, and after that, she just kept putting one foot in front of the other.

CHAPTER SEVEN

Tessa Simmons had just poured the hot water over her tea bag to steep when someone rapped on the door. She turned that way, a wave of PTSD engulfing her, leaving her panting and feeling like she really had just been washed under.

She had no idea how long she stood there, but it was long enough for the visitor to knock again, louder this time. Her natural instinct had her hurrying across the kitchen and living room to open the door. Instead of throwing it wide the way she would've in her suburban Pennsylvanian home, she cracked it and peered out onto the porch.

A dark-haired woman stood there, wearing a pale pink blouse that the wind kept grabbing at with its relentless fingers. She'd cinched her arms across her midsection as if trying to stop it, and her dark eyes found Tessa's easily.

It was like looking into Janey's eyes, and Tessa took a sharp breath. "Can I help you?"

She'd never met this woman before. She wore a pair of sensible denim shorts that went all the way to her knee, as if she knew her age and was content to dress to it. She had to be Tessa's age, if the lines around her eyes meant anything, though she didn't have a speck of graying or white hair in all that dark yet.

Janey didn't either, though, and Tessa couldn't help comparing the two of them even more closely. Janey did a lot to accentuate the high cheekbones she'd been given, and even she'd admitted she didn't know what her natural hair color was anymore. Right now, it was black and blue, and she wore enough jewelry to hide any other imperfections.

Tessa had seen her without makeup, but if Janey left the house, she painted herself up first. Even just to go to the beach, she'd put on mascara and lip gloss. Since moving to Nantucket permanently, Tessa couldn't remember the last time she'd put on makeup.

Perhaps when she interviewed for the docent position at the Nautical Museum in downtown Nantucket. She'd gotten the job, but she hadn't started yet, and Tessa supposed she would add some color to her cheeks and smooth out any blemishes before she went to the museum next week.

The other woman still hadn't answered her question,

her eyes sizing up Tessa as completely as she'd been assessing her.

"I couldn't help overhearing part of what you said on the beach." The woman looked to her right, out toward the beach. Tessa simply watched her. She'd been talking to a friend back in Pennsylvania—a private investigator.

She liked and trusted Sean, but he was quasi-dating Janey, and he hadn't wanted to get involved with trying to dig up information on her biological father. Not only that, but he was a lawyer, not a private investigator.

She'd thought she wouldn't be overheard out on the beach, and she still didn't trust the cottage to be bug-free. Bobbie and Riggs Friedman had really done a number of her psyche, and her skin crawled with the very idea of talking to this stranger.

"I didn't hear much, I promise," the woman said, and she even spoke like Janey. "It's just that...you said Ryan Harper."

Tessa wasn't going to confirm or deny it. She also didn't think this woman had a knife or any weapons, and she let the door open further. She'd been planning to ice her tea after it had steeped, so she didn't have anything to get back to. She was ripping out all of the old carpet on the second and third floors, but this woman had saved her from back-breaking work.

"I just wondered..." The woman let her eyes go back to the beach. "I'm sorry." She gave a nervous laugh and focused on Tessa again. "I must sound crazy to you."

"Not yet," Tessa said, trying to be as kind as possible. She had the very real feeling that this woman was about to introduce herself, and she already knew who she was.

"I'm Julia Harper."

Harper.

"Ryan Harper is my father."

Tessa's pulse beat like a big bass drum in her chest, the sound echoing and vibrating up into both ears. Even though she'd expected her to say that, the words landed with the strength of bombs, blowing up Tessa's finely crafted world where this man that neither her sister nor herself knew stayed inside his own bubble, safe somewhere in New York.

She stepped further back into the house, cursing herself for assuming the beach was a safe place to have a conversation. "Would you like to come in? I have hot water ready for tea. I think my sister—" She very nearly choked on the words. "—has some instant coffee here. I've got ginger ale too."

Tessa kept facing Julia until she stepped inside. She seemed to be two opposite things wrapped in the same package. Timid and yet determined too. Well-dressed but clearly discombobulated. Sophisticated but without shoes on her feet.

"I'm Tessa Simmons," she said. "Do you live around here? Just visiting?" She needed to know how long she'd have to deal with Julia, and that would determine how much she told her. She gestured for the other woman to head toward the kitchen.

"These floors are great." Julia actually bent down and ran her palm along the bamboo Janey had installed over the summer. "What is this?"

"It's bamboo," Tessa said. "Bleached or whitewashed. I can't remember. My sister picked it out."

"It's very nautical." Julia stood and offered Tessa a smile that trembled along the top edges. There was that duplicity again. "I just moved into The Lighthouse Inn. I'm one of the caretakers." She turned away as if she knew this news would stun Tessa, so she didn't see the wide eyes or the way Tessa's mouth gaped slightly.

She lived here. Not only that, but she lived only a hundred yards away from Tessa's front door. She'd never been happier that Janey had moved to the southern side of the island to live with Viola Martin and the live-in butler, Miles Greene.

Even as she tried to tell herself that Janey would never have to know about Julia, Tessa knew she wouldn't be able to keep the other woman a secret. Janey came to the cottage all the time. She'd been thrilled to see the job notice disappear from the doors at The Lighthouse Inn.

That means they hired someone, Tess. The inn will be open soon enough.

For some reason, the inn closing had bothered Janey, but Tessa wasn't sure why.

"Do you live here full-time?" Julia asked, twisting back to Tessa.

She managed to snap her mouth closed and nod. "Yes," she said. "I just moved in this summer." She cleared her throat and edged around Julia to get another cup out of the cupboard. "My mother owned this cottage. We came here every summer growing up."

"How coincidental."

Tessa glanced at Julia and saw something calculating on that pretty face. It didn't fit, and she backed away from her in a pretense to get to the hot water kettle. "What do you mean?"

"My family came to the Point every summer too."

"Lots of people do that." Tessa gave her a smile and held the hot water in front of her. If she had to, she'd throw it at Julia and run for the front door. She'd gotten very good at making escape plans since being drugged and kidnapped by the two older people who'd lived next-door to her mother for decades.

"Did you have a cottage?"

"We rented one," Julia said, her eyes sweeping the kitchen and even going down the hall. She seemed less menacing now, but Tessa still positioned herself next to the knife block. She'd been overcome once in this kitchen, and she wasn't going to let it happen again.

"Sometimes down the road a little, on Bakery Avenue?" She made the words into a question, and Tessa nodded. She knew it. She'd been to the beachside bakery, which was a converted cottage, just yesterday morning. The line on Labor Day had been strewn down the sand, but the peanut butter and jelly doughnut had been worth it. She'd bought a couple of éclairs too, and they still sat in the refrigerator for dessert that night. Janey was supposed to come tell Tessa about her first day of working in Sean's office.

Her sister had decided to take the job, and he'd told her to drop by and start learning the ropes from his current secretary-slash-assistant.

"Sometimes we'd rent a house on the west end of the island," Julia said. "But the Point has always been my favorite part of the island." Her smile reminded Tessa of all the sugar in the doughnut she'd eaten yesterday. "Downtown is so busy, you know? And Wainscott feels stuffy."

"I know what you mean," Tessa said, just to have something to say. "Did you want tea?" She lifted the kettle and cup.

"Sure." Julia sat at the kitchen-table-for-two, and Tessa poured the hot water into the cup and set it in front of her.

"Bags are right there in front of you." Her teacup still sat on the counter where she'd left it, and after she replaced the kettle on the electric burner, she collected the tea and put it on the table too. "I was going to ice mine. Do you want ice?"

"Great idea."

Tessa filled a small bowl with ice cubes and finally

joined Julia at the table. She certainly didn't want to tell her that she'd hired a PI to get the goods on her father. She was staring at a source, and Tessa couldn't help wondering if she could save time and money by simply asking Julia a few questions.

She'd already brought up her father's name, so Tessa dunked her tea bag a few times and let the silence prompt Julia to speak first.

"Do you know my dad?" Julia asked, stirring her own tea bag around with a spoon. She watched the swirling liquid as if it were the most fascinating thing in the world.

"No," Tessa said truthfully.

"Why were you talking about him then?"

"Ryan Harper is a very common name," Tessa said, deciding the water had enough flavor. She deposited the tea bag on the saucer and reached for the ice. Julia's eyes on her face felt like lead weights, but she didn't look up until she'd put a healthy number of ice cubes in her tea.

Julia's eyes flashed in annoyance, in the exact same way Janey's did. Tessa blinked, trying to get the parts of her that were different to come forward. Julia had a narrower face than Janey, and her shoulders and torso weren't nearly as barrel-like as Janey's. They seemed to possess the same air of importance though, as if Julia expected all of her questions to be answered instantly simply because she'd asked.

"You've mentioned a sister," Julia said. "I think I met

her. Janey Fonsbeck? Fore... I'm sorry. I can't remember the last name. She stopped by on my first day."

"She did?" Tessa couldn't hide the surprise in her voice.

"Yes, on Friday."

Tessa cocked her head like she could only examine her memories if she held her neck at such an angle. "Friday..." she mused. "We went to lunch with someone new Janey had met."

"She came to the inn just before lunch," Julia said, lifting her teacup to her lips without removing the bag or adding any ice.

"She didn't say anything," Tessa said, though that didn't surprise her. Not really. Janey liked to keep things close to the vest until she understood them. At lunch, she'd told Sean she wanted to start at his law office at the end of September, and they'd chit-chatted with Helen Ivy, a woman Janey had run into on her way from the shuttle station to the cottage. She loved meeting and talking to new people, and Tessa hadn't been surprised to find "her new friend" in her seventies.

Julia put her teacup down. "She seemed a little rattled." Her dark eyes trained on Tessa and wouldn't let go. "Just like you, and I heard you say my father's name, and I know it's the same man. I just want to know how you knew him."

"I don't know him," Tessa said. "I've never met him." The truth surged to the back of her tongue, and she put herself in Julia's shoes. Would she want to know her dad had another daughter, close to her same age? What would that do to Julia Harper?

"Are your mom and dad still married?" Tessa asked.

"Yes," Julia said. "Going on forty-eight years."

Tessa smiled and nodded, her heart turning into that bass drum again. Everything inside her told her to tell Julia. She'd wanted Janey to go to Southampton and meet her biological dad too. She was tired of secrets, and after her summer spent chasing them, she'd had enough of them to last a lifetime.

"I don't think you'll like what I say. It's...not easy to swallow."

Julia leaned away from the table and folded those bony arms again. "Try me."

"I recently learned of your father," Tessa said, searching for a voice or the prick of her conscience that would tell her to stop talking. None came. "His name came up when my sister and I were settling my mother's estate."

Julia's eyebrows went up, but other than that, she didn't initiate any other muscles to do their job.

"We discovered that he's my sister's biological father, not my dad the way we'd thought."

Shock coursed across Julia's face then in waves large enough to catalog on the Richter scale. "How old is your sister?" she whispered.

"Forty-six," Tessa said in an equally quiet voice.

Julia jumped to her feet. "That's impossible. *I'm* still forty-six." She threw her the dirtiest, foulest look Tessa ever did see and spun. She marched toward the door. "You don't know what you're talking about."

"He and my mom met here on the Point," Tessa called after her. "It was a summer fling."

"You're wrong." With that, Julia opened the door and left the cottage, bringing the door slamming closed behind her.

Tessa sat in the ringing silence, a sense of numbness moving through her that reminded her of the drugs Bobbie had injected into her neck. "Janey's going to kill you," she whispered. Her sister had made it clear she wasn't ready to go to Long Island and meet her father. They didn't even know if he knew about her.

That was only one reason Tessa had hired the private investigator. She should cancel Terry's services, but before she could reach for her phone to do that, the front door of the cottage opened again. She jumped to her feet, expecting it to be Julia, returning with reinforcements.

Instead, Janey entered the cottage. "Hey, sissy," she said cheerfully. She wore the tailored, sophisticated clothes of a law assistant, and she looked like she belonged in any professional office. "I'm dying for that éclair you promised. I haven't heard so many terms I don't understand in a long, long time." She let out a peal of laughter, and Tessa had no idea how to burst this bright bubble of Janey's.

She wouldn't, at least not right now. The news of Julia Harper's visit could wait. After all, Janey hadn't told her about stopping by The Lighthouse Inn.

She stepped over to the fridge and opened it to get out the bakery box of éclairs. "Right here."

"Who was here?" Janey asked, and Tessa spun back to the table. As if in slow motion, Janey reached out and picked up Julia's teacup before turning to meet Tessa's eyes.

CHAPTER EIGHT

"Okay, Dad," Maddy said, looking at the clipboard on the desk. She'd put in a full day's work, and she didn't have to burn the midnight oil. Nowhere had that been specifically stated in her contract here at The Lighthouse Inn. "I'll be over in about a half-hour, okay? I just need to change and make the drive."

"I'll put some hot dogs on the grill."

"No, Dad," Maddy said quickly. "If you're not feeling well, we don't need to add fire to that, okay?" Worry gnawed at her, and she once again wondered how much longer her father could live alone. Now that she'd signed her contract, she couldn't move in with him, and he certainly couldn't move into the inn with her. He'd never be able to get up and down the stairs, for one.

The old inn had an elevator that went up the back—or

rather the front—of the building, but neither she nor Julia had been able to get it working that day. She'd noted it as an item they needed to speak to Vivian about. An elevator from the first floor to the second seemed like a necessity to her, if only for their mobility impaired guests.

"Okay," her dad said. "I'll just wait."

"Get out your knitting," Maddy said, and while she'd always smiled about her dad's knitting in the past, it seemed that Chris and the divorce had stolen the ability to do so from her. "I'll be there before you even finish a mitt."

Behind her, the door to the inn slammed open, and she spun toward the thunderous sound, expecting the glass to break and fill the air with high-pitched shatters.

Thankfully, it didn't. A sob did fill the void after the crash, and Maddy made it to the doorway just in time to see Julia race around the check-in desk and fly down the steps leading to the caretaker's rooms.

"I have to go, Dad." She hung up while her father started to say "Okay," and she followed Julia. She paused at the top of the steps, wondering if she should go down and knock on the other woman's door. If she'd just entered the lighthouse in a sobbing, panicked state, she wouldn't want someone she didn't know anymore and had spent most of her life disliking to come knocking.

Her mind raced. She couldn't just leave her here as distressed as she was. What if she was hurt? What if she needed help?

Her mind flew back twenty-five years to when she was

the one on the other side of the door, sobbing. She hadn't wanted anyone to see her. She'd fled the diner where Alan and Julia had been, and she hadn't told their other two roommates where she was going.

She'd gotten into the first cab she'd seen, and she couldn't remember how she'd told the driver where to take her. She'd hurried into the building, everything caged behind a thin veil that had broken the moment she'd crossed the threshold into her bedroom.

Or what she'd thought was her bedroom.

It had been the wrong apartment, on the wrong floor even. The door hadn't been locked, because the world was a different place in the nineties. She should've been able to pick up the differences in smell and décor, but Maddy barely remembered them even now.

Can I help you? a man had asked.

She'd spun toward him, her heartbeat ricocheting around inside her chest in a strange, military beat that only made her cry harder. She'd collapsed on the floor, and the twenty-something boy had tried to help her.

That boy had been Christopher Lancaster, and he'd been older than Maddy. Kind and gentle, though his agenda to be the man with the highest political power in the modern world had already been cemented.

He'd let her cry and cry, and he'd even left her alone in his bedroom, where she'd slept the night. She'd found him on the couch the following morning when she'd made the Walk of Shame, her ballet flats pinched between her fingers to stay silent as she snuck past him.

A completely different Walk of Shame than she made three months later, when she'd once again slept in his bed, his very male, very warm body beside hers. He'd tracked her down after the first time to be sure she was okay. He'd called her after the second, and he'd met her after class the next day so they could sneak into his professor's unused office and make love again.

Maddy's chest rose and fell as if it were two breaths away from sticking to itself. She needed to keep the air moving, or her ribs wouldn't be able to keep her lungs inflated, and she'd suffocate and die.

She'd felt this suffocating, sobbing, sadness only three times in her life: Once, when she'd seen Julia with Alan at that diner. Once, when her third child had been stillborn. Once, when Chris had announced he wanted a divorce.

It's about power, Maddy. You understand.

Right, Maddy?

You understand?

She pulled herself from her memories and went down the steps after Julia. She did understand the depth of that pain and anguish, and she didn't wish it on anyone.

Not even the woman who'd caused it for Maddy the first time.

"Julia?" She went right to where the door met the jamb and leaned her ear in close. "Are you okay?" She rapped her knuckles against the ivory-painted door, noticing the faint pink and green and purple of a flower that had long-since been painted over.

"Go away," Julia said, her voice rough and torn at the same time.

"I will," Maddy said. "But not until you open the door and *show* me you're okay." She'd never truly been able to face her after the diner. After her initial Walk of Shame out of a fourth-floor apartment when hers sat on the seventh floor, Maddy had boxed up everything she owned while the rest of her roommates had been in class that day.

She'd lived out of a hotel for the rest of the semester, and then she and Chris were so madly in love, they'd moved in together before the wedding. Everything she'd done could be considered a scandal now, and it was no wonder, her name—and Chris's and their children's—had been dragged through every sticky substance known to man during his first run at governor.

"Julia," she threatened in her best Mom-Tone. She never got to use it anymore, and she found joy in hearing it still had plenty of bite.

The door flew inward, and Maddy nearly stumbled after it. Julia stood in front of her, tears staining that olive skin. "I'm fine. Go away."

Maddy took in the rumpled hair, seeing the other woman's fingers in it as she pulled against it, trying to work through a problem. She saw the younger woman who chewed on her eraser as she did complex math problems. She saw the paleness of the girl who'd once stayed up all night to study for her biology exam—and had then scored the highest in the class on it.

There was so much that had happened between all of the things Maddy remembered about Julia and this moment, and her heart pulsed out compassion and... She pulled back on the forgiveness.

"Where did you go?"

Julia pressed her lips together and shook her head.

Maddy's phone chimed out a *snicker-snicker-boop*, and she looked down at it gripped in her hand. "That's my dad. I have..." She looked over her shoulder, but of course no one stood there.

She faced Julia again. "He's not super-well, and he lives over in Wainscott. I'm going to spend the evening with him and make sure he eats more than boxed macaroni and cheese for dinner." She cleared her throat and held her head as high as she could possibly get it. "Would you like to come?"

The last thing she wanted was for this woman to come see her aging, ill father. Maddy simply felt like it was the right thing to do to offer.

"No, thank you," Julia whispered. "I'll be fine here."

"I can bring something home," Maddy offered. "I'll probably make something like a turkey sandwich or a salmon BLT."

Julia shook her head, dislodging a single tear, which she swiped away before it truly touched her cheek.

Maddy nodded, a silent acknowledgement that she

was only a phone call away, and then she turned and walked away. Behind her, instead of the door slamming and the old lighthouse filling with tension from rafter to roof, and floorboard to foundation, only the quiet *snick* of the door catching reached her ears.

"Here you go, Dad," she said an hour later, sliding a plate with a hot ham and cheese sandwich on it in front of her father. He rarely got up from the recliner or the bed these days, but he could get himself into the restroom and out onto the deck. She'd forbidden him from driving, and in order to enforce it, she'd taken his car keys the moment she'd arrived in Nantucket last week.

Exhaustion poured through her, and she let the sigh out in measures as she turned to get the bag of thick, rippled potato chips he liked so much. With that bag on the small coffee table beside him, and her own sandwich plated, she joined him in the living room.

Dad adored old game shows, and his house looked like it had been decorated with the prizes from one. Not a single thing matched, and he said that gave it part of its charm. Maddy disagreed most vehemently, but she didn't have to live here full-time. She didn't have to see the mounted swordfish above the front door and part of the front window every time she left to go to work.

Her father didn't leave to go to work either, though

he once had. Early too, and Maddy closed her eyes and said a quick prayer of thanksgiving that she was in a position to be able to take care of her father as he aged. He hadn't been young when he'd married and started having kids. His first wife had died in childbirth, along with the baby, and it had taken him a decade to heal and start again.

Maddy had a younger sister and a younger brother, the three of them coming along in only seven years. Brittany had a daughter still at home, her two oldest boys out of the house now. Tony worked at a prestigious law firm in Boston, and as the youngest and wanting to be finished with school before he started a family, his wife and kids were quite a bit younger than him.

Maddy adored her nieces and nephews, even if fifteen-year-old boys made the strangest noises with their mouths and twelve-year-old girls could break down into tears without any warning at all.

Maddy knew; she had a son and a daughter too, albeit grown now.

"Thank you, baby," Dad said, his voice rusty but warm. It had always made her smile, and she gave him the gesture now too. He ate, and not fifteen seconds after he'd polished off the bag of potato chips—she was going to have to put the next bag higher up in the cupboards, so he couldn't get to it without help—his soft snores started to fill the room.

Dad's still alive, she sent to Tony and Britt. *Doing*

well, it seems. He just ate and fell asleep. We really do turn back into babies when we get old.

She looked at her father with fondness, pure gratitude for him filling her. He'd let her come to Nantucket the moment she'd asked, and that was more than she could say for her mother.

Her parents had been divorced for twenty years now, and Pam had remarried a man who ran a commercial boating operation out of Cape Cod. They had a ginormous beach house there that Pam probably hadn't seen all of in five years, but she'd been "too busy" to have Maddy come when she'd needed to. Something about a garden party and then a clambake that simply couldn't be put off.

She certainly knew what it was like to think events and the public perception of them meant more than the people inside them, so she tried not to judge her mother too harshly.

Thank you for being there, Tony said, ever the diplomatic one who really wanted the three of them to get along and have a close adult relationship. He'd been the first to call Maddy after he'd heard of the divorce, and he'd offered her a room in his home.

She'd taken it too, though she hadn't told Britt. It would've hurt her sister's feelings, and Maddy told herself the little white fib she'd told Britt about where she was staying in those first few days didn't hurt anyone.

How was your first day at the inn? Britt asked. *Do you have any pictures? You should do that Before and After makeover thing for Elios, and you could win a bunch of money!*

Britt loved to enter contests and sweepstakes. It was almost like a full-time job for her, and she *had* won quite a few things over the years. Trips to Atlantic City and Galveston Island. Tickets to the New York Yankees game. A year's supply of steak once, from a steak-of-the-month club.

That made Maddy smile more than anything, because Britt didn't even eat meat. *Curtis does*, she'd said in her defense. *Judd and Forrest too.* Her husband and sons.

As far as Maddy knew, all of that steak had been thrown away eventually. Curtis had done that too, because Britt rarely cleaned out anything, her old packrat tendencies alive and well.

Maddy had to press against them herself, and she looked around her father's postage-stamp-sized house. This thing could use a good cleaning, but she wasn't going to do it today.

First day was good, she told her siblings. *We did a walk-through of the property, and we'll start to make some decisions, order supplies, and get companies booked tomorrow.*

She honestly had no idea if any of that would happen, but it sounded upbeat and positive. Right? She read over it again, and yep, it sounded like everything at The Lighthouse Inn was cotton-candied-narwhals. The plush kind.

She sent the text and swiped to open her social media.

Chris had taken everything in the divorce—except her alimony, her clothes, and her car. The kids—that precious boy and girl Maddy had mothered for decades now—had gone with him. Their friends had been forced to choose sides, and no one wanted to be associated with the downtrodden, made-out-to-be-crazy divorcée when they could be aligned with one of the most powerful men on the Eastern Seaboard.

She knew she shouldn't, but she couldn't help checking on Kyle and Chelsea every few days. Maybe every other day. Fine, every single day. She couldn't sleep without knowing if her children had posted that day and what it was about. In some small way, she could cheer them on from across the water and the miles between them, and she believed they'd feel her spirit and know she still loved them.

Pictures could be so misleading, and the human face was a marvel never before seen to mankind, because it could hide so much.

Chelsea hadn't posted, but she should've started a new job recently. Perhaps Maddy had checked too soon. She didn't think so, because Chelsea liked to post about things *after* they happened. She'd learned to do that in an online safety class in high school, so predators and kidnappers wouldn't know where she was in the moment, only where she'd been.

Kyle, the oldest, had posted, and Maddy's eyes couldn't absorb the few sentences fast enough. A picture accompanied them, and he and Bea, his girlfriend of about a year, looked like they'd just won one of her sister's huge, million-dollar sweepstakes.

Bea and I are THRILLED to announce that she's due with a baby at the end of January! We're getting married before then! Hit one of us if you want an invitation.

His bright blue eyes broadcast true happiness, but Maddy had seen herself in pictures where she looked this same way, and she'd actually been scared to death. Unsure. Nervous beyond belief.

Bea had large brown eyes, a smattering of freckles across her nose, and a smile as yawning as the Grand Canyon.

Maddy sat stunned, sure her son had not posted this on social media first. Not before he at least sent her a quick text with the same words.

Her heart started to turn itself inside out, flowing through her veins with her blood, where it would all leak to the floor by morning. The world around her cracked, the blaring sound of a cereal commercial the symphony to accompany it.

For the fourth time in her life, the suffocating, sob-filled, sadness crashed upon her. This was far worse than having a baby who'd never taken a breath. This was her oldest child, the one she'd devoted her whole life to raising and loving, choosing *not* to include her in the biggest event of either of their lives.

This was that child sawing her away from the joy of being a grandmother.

Her sobs shook the air, her awareness, and the very atmosphere above the house. She'd thought nothing else could possibly surprise her. She'd been wrong about that twice tonight, because her father slept through her anguish in a way Maddy couldn't comprehend.

CHAPTER NINE

Julia showered, spending a very long time in the hot spray before she got out. The Lighthouse Inn produced wonderful warm water, because she never came close to running out. After she'd dressed and stepped out of the garden room, she knew Maddy had gone. The building sat in silence, the kind the brownstone had been steeped in once Alan had packed his things and moved out.

She'd stayed for another month before this job here had started, and since he was the real estate expert, she'd left the sale of their home to him. Before, whenever she thought about losing the five-story, rich-with-history brownstone where they'd raised their children, tears would prick her eyes. Today, they didn't. Today, she simply wanted the silence to give way to some party music.

In the office upstairs, she turned on the Internet radio on the computer and cranked the volume. The silence disappeared and while Julia had once been a dancer in her youth, she simply used the beat of the pop song to take the steps up to the second level in sync with the rhythm.

She collected the photo album from the bedroom in the corner and took it down to the kitchen. It mocked her through her preparation of the banana bread, and once she had that in the oven, baking, she grabbed the plastic container of chocolate-covered raisins and faced the photos.

"All right," she said, pulling out the barstool and throwing back a couple of raisins. They could make any chore more palatable, and she had fond memories of receiving them from all three of her children each year for her birthday. As her three sons had matured, they'd branched out a little bit, and Julia got her favorite tea, the chocolate-covered raisins, and a new pair of fuzzy socks from someone every year.

Her life felt so simple in that moment, and she paused, wondering what Alan had hated so much that he couldn't stay. A sigh filled her soul and came out of her mouth, her mind recalling some words her eldest son, Will, had said to her as she was going through the divorce.

All of the kids had gone through it too, and now they had to choose where to spend their holidays. Mom's or Dad's? Would she even get every other year, especially once her boys found wives and started families of their own?

She shook the unpleasant thoughts from her head and opened the photo album, barely touching the cover or any of the pages.

It wasn't that he was unhappy, Mom, Will had said. "He's just bored."

Julia could admit to being boring. She and Alan had enjoyed very common beach vacations, trips to see her parents in Southampton and then his in Baltimore. Will played in the band; Spencer played rugby; Andrew did theater. Nothing out of the ordinary or too exciting.

The most dangerous place they'd made love was in the shower, and she couldn't remember the last time they'd done anything that wasn't just straight-up missionary-type sex.

Maybe that was what Will meant. Alan had been bored. Perhaps he'd wanted a woman who could please him more in the bedroom. Someone who wanted to jump on a plane and go anywhere it was flying. Someone who got crazy and served dessert before dinner.

She honestly didn't know. She only knew how to be herself, and he'd never complained about her strait-laced lifestyle before.

Without Maddy breathing down her neck, Julia took her time with the photos and papers in the album. She didn't recognize anyone in the years leading up to 1974, and she once again stalled at that picture in the bottom right-hand corner. Her fingers still itched to rip the protective covering back and take it out, but she flipped the page instead.

That same woman stood with another man, and then a trio of them. Her father didn't appear again. The woman exuded pure joy, and it was no wonder with her long, dark hair, plentiful curves, and youthful smile. Each and every one of the men in these pictures was clearly in love with her, and Julia was once again shocked at how well cameras could see things the human eye couldn't.

There weren't pictures every year, but they at least went sequentially. She pulled in a breath on 1977, because there she sat on her mother's hip, her chubby cheeks pressing against her three-year-old smile.

Her father stood next to her mom and her, that same glorious smile on his mustached face as from three years previous.

"So she could've just been a former girlfriend," she told herself. She glanced at the timer on the banana bread and then toward the door that led out of the kitchen. When Maddy didn't walk through it and demand she stop what she was about to do, Julia reached for the plastic covering and peeled it back.

She took out the picture of her with her mom and dad. Annie was only three years younger than her, and she'd have been born already when this picture was taken. "Most likely," Julia said, squinting as if that would help her see off the edges of the photograph to see who'd held Annie for her parents as they took this picture.

The previous caretakers of The Lighthouse Inn had been Phil and Margo Michaels, and Julia had half-expected to get some sort of letter or instructions from them. Of course, Vivian and the Nantucket Historical Society had provided those handbooks of procedures that Julia had barely looked at, so the Michaels didn't need to leave anything.

With the picture free, she set it on the counter above the album. She flipped back and peeled out the pictures of that woman—Tessa Simmons and Janey Forsythe's mother—and then she completed the job she'd started in the bedroom earlier that day.

Some of the color on two other photographs came off with the plastic protector, and Julia cursed under her breath. Maddy had been right; she'd ruined some of the other pictures.

The one of her dad and the mystery woman seemed glued in, and Julia worked her fingernail around the edge of it over and over before it popped free.

She instantly flipped the picture over to see if anyone had written on it.

Ryan Harper stared back at her. *Lydia Lyons*.

She looked at the backs of all the pictures with Lydia. She was listed in each one, along with Gregory Clarke, Dale Harton, and Rick Fry. The summer of 1974 sure had been busy for Lydia. It was entirely possible that she was simply friends with all of these guys. The picture of the four of them, and then the single of her and Gregory Clarke seemed to have been taken on the same day.

The one of Lydia and her dad had been taken a different day. Lydia wore her hair up, as well as a different swimming suit. The sun shone from a different place in the sky too.

Tessa said her mother owned that cottage and they came to Nantucket all the time. Julia closed her eyes and tried to find any memories with either of the dark-haired women she'd met that day. She couldn't. Their family beach vacations had been carefree and filled with sailing, sun, sand, and seafood.

Her father had worked from time to time when they'd come to the island, and her mother had taken Julia and her siblings to the beach alone. Once, he'd had to return to Southampton to take care of a client, and Julia's mother had kept the kids for the week alone.

She couldn't help the track her mind went down, because Tessa Simmons had said that Janey was her father's daughter. That made her Julia's half-sister. They shared the same father.

She gathered up the pictures and took them into the office. The Internet was an amazing thing, and she started searching for the names of the three men. Gregory Clarke had passed away years ago, if the obituary in the Nantucket Point Times had reported on the same Gregory that smiled from the picture.

"He's survived by his wife, Lydia," Julia read. "And daughters, Janey Forsythe and Tessa Simmons. Definitely the same guy."

Dale Harton was a doctor in Maryland, retired now, of course. He and his wife, Joan, had really made a name for themselves in their community, and an article of her illness had been published recently.

It wasn't hard to see a connection between Dale and Gregory. Both doctors, both graduates of the same college. Both well-off, with plenty of Eastern Seaboard upbringing. They'd probably come to Nantucket as boys too. By all accounts, with their prestige and intelligence, her father would've fit right in with them, though he was a lawyer and not a heart surgeon.

Her mother and father had plenty of friends, and they always had. Dale and Gregory weren't two of them.

She glanced down at the picture and the third name there. "Rick Fry." Her fingers clickety-clacked over the keyboard, and she slapped the enter key.

Grim-faced mugshots came up, along with headline after headline with words like *fraud*, *wanted for questioning*, and *police have seized all boats at the repair shop where Fry was last said to be working*.

She looked from the images online to the decades-old photo. It was definitely the same man smiling on the beach without a care in the world as the man who'd been taken in for questioning. Julia couldn't tell which one had been taken first, and she checked the dates on the headlines.

Late 1974 through 76, so a few years of varying degrees of trouble with the police, though they never had seen him again after he'd run in late 1974.

One headline read, "Fry disappears without a trace / Possible new identity assumed." The article contained a half-dozen pictures, all of them drawings or renditions of what he might look like. One with glasses. One with a beard and mustache. One with sunglasses and a hat.

Rick Fry was still wanted for crossing international lines with drugs onboard a vessel, connections to the Mexican drug cartel, and for questioning involving the disappearance of a young girl named Louisa Fry.

Julia sucked in a breath. "His sister."

Her mind whirred and whistled like a kettle coming to a boil. She closed the browser windows and stacked the few photos on top of one another. The pop music still blasted through the inn, and that was the only thing keeping her from fleeing this place and never coming back.

Rick Fry had been here, at this inn, possibly while he was wanted by police. Had he hidden out here? Where had he gone? Was he still on Nantucket somewhere?

She looked down at the pictures, the top one of Lydia and her father. She'd run out on Tessa earlier today, and she shouldn't have. She should've stayed to ask a few more questions. Now that she had a few more answers and some of the blanks filled in, she thought perhaps she'd be brave enough to cross the dunes to Seagull Lane and talk to the women in the blue cottage again.

CHAPTER TEN

Janey walked past yet another delivery van parked in front of The Lighthouse Inn. They'd been getting things for the past week, and a giddiness bubbled inside her she hadn't anticipated.

She eyed the double-wide glass doors as she passed them, her destination not inside the inn today. She'd vowed not to go inside and talk to Julia Harper again. She'd told no one about the incident, and she'd started at Sean's law firm this past week. She barely had time to eat, sleep, and get to work, let alone stew about the half-sister that had come to Nantucket Point and now lived and worked only a football-field-distance from the cottage.

Tessa had been branching out too, having tea with a woman who lived in Nantucket full-time on the next street over. Janey had barely missed meeting her, but she was glad Tessa was starting to make a real life here.

After crossing the sand to the little blue house, she arrived back on asphalt just as someone turned the corner down at the end of the street. The road went straight for about another half-mile, little fingers of lanes branching off from it, and cottages sat on both sides of those fingers.

Janey grinned when she recognized Helen Ivy's gait, and instead of continuing straight and going up the front steps to the cottage, she pivoted and started down the lane. She lifted her hand and called, "Hey, Helen."

The older woman raised her head, her smile coming a moment later. "Afternoon," she called. The two of them reached one another, and Janey embraced the older woman.

"Right on time, I see," she said.

"Nothing keeping me," Helen said, her eyes seriously the brightest blue Janey had ever seen. "Besides, Tessa said she was picking up the carrot cake bars from the bakery. I can't be late for those."

Janey laughed lightly, glad she'd made it through her first week at a new job. "No, you can't."

"Is Sean joining us again?"

Janey started back toward the cottage, basking in the September sun and recognizing the crisp quality of the air despite it. "Not today," she said. "He went to see his sister this weekend, actually, and the office is closed today. That's why I'm able to sneak over here for an afternoon carrot cake bar."

Tessa better have something to drink too, but Janey

kept that to herself. Helen acknowledged that Janey had spoken, and they finished the walk back in silence.

When she reached the door and opened it, she called, "Tess," into the cottage.

"On the deck," she said, her voice coming in from the window to Janey's right. She stalled and Helen bumped into her from behind.

"Oops," Janey said. "She's outside." They turned around and went back the way they'd come, moving along the front of the house and then making a left to wrap around the porch with the deck. Tessa sat down at the end of it, a square table laden with a bakery box, an assortment of soda pop cans, and a single bottle of red wine.

Janey sighed at the sight of it, though she wasn't a huge drinker. Something had been hanging over her ever since she'd gone crazy and stepped inside The Lighthouse Inn almost two weeks ago now. She leaned down to hug her sister before sinking into the chair next to her. On the other side of the table, Helen took the closest chair, already reaching for a carrot cake bar.

"Are these the raisin ones or the non-raisin ones?"

"Janey doesn't like raisins," Tessa said, as if that answered the question.

Janey went for the wine first, offering it to the others, who both declined. She poured herself a small glass of it, vowing to only have the one. Then she too reached for a non-raisin carrot cake bar.

Helen had already moaned her way through one, and

she popped the last bite into her mouth with, "I love these so much."

"They are delicious," Tessa said, facing into the wind and letting it blow her hair back off her face.

Janey adored afternoons like this, where the world seemed unfettered and at peace. She closed her eyes and let the power of the universe flow through her. When she opened her eyes again, she saw blue sky, teal water, and golden sand. This was the stuff dreams were made of, that was for sure.

A few minutes passed, or maybe ten, Janey wasn't sure. She did know the wine had started to soften her, and her taste buds were quite happy with the two bars she'd eaten, when the doorbell rang from inside the house.

"We're on the deck," Tessa called, getting to her feet. Janey let her, because she technically lived here and Janey did not. She looked in that direction, not sure who would come calling at the blue cottage. Helen did too, and they all saw the tall brunette as she rounded the corner. She paused.

The spinning of the world paused for Janey.

The breath paused in her lungs.

"Come on," Tessa said somewhere outside all the pausing. She stepped over Janey's legs and toward Julia Harper. "We won't bite."

We won't? Janey wondered, and the Earth pitched forward again, hurling her with it. She jumped to her feet and had to reach out and grab onto the railing in front of her as everything spun too much now.

"Come meet everyone," Tessa said from further down the deck. She turned back to Helen and Janey, a bright smile on her face. Side-by-side, Tessa and Julia looked so much alike it was freaky.

They didn't share any of the same blood, and perhaps the wine had muddled Janey's mind more than usual. She looked at the glass she'd poured, and a swallow remained, so she hadn't even drunk that much.

She reached for the glass now and threw back the last bit as if it were a shot. As she replaced the glass on the table, Tessa said, "This is Helen Ivy. She lives on the same street as the bakery."

Her eyes flew to Janey's. Time slowed, and Janey watched every minute movement in Tessa's neck as she swallowed.

"This is my sister, Janey Forsythe." Tessa had her hand on Julia's lower back, and it sure seemed like she was pushing Julia toward them. "Janey, Helen, this is Julia Harper. She's one-half of the new caretakers at The Lighthouse Inn."

Helen didn't get to her feet, but she was old, so she had a valid reason. She did extend her hand and say, "So nice to meet you. I've loved that inn over the years."

"Nice to meet you too," Julia said, her eyes leaving Janey's for only a moment to look at Helen.

Thunder struck Janey in the heart. Julia knew who she

was. Her pulse skipped through her body, leaving holes where it should've landed but didn't.

"Janey," Tessa said, her voice that placating, motherly type that Janey loathed. "I invited her this afternoon, because she said she has something to show us."

In that moment, Janey saw the manilla folder in Julia's hand. Fear gripped her lungs and squeezed the air out of them, making her light-headed and breathless. She couldn't speak with lungs like that, and she collapsed back into her chair.

Tessa took that as some sort of good sign, and she pulled the last chair into a closed semi-circle and retook her seat as Julia sat down. "Pull the table out, Janey," Tessa said, and Janey, in her stupor, did it.

Helen removed the drinks and carrot cake bars, and Julia cleared her throat as she set the folder on the now-available table. "I found these pictures in an album in the inn."

Janey looked at Tessa. "More pictures?"

"I haven't seen them yet," Tessa said, keen interest in her voice and her gaze as she looked past Janey to the table.

Julia took out four square pictures, what looked like old Polaroid shots. "This is your mother," she said, pointing to the young woman in her twenties that was definitely Lydia Clarke. "Lydia Lyons."

Janey hadn't heard her mother's maiden name used in a long time, and she blinked.

"Oh, look at her," Tessa said, reaching for the pictures. "Can I touch them?"

"I put them in an acid-free plastic," Julia said. "You can pick them up."

Tessa picked up the one with Mom and Daddy—at least the man Janey had known as her father. "It's them, Janey. Look."

I see it, she wanted to scream. No sound came out.

Tessa didn't tilt the picture toward her anyway. She looked at the one with Mom and three men, one of them Daddy—Gregory Clarke. The other man was Dale Harton; Janey recognized him as she'd seen younger pictures of him recently, as well as the man in-person too.

The last man in the picture of all four of them was Riggs Friedman. Janey's body reacted to the sight of him, and as a younger man in his twenties, he was quite good-looking. All three of them were, and while Janey didn't like thinking of her mother sleeping with all of them, she knew that had happened.

"This is my father," Julia said. "Ryan Harper."

Janey met her eye, and this time, she was the one who couldn't look away. "I'm sorry," she said for some reason. The words had just come out. She felt Helen's gaze on her too, and then she looked back at the pictures.

"It's not your fault," Julia said, her voice so quiet it nearly got whipped away in the wind. "Before I knew much, I looked up the names on the backs of the pictures." She started to pull something else out of the folder.

Helen picked up the picture of Mom with her three summer boyfriends. "I remember these people," she said. "Of course I knew your mother and father." She flipped the picture over. "Yes, Dale, of course. He was never far from Greg."

Janey managed to look away from Julia and at Helen. She wore a fond smile that suddenly turned dark. "Oh. Rick Fry. Of course."

"Wait," Janey said at the same time Tessa asked, "Who?"

"Rick Fry." Helen held up the picture as if they were having trouble seeing it.

"That's not Rick Fry," Tessa said. "That's Riggs Friedman."

Helen frowned and shook her head. "It says Rick Fry right on the back of it." Pure confusion rode in those sapphire eyes now. "Riggs Friedman? He lived next door."

"They're the same person," Janey said.

"No," Helen said as she peered closer at the picture. "I don't think so."

Janey wanted to rip it from her hand to examine it herself, but she refrained.

Julia said, "They could be, I suppose. Rick Fry has been wanted by Maryland police for decades."

"What?" Tessa and Janey said at the same time.

Julia smoothed a couple of pieces of paper on the table, over the remaining pictures. "I looked up the names. I learned a little about your dad and Dale. There wasn't much. Where they went to school, the obituaries of your parents." She ducked her head and ground her voice through her throat again. "But Rick Fry had a ton of articles written about him."

Helen clucked her tongue. "Oh, yes, I remember that," she said. "Bad business that was. His family came here all the time, and then one day, he abandoned his boat shop on the mainland. The police thought he'd had something to do with his younger sister's disappearance." She picked up the printouts Julia had brought. "He seemed like such a nice man. I didn't believe the articles. But he never came back to the Point."

"They've still never found him," Julia said.

"I met little Louisa the summer before she disappeared." Helen sounded so dejected now. "I don't think they ever found her either." She looked at Julia, who shook her head.

Janey's was spinning. Spinning around so many things at once. Spinning around the fact that Riggs Friedman had disappeared from right here at this cottage a little over a month ago...and still hadn't been found.

She and Tessa had managed to detain Bobbie until the police arrived, but Riggs had run. They hadn't found him yet. If he was Rick Fry—and in Janey's opinion, there was no *if* about that—he knew how to hide in plain sight. He could still be on the Point, though numerous people from the Sheriff of Nantucket to Sean had assured her over and over that he wasn't. No one would be that stupid.

She picked up the picture of Mom with the men that Helen had put down and peered at it. She had some experience with old photos of Riggs too, and this was definitely the same man. She flipped over the picture and saw the old-fashioned, loopy handwriting.

Rick Fry.

Tessa had gotten hold of the articles, and she said, "I can't believe this."

"It sounded to me, from what I read," Julia said. "That they're not really sure if he has anything to do with anything. They only issued a warrant for his arrest *after* he fled, for example."

"Him running away speaks a little bit about guilt," Janey said, though she knew it didn't always mean a person was guilty. Fear drove people to do a lot of strange things.

"This says fraud, drug charges, and the possibility of him being involved in the disappearance of his sister." Tessa thrust the papers toward Janey, but she didn't want them. She took them anyway and put them back on the table.

"What happened to his sister?" Janey asked, looking at Helen to tell the story. Julia didn't seem to have any more papers in her folder anyway.

"Her parents said over and over that Rick didn't have anything to do with it," Helen said. "They claim she was taken from the beach while they were here on holiday." She glanced at Julia. "At The Lighthouse Inn."

Julia nodded. "That's what they say."

"It's not true?" Tessa asked.

"I don't know," Julia said. "There's a record of their stay at the inn, yes, during the dates they say they were here. But they didn't check out early. No report was filed with any Police or Sheriff's Department here until they'd been home in New Jersey for two days. Once they did that, then the police started asking questions. We have them checking-in to the inn through the logbook that sits on the front counter and everything."

"The police?" Tessa asked. "They checked in through the logbook?"

"Yes," Julia said.

"There were a lot of police here after the story came out that Louisa had disappeared," Helen said. "I do remember that. I think that's when they went to talk to Rick, and he ran away."

"You haven't seen him since?" Tessa asked.

Janey didn't understand how Helen wouldn't have recognized Riggs as Rick Fry. She'd known it was him right away, and he'd only left Nantucket for several months before returning with Bobbie as his wife. They'd lived less than a half-mile from Helen for decades. How could she *not* know?

"No," Helen said, looking from Janey to Tessa. "No one's seen him or Louisa ever again."

A sob worked its way through Janey and burst out of her mouth. "My goodness, Tessa, they had you. You're so lucky and blessed to have gotten away from them." She jumped to her feet and practically knocked the table down. "Excuse me."

"Janey," Helen said, but Janey flew past her, crashing toward the chairs where she and Julia sat. She had to get out of here. Now.

Julia stood up and blocked her way. "Don't run away," she said. "I did that last week, and it did no good. Stay. It's okay. You're safe here."

Janey glared at her, fire licking over the panic now and turning it all into dangerous fury.

"Janey," Tessa said, her voice thick and tinny at the same time. "She's right. We need you to stay and help us figure out what to do."

"What to do?" Janey rounded on her sister. "We need to call the cops, that's what we need to do." She spied the bottle of wine. She'd call the police—heck, she knew a lot of them by their first name now—and then she'd drink the rest of the wine. That was what she was going to do.

CHAPTER ELEVEN

Julia watched Janey pour another glass of wine, her hand shaking this time. No one said anything, but Tessa stacked up the pictures, put them with the printouts, and tucked them all into the folder Julia had brought. She left it on the table in the middle of the four women and shot a glance at Helen Ivy.

Julia hadn't known her before this afternoon, but she didn't mind the older woman's presence. She wore kindness in the deep wrinkles around her eyes, which shone with one of the brightest lights of wisdom Julia had ever seen. Helen reminded her of her mother, and a stab of missing ran through her.

She hadn't called her parents after finding the pictures, almost a week ago now. She didn't know which words to say to her dad, and that left nothing for her to say to her mother. Had she known? If she did, Julia didn't want to bring up possibly painful memories. If she didn't... Julia did *not* want to be the one to tell her about her young husband's infidelity while she'd been three months away from delivering their first child.

Her parents were still married. They still lived in the sprawling home in Southampton; her mother still hosted luncheons for the library board, attended their literature tea parties—complete with parasol and Regency ballgown —and influenced the naming of the beaches with her bank account.

Julia's divorce had been a personal blow to Sandi Harper, who hadn't understood what Julia had done wrong. Julia had told her to "join the club," last time they'd spoken about Alan, and her mother had literally said, "You must've done something, Julia. A man doesn't just divorce his wife for no reason."

They hadn't spoken much since, because Julia didn't need to be reminded of all of her shortcomings. She couldn't stand playing the what-if game or spinning the maybe-I-did-this-that-one-time wheel of roulette. She felt bad enough about the situation which she found herself in, and going back over all of the things she'd said or done in the past two decades didn't help anything.

Janey took a huge swig of her wine and set the glass right on top of the folder. "Who's going to go first?" She looked at her sister, though Julia supposed she had the same amount of common blood flowing through her veins as Tessa did.

"Should we talk about my dad? Or Riggs?" She turned her sharp-as-fishhook eyes on Julia then. "We just found out about Ryan Harper, what? Tess? Six weeks ago?"

"Sounds about right," Tessa said, her voice filled with more gravel now than before.

Julia found that comforting for some reason. She couldn't stand the thought of these women being out there her whole life, knowing things she didn't know about her own father. She didn't know what to say, so she simply nodded.

"I don't want to contact him or anything," Janey said. "I don't know if Lydia ever did, and if she didn't, she had reasons."

Julia cleared her throat. "She never mentioned it while she was alive?"

"Never," Tessa said. "She didn't even mention it after she'd died. She gave us all these clues we had to riddle through."

"It *was* pretty ridiculous," Janey said, reaching up to touch a lovely, silver starfish necklace at her collarbone. Julia remembered her wearing it when she'd stopped by The Lighthouse Inn before Labor Day. She hadn't commented on it then, and something told her not to now either.

"I also want the record to show that I didn't know who you were when I stopped by the inn a few weeks ago."

"It was like ten days, Janey," Tessa said quietly.

"Whenever," Janey said, throwing her a dark look. "I

didn't know who'd they'd hired. I love the inn, and I saw people moving in, and we live so close by..." She let her voice trail off into nothing, and Julia just nodded.

Something about Tessa and Janey seemed so authentic, and she didn't think they'd lie to her. Of course, she'd thought everything in her marriage had been fine, so she wasn't sure what to believe and what she couldn't.

"I live nearby," Tessa said, giving Janey a smile she did not return. "You live way down in Wainscott."

"Yes, and I'm thinking of trying to find something downtown," Janey quipped. "The commute to the law office isn't that fun when you don't have a car."

"How has the first week been, dear?" Helen asked.

"Good," Janey said, her voice pitching up in a way that indicated it hadn't been made of only good. Julia supposed few things in life were. "Sorry, Helen." She reached over and took the older woman's hand in hers. "I don't want to talk about work right now."

She took another long drink of wine and surveyed the group. "Should I call the police?"

"I think if any of us should," Julia said. "It should be you." She glanced at Tessa. "Or Tessa. You two have the most experience with Rick...or Riggs. Whoever he is."

The two sisters looked at one another, and Julia felt like her time on this porch was just beginning, but also ending. "I should get back to the inn," she said. "Maddy and I were just taking a quick break." She got to her feet, the words she'd practiced over the past several days catching in her throat. They made her heart reverberate through her body like it was an empty plastic bin and someone had banged on it. Over and over, they pounded it, sending shockwaves through the whole of her being.

"I'd like to... Maybe we could go to lunch one day. Or dinner. We usually work through lunch." A smile moved across her face, and she felt it disappear as soon as it had arrived.

"I'm always up for dinner," Helen said.

"As am I," Tessa said.

Janey said nothing as she drained the last of her wine glass. "Why not?" she asked, her voice made of sarcasm. "We can talk about Dear Old Dad."

"Janey." Tessa shot her sister a look.

"What? You wouldn't let me leave. You knew she knew we were related, and you didn't tell me. You lured me here with wine and carrot cake bars after a long week at my new job, and I'm supposed to be like, yay! Let's go get lunch with my half-sister I didn't know about until a month ago?"

She set her glass down, and Julia thought it probably should've shattered for how hard she gripped it. As she got to her feet again, her elegant caftan billowing around her, she said, "I'm leaving. I've got to eat something to go with this wine, and I saw The Holiday House has a garlic shrimp pop-up tonight."

"I'll come with you," Helen said, pressing both palms

against the arms of her chair to get to her feet. "I love Shrimp and Olive's."

"We'll all go," Tessa said, looking to Julia for confirmation. While garlic shrimp sounded better than a spaghetti and meatball microwavable meal—what Julia had been planning to eat that evening—she shook her head.

"Sorry," she said. "I can't. Maddy and I are painting the dining room right now, and it's huge. I really need to get back to her." She spoke Maddy's name as if they were the best of friends. The past week of working with her hadn't been terrible. She had a great eye for design and color, and Julia hadn't argued about which paint to buy. They'd ordered dozens of items, from curtains to towels to paintbrushes, and they'd been bringing in packages daily for a few days now. Sometimes more than once per day.

"Next time," Helen said, linking her arm through Janey's. "I want to hear why you live in Wainscott, dear. I seem to remember you telling me the first time we dined that you couldn't afford anything on Nantucket."

Julia let them go by her, her eyes trained on Janey, who didn't even look at her. She met Tessa's eyes, and she said, "I'm sorry. I should've told her more, but I didn't think she'd come."

"It's okay," Julia said. "She reminds me of Annie a little bit. She's so headstrong, and so sure of herself."

Tessa nodded and picked up the wine glass and then the bottle. "Thanks for bringing this stuff. It's..." She sighed and looked out toward the beach and waves and wind. "I don't know what it is. Too crazy to believe."

"I'll leave it with you," Julia said. "You might need it for the police."

"They'll want to talk to you." Tessa brought her attention in from the Sound.

"You know where to find me." Julia put her bravest smile on her face, nodded, and turned to leave the blue cottage's porch. Her mind tumbled like the wind as she made the short walk across the sand to The Lighthouse Inn, and the pungent scent of wet paint met her nose the moment she opened the door.

She wanted to do an about-face and walk right back outside. Instead, she continued toward the office, calling, "I'm back."

The other woman didn't answer, and Julia came to a screeching halt when she saw the golden blonde standing at the window, her phone at her ear. She turned toward Julia, who held up both palms as if to say, *Sorry, I didn't know you were on the phone.*

"I understand that," Maddy said, clear unrest in both her expression and her tone. After a few more beats of silence on her end, she added, "You're my son, Kyle. I want to be there." She sank into the desk chair, a sigh leaking from her mouth that felt...painful more than frustrated. "Think about it, please," she said in almost a childlike voice. "I will do whatever you want, and I am content to sneak in the back and go up the stairs to the balcony. No one will even know I'm there."

She lifted her head and met Julia's eyes again. Hers went from regret-filled to fire-filled, as if she hadn't truly realized that it was Julia who'd entered the inn. Maddy never showed emotion to the wrong person, and Julia watched her box it up and lock it down tight.

"Let me know," she said in the same brisk tone she'd used with the pillow supplier only yesterday. The call ended, and she set her cell phone on the edge of the desk. "Sorry, that was my son."

"Kyle," Julia said, her body vibrating like that plastic bin again. "I heard." She took the remaining few steps to the chairs facing the big desk and sat down. "What's happening with him that you want to attend?"

Maddy wore resentment in her eyes now, covered only thinly by pure strength. She could only hold it for a few seconds before she cracked. Her shoulders slumped. That sigh came out of her lungs again. She ran both hands through her hair, gathering it into a high ponytail before letting it all drop again.

"He's getting married, and his girlfriend is pregnant."

CHAPTER TWELVE

Maddy wanted to recall the words as they flowed from her mouth. When she said, "I found out on social media," she felt like she'd kicked herself in the stomach. Every time she thought of Kyle's announcement, she felt winded and weak. She couldn't believe she sat across from the woman who'd once stolen everything important to Maddy and flaunted it in her face, telling her any of this.

Julia looked truly horrified. Her mouth moved a few times before she said, "I'm so sorry, Maddy."

Maddy opened her mouth to say something—what, she didn't know. *Thank you* maybe. Or *It's fine,* though it wasn't fine. Nothing about her son getting married and becoming a father without her in attendance was fine.

"I think that's the first time you've said my name," Maddy said, glancing away from Julia.

"I—probably," Julia said.

"I only said yours when I was worried about you." Maddy swiveled in her chair and looked out the window. The view was just a strip of sand and then a parking lot, but it was better than inhaling paint fumes as she tried to turn an ugly dining room into one with personality and charm.

She realized in that moment that she'd been trying to do that with herself for decades. Turn herself into something she wasn't. A politician's wife. The perfect woman, who had perfect clothes, hair, nails, and teeth at all times. Along with this version of perfect came the perfect children, and of course, hers were no exception.

Never mind that Kyle hadn't gone to college. Rather, he had, but he'd dropped out to help his father run for governor. Chelsea, her nineteen-year-old daughter had wanted a year after high school to "find herself," and when she'd returned from her backpacking trip to Chile, she'd promptly moved in with Chris to be on his public relations team. No mention of schooling, training, or anything had happened.

At least that you know of, the thought like poison in her mind. There was so much she didn't know that Maddy's eyes started to throb. "I'm sorry," she said. "Everyone has problems. Let's get back to work."

"I found out that my dad had an affair with that woman in the picture," Julia blurted out. Their eyes met, and Julia now held caged fear in hers. Maddy knew what that kind of fear felt like, and it wasn't pretty. "My mom was nearly due with me, and that other woman was almost three months pregnant with my half-sister. Not only that, she lives right here on the island. In that blue cottage at the end of the very first street. You can see it from the shipwreck room."

Maddy blinked, trying to catch up to the conversation. Shipwreck room? They hadn't officially named the rooms yet, though they had spent almost all of their time last week ordering supplies, paint colors, and linens. The final touches of décor would go in last.

All of the tightness in Julia's shoulders melted out of her, and she sank further into the chair. "So yes, we all have problems. But we don't have to go through them alone."

Maddy's first inclination was to buck against any idea of working together with Julia. Truly working together. She could hang some curtains and paint some walls. She didn't want to discuss her broken marriage, her disjointed relationships with her children, or how devastated she'd be if her father passed away.

"I'm sorry," she managed to say, because she had spent years in fancy halls and attending fundraising dinners with the rich and important.

Julia reached up and brushed at her eyes. "You met her too. She came in the very first day we were here. Janey Forsythe."

"Oh." Maddy didn't know what else to say. She did

remember the brunette with blue in her hair who'd come in. She'd been all smiles and excited to see The Lighthouse Inn open again.

The two women sat there and looked at one another, and moment by moment, a tether grew between them. Turned out, sometimes words weren't needed to build a bond, and simply existing in tough times or emotional turmoil spoke loud enough for any voices that couldn't quite work.

Maddy stepped from the dock to the deck of the boat, the water rolling beneath her actually welcome. She smiled as she reached for the lifejacket and put it over her head. "It's the perfect weekend to go out," she said to Julia, who stood along the rail of the yacht.

The inn owned the boat, and Maddy had been tending to it all week. She'd cleaned out the old crates of supplies, torn down the curtains that looked like they'd originated in the seventies, and spent a good half-day in the kitchen, scrubbing it clean.

She'd rented a power-washer, and the strength with which the grime had come off the deck and sides of the boat had infused right into her. She'd had no idea that using something as simple as a power-washer would make her feel so alive. So worthwhile. So accomplished, like she'd done something amazing by holding that hose and aiming it at the orange stains and watching them disappear.

"The wind is blowing," Julia said, her face turned into it. She hadn't said anything else about her father or Janey Forsythe, and Maddy had decided to let her bring it up. If she wanted to talk, they had plenty of opportunities for that. Maddy hadn't said anything more about Kyle and Bea either, and she'd returned to her social media, found her son's post, and filled out the form to get an announcement at least.

She'd spoken to him, and he'd sounded the tiniest bit sympathetic. Chelsea had been with him, because Maddy had heard her voice in the background. *Let her come.*

Maddy had been clinging to those three words for the past five days. Those three words, and the rush of the power-washer.

"It'll be okay," she said to Julia. "I'll get us out in the Sound, and we can talk about possible boat tours to offer through the inn." Part of the requirement to run The Lighthouse Inn was to have an operational boat captain's license. Maddy's had expired, but she'd taken the needed courses and tests to get it active again, and being out at sea had boosted her confidence in a way she hadn't anticipated.

She'd always loved the water, and as she walked to the front of the boat to take the cooler down to the kitchen, she smiled at the gentle waves lapping against the vessel. Then she went up to the captain's control panel and pressed the button to get the boat started. It purred as it came to life, and Maddy smiled.

"Ready?" she called over her shoulder to Julia. "There's room up here, out of the wind." She stood above the deck, the long, sleek nose of the yacht pointing the way in front of her. The sky above them held the purest form of blue, and the waves and ocean beyond Nantucket Sound called to Maddy in a way that pulled hard on her heart-strings.

"Coming." Julia joined her in the control room, sighing as she sat in the chair on Maddy's right. She carried the clipboard today, and while it had been hard for Maddy to relinquish control of it to her, she'd done it. She could do new things, as she'd been learning since officially starting at The Lighthouse Inn two weeks ago.

"All right," Maddy said, pressing forward on the controls. The boat started to ease away from the dock, and joy filled Maddy from top to bottom. "Here we go."

Julia looked at her, and while Maddy's first instinct was to erase the smile from her face, she couldn't. "You always did love boats."

"I have," Maddy admitted.

"Did you and Chris do a lot of sailing?"

Maddy's smile did hitch then, though it didn't fall completely. "Not really," she said. "Chris is more of a land-man." She ground her emotion out in her throat and threw Julia a glance. "What about you and Alan? I remember he used to like sailing."

"He did," she said. "I'm the one who gets seasick." She looked out the wide window again. "He'd go out from time to time with Jason."

His brother. Maddy nodded, her throat narrowing to the width of a straw. Irritation filled her, because it had been so long since Julia and Alan had started their relationship, which had gone on to marriage.

Perhaps it was time to let it all go. Truly let it all go.

"You two seemed so happy," Maddy said. "I'm sorry it didn't work out."

Julia remained silent so long that Maddy glanced over to her again. She nodded and reached up and swiped at her eyes quickly. "Me too."

The scar on Maddy's heart that had seemed so thick once, that had expanded to other parts of her body—her stomach, which tightened whenever she thought of her college days, her mind, whenever she thought of what life might've been like with Alan instead of Chris, her lungs, which seemed plagued by the inability to breathe—thinned. It stretched and tore, and then it was simply gone.

She took them away from the island and around toward the operational lighthouse on the true Point of Nantucket, the wide waters expanding in front of her. "We can go all the way to Five Island Cove on this boat," she said. "Just like the Nantucket Clipper."

"The Clipper is fast," Julia said. "Far faster than this boat."

"Oh, definitely," Maddy said, reaching to open the vent in her side of the window. In her opinion, the sea air should be breathed into one's soul, where they could access it later should they need to. Right now, she needed all the oxygen and clarity she could get. "But this boat holds enough fuel to get there. We'd have to refuel before returning, but that's easy in Five Island Cove."

"Are you thinking you want to have day excursions to Five Island Cove? They have nice golf courses there."

"It's twelve miles," Maddy said. "It would take an hour, minimum, to get there. I suppose we could, but that would be the only thing we could do with the boat that day."

"They have festivals and things," Julia said, holding up her phone. "A hot air balloon thing. A big food and wine festival in the summertime."

"Nantucket has all of that too," Maddy said. "I don't know if we need to be taking people away from the Point. It's magical enough as it is."

"I agree," Julia said. "We could do easy rides around the island."

"Yes, a full-island circle," Maddy said, steering the boat to do that. "Let's time that. We left, say five minutes ago." If it was her, she'd use her phone to time it, but Julia just nodded and wrote something on the clipboard.

"Do you think both of us should lead the tours?"

"I don't think so," Maddy said. "That would take us

both from the inn, and surely there will be work there to do once guests arrive."

"I'm the one with the marine biology degree," Julia said. "We could do little tours of the animals that live in the sea surrounding Nantucket, but you won't know that stuff."

"Maybe those could be land tours," Maddy suggested. "You could take them to the tide pools down by the lighthouse. Or over to the south side of the island when the whales go by. That kind of thing."

"I'm noting it," Julia said, and Maddy noted that she hadn't said "good idea" or anything of the sort. She rarely did, and Maddy knew she hadn't really been giving Julia that kind of feedback either.

"You could teach me," she said next, her voice taking on a higher pitch. "About the things I could tell people as we go around the island."

"I think we could do a Nantucket History Boat Tour," Julia said. "You'd point out specific landmarks from the boat that people can see and talk about Nantucket. It'd be an hour or something."

"I like that idea," Maddy said, and she looked at Julia to see how she'd react to more obviously-stated praise. A smile touched her mouth as she wrote. "And a Nantucket Marine Life Tour. Same idea, but talking about the marine life they might find on or around the island."

"Yes," Julia said. "That would be seasonal, I would

think. You're not always going to see the same animals here."

"Harbor seals and gray seals are here year-round," Maddy said. She'd been to Nantucket enough to know that.

"There are two more species that come too," Julia said. "The hooded seals and the harp seals will be here in the winter and spring."

"I'm not sure about boat tours in the winter," Maddy said. The water didn't freeze or anything, but it certainly wasn't warm. People would need coats and hats for sure, as water sprayed off the front of the boat. In the summer, that was fine and dandy, but winter seawater would be like a punch in the face.

She'd just eased the boat around the last of the point, turning it from south to more of a south-western path when something stuttered beneath her feet. Adrenaline pounced through her, and she looked at the control panel just as a blue light started to flash.

"It's the bilge pump," she said. "I'll be right back."

Julia jumped to her feet. "Wait, wait. You're leaving?"

"We're going straight," Maddy said. "You stand right here and keep us going in that direction. It's like a car, Julia." The name came out of her mouth without much thought, and Maddy didn't trip over it at all. "I'll go check the pump—it just didn't come on after two minutes, and it should've—and we'll be fine." She gave Julia a reassuring smile and bustled down the few steps to the deck.

She went down another level and then another to the engine room, where the same blue light flashed above the bilge pump. When it had done this a couple of days ago, she'd manually opened the release, and the water had been evacuated from the boat. No big deal.

Today, she stepped over to the button and the window next to it. Water lapped there, so they'd taken on a little bit of water. Nothing that would compromise a yacht of this size. Still, she wanted her bilge pump to be operational. It was one of the most important safety systems on a boat.

She pressed the button, and nothing happened. A frown creased her eyebrows, because she wasn't sure what to do if the system failed on its timing to release the bilge, and the manual override didn't work.

"It's fine," she told herself, her voice barely loud enough to reach her ears over the sound of the engine growling. "You don't need a bilge to make it around the island." She could release it once they returned to land, find a manual on this boat, and figure it out then.

She turned to go back up top when the boat lurched to the right. She fell left, as an object in motion wanted to stay moving in that direction. Her ankle twisted, and she rammed her knee into a knob on the way down.

A cry spilled from her mouth, and pain shot through her leg and back. Irritation spiked too, and she grumbled, "What are you doing, Julia?" They seriously should've been able to simply sail straight for a while. The bottom edge of Nantucket wasn't hard to navigate, for crying out loud.

Once they reached the west end, she'd have to decide if she'd go between Nantucket and Tuckernuck Islands, but she'd probably go around the smaller land mass. Include it on the tour. Why not? People wanted an hour-long tour, and they didn't need to cut corners unless there was something to see on the east side of Tuckernuck.

She tried to get to her feet, but the boat lurched again, keeping her on the ground and gripping a knob that Maddy probably shouldn't even be touching. In the next moment, the engine sputtered, coughed, and died. The silence around her brought foreboding, and Maddy's ears rang with the absence of the growling.

Then she heard, "No, I swear. She's right down here, and she'll know the answer to all your questions."

Heavy footsteps on the stairs met her ears, only drowned out by the pounding of her heart. Maddy got to her feet, using the wall of controls as support. Somewhere in the back of her mind, she recognized that those steps belonged to a man, which only sent another dose of adrenaline rushing through her.

Her left ankle and knee ached and protested the movement, but when a uniformed Coast Guard officer filled the doorway, the pain faded into the background. He wore a frown between those ocean-blue eyes, which quickly turned to alarm. His light brown hair was shaved close on the sides and swooped up on the top, though he couldn't be in his twenties and wear so many stripes on his chest.

"Ma'am," he said, which she didn't like. *Ma'am* was a nicety for older women... Maddy hated feeling old, and she reached up to tuck her errant hair behind her ear, embarrassed she was attracted to this man. He had muscles in his arms and chest, his shirt bulging with them, and not an ounce of body fat anywhere else.

Along her hairline, her fingers smeared through blood, and when she saw the brightness of it on her fingers, the world swayed again. A groan came from her mouth, and the last thing she saw was that handsome man rushing toward her as she crumpled to the ground.

CHAPTER THIRTEEN

Julia looked from the Coast Guard ship to the stairs that went down to the control room when a crash filled the air. "Maddy?" She got moving in that direction, and when she arrived at the bottom of the stairs, she braced herself against the doorway.

Captain Benjamin Downs was down on his knees, Maddy cradled in his lap. There seemed to be blood everywhere, and Julia's eyes landed on it on the front of the controls, the floor, Maddy's face, hands, clothes, and Captain Downs.

"I need you to get my health services technician," he said, his voice a barking command. He twisted to look at her when she didn't move. "Now, Julia."

She flinched at the use of her name in that irate tone. The captain needed to take his attitude down about ten notches. They'd been sailing along the coast of Nantucket, doing nothing wrong, when he'd pulled her over.

"I just start waving my arms?" she asked.

"Yes," he said. "My lieutenant will be watching the yacht. Or get my radio here and press the top two buttons." He nodded to his waist, where a radio had been clipped to his belt. "I've got a doctor on board, and I need him over here right now."

Julia could not sail this boat back to the dock at The Lighthouse Inn. Maddy better wake up to get that job done.

"Julia," Captain Downs clipped out. "Now."

"Oh, right." She lurched forward, the boat not completely stationary though the engine had been cut. It had taken her several seconds to figure out how to do that, and Captain Downs had not been happy about that.

She fumbled along his waist, embarrassment filling her for how groping she seemed. She finally got the radio off his belt and pressed the top two buttons. "Hey, uh..."

"Hold it in front of my mouth," the captain said, obviously annoyed with her.

She did, he said, "Yacht 8344 to MLB 47219, this is Captain Downs. I need HST Davidson over here. I've got a woman passed out and bleeding." He looked up at Julia. "Let go of the buttons."

She did, foolishness rushing through her. She wanted to tell this arrogant captain that not everyone knew how to be a Coast Guard member. She loved the beach, yes, but she didn't spend time radioing her friends. She thought of the movies she'd seen with boats, and she commanded herself to *think*. She was so tired of feeling out of her element or like she could only be a support to her husband and a housewife.

"MLB 47219, sending over HST Davidson," chirped through the radio. The speaker almost sounded bored.

"Leave me the radio," he said. "Go meet HST Davidson and get him down here."

"Yes, sir." She stooped to put the radio on the ground beside him, noticing how focused he was on Maddy. He didn't check her pulse, but even Julia could see she was breathing and alive. Comforted by that at least, she hurried upstairs just as another man, this one carrying a big red bag with a white cross on it stepped onto the yacht.

"Down here," she said, waving to him. "My friend is hurt." Her throat closed around the words "my friend," and she couldn't get a proper breath. She and Maddy were definitely not friends. At the very best, they were co-workers who'd figured out how to get along. They'd been working together for a couple of weeks now, and while not everything could be healed quite so quickly, they had made some progress.

They were above tolerating each other. Julia had told Maddy a few things about her life, and Maddy had shared too. They might be acquaintances now, bordering on *becoming* friends. Julia wasn't even sure such a thing was possible, but she wanted to believe in forgiveness and redemption, so she held fast to it and turned to go back down the steps.

She wasn't needed down there, and the space was too small anyway. She retreated to the main deck, where no less than five other men surveyed her from the Coast Guard boat that had blooped at her and told her to stop. She'd never been particularly good at handling conflict, especially with law enforcement, and she hugged herself and wished she could get out of the wind.

Movement behind her caused her to turn, and she really didn't like sight of Maddy appearing on a stretcher. Where that had come from, Julia had no idea.

"We're putting her on our boat," Captain Downs said. "You can follow us back to the Brant Point station."

"And then what?"

"She might need to go to the hospital."

Julia watched them go by, silent. Her life jumbled together, and she had no idea how to tell anyone on that lifeboat that she couldn't actually sail. She told herself she didn't need to sail, at least not with actual sails and what-not. She needed to be able to push a button to start the engine. Drive the boat. She could steer a car, and she'd been going along fine before the Coast Guard had flagged her down for having expired tags on the hull.

Maddy had said she'd checked the registration, but that was one more thing Julia didn't know where to find.

Captain Downs and HST Davidson moved from one boat to the other as if they were on dry land, and Julia marveled at that. Their boat started to swing around, and Julia's pulse lurched against her ribcage. She hurried up to the bridge and got everything up and running again. The blue light that had drawn Maddy down to the control room flashed on the panel, but Julia didn't know what it meant or how to fix it.

She did know how to pray, and she sent up a quick murmur of, "Please help me get this boat back to The Lighthouse Inn without killing myself or sinking anything."

Please, she added mentally, and then she eased the throttle forward the way she'd seen Maddy do. The motorboat in front of her didn't go too fast, and she kept pace behind them. If she just followed their trajectory, she should be fine. She didn't see the captain, the doctor, or Maddy, and her eyes ached by the time she pulled into Brant Point.

Several guardsmen helped dock the yacht, thankfully, and all she had to do was get close enough for them to throw ropes and secure the boat. She knew how to turn it off now, and once done and tied down, she hurried toward the dock.

Captain Downs had disappeared, which irritated Julia. "Sir," she said to the nearest man, though he hadn't been on the motorboat. "Where can I find my friend?"

"They took her to the infirmary," he said, barely looking up from the tablet in his hand. "Right in there, to your left." He pointed to the quaint, white building that looked homey but certainly couldn't be mistaken for anything but a military unit. Julia steeled herself and strode toward it.

Inside, everything stood at right angles, not a stitch or even something simple like a pen out of place. It screamed Captain Benjamin Downs, who she found leaning against the doorway, his arms folded. He looked over his shoulder at her, that frown between his eyes back again.

"She's awake," he said, nodding further into the room.

Julia joined him in the double-wide doorway and found Maddy sitting up on a doctor's table. HST—which Julia had no idea what that stood for—Davidson stood in front of her, asking her questions. Fire lit those blue eyes of hers, and she clearly didn't want to be fussed over any longer.

A bandage about as long as Julia's pointer finger ran along Maddy's forehead, right at the hairline and cutting down diagonally toward her ear.

"I'm fine," Maddy said, her eyes flicking to where Julia stood. Relief filled her gaze. "My friend is here, and she'll get me home just fine."

Two fines, Julia noted. The more times a woman used *fine*, the more upset she was. Julia also heard the words "my friend," and she was glad she and Maddy had come to some sort of unspoken agreement to put on the public appearance of getting along.

"You two run The Lighthouse Inn?" Captain Downs asked, only his mouth moving. He studied the scene in front of him as if it puzzled him, even when Julia stared at him for several long seconds.

"Yes," she said, the word lodging in her throat. She cleared it away. "Kind of. We're renovating it right now. We hope to reopen before the holiday season."

He nodded and pushed away from the wall as the doctor stepped back and offered his hand to help Maddy down from the table. Captain Downs joined them, putting his hand on her right elbow, the two men flanking her.

She glared at him too, but the look softened considerably, and Julia watched as the scene froze and she got thrust behind a sheer, plastic wall that magnified everything. Captain Downs had a soft touch with Maddy. Her eyes held vulnerability and interest, and as he turned his head to look forward—everything happening in super slow-motion—Julia found the attraction in his gaze too.

"All right," Captain Downs said, and the wall disappeared. Time rushed forward again. Julia blinked at how whiplashed she felt. "I'm going to release her to your care. Davidson?"

"If she acts confused, she needs to go to the hospital. She could have a concussion."

"I don't," Maddy said, glaring at him as he stepped away. "I just don't like the sight of my own blood. That's why I passed out."

The doctor looked at her dubiously, his dark green eyes clearly full of disbelief. "If she throws up, hospital. If she sleeps forever this afternoon, hospital." He continued to talk, but Julia stopped listening. Her second son had suffered a concussion during a rugby game in his senior year of high school. She knew what to watch for, and she agreed with Maddy. She didn't seem to have any symptoms of a concussion.

She also noted that Captain Downs didn't release her arm, though the doctor had stepped away ages ago.

"Okay," she said once he stopped talking. "Thank you so much." She extended her arm for Maddy to loop hers through, and time stilled again.

Maddy simply stared at her arm, and Julia wanted to pull hers back, tuck her hair, and run away. Her face heated while she tried to figure out what to do, and then Captain Downs, in all his sensitive glory, transferred Maddy's arm from his to Julia's and said, "You ladies take care of each other, okay?"

"Yes, sir," Julia said while Maddy turned her stare to the captain. Something popped and crackled inside Julia, but she managed to keep it dormant until she and Maddy had boarded the yacht and pulled away from the Coast Guard station.

Then she started laughing, the sound filling the small bridge room where Maddy stood at the wheel again.

"What?" she barked, very much like Captain Downs would.

"I think that captain liked you," Julia said between giggles.

"Don't be ridiculous." Maddy tossed her hair over her

shoulder in a classic *I'm-not-talking-about-this-because-you're-right* move and groaned. "Oh, I can't do that with my headache."

"Headache?" Julia asked. "Maddy, are you sure you're okay?"

"Yes," she said, giving Julia a glare. "The doctor gave me some painkillers. They just haven't kicked in yet. We'll get back to the inn and I'll take a quick nap. I'll be good as new." She spoke with confidence, but Julia knew that just because she wanted something, didn't mean it was going to come true.

She did get them back to the dock at the inn. Julia didn't touch her as they went inside. Maddy disappeared into her room, but Julia went into the kitchen and filled a bucket with hot, soapy water and returned to the boat.

After all, the blood in the control room wasn't going to clean itself up.

As Julia got the job done, she found herself praying that Maddy would be okay, and not because Julia needed her to be well. But because Julia *wanted* her to be healthy. She knew how to check on people discreetly, as she'd raised three boys who would insist to the death that they were fine, even if their leg had been chopped off.

Once she finished cleaning up the yacht, she rinsed out the bucket and went down to the basement level of the lighthouse. Maddy's door around the corner stood shut, and Julia didn't knock on it. She eased it open and found

Maddy lying in bed, her eyes closed and her chest rising and falling in an even rhythm.

Fondness filled her, because they'd once been such great friends. Julia remembered checking on her like this in the past, when Maddy had come down with the flu. "I'm sorry," she whispered into the silence, and then she eased the door closed.

CHAPTER FOURTEEN

"I wanted to." Tessa set down the bundt cake she'd picked up from the pop-up dessert shop that had come to The Holiday House that day. "I got four of these from Beauty Bundts. This one is white chocolate raspberry." She beamed at the cake in the middle of the table and then looked at Julia, the dark-haired woman she'd started to feel close to.

On her right sat Madelynne Lancaster, who'd been injured that morning on the inn's yacht. When Tessa had heard about it, she'd immediately selected a cake and said she'd be by that afternoon to check on the two women working on the inn to get it reopened.

Maddy had just said Tessa didn't need to bring the cake, but she did take a slice after Julia plated one and handed it to her.

"Janey said she'd bring dinner," Tessa said, sighing as

she sat down. Julia exchanged a glance with Maddy, but Tessa couldn't read their unspoken language yet.

"Janey's your sister, right?" Maddy asked, delicately putting a bite of cake into her mouth. She clearly came from money or at least had attended plenty of high-society functions, because a bite like that meant the food would be gone in less than two seconds. That allowed her to converse with the appearance like she'd eaten something, when in reality, she'd only eat a few bites of cake before she pushed it away.

"Yes," Tessa said, shooting a look at Julia.

"She's my sister too," Julia said. "I told her about Janey and my dad and everything."

Tessa nodded, her chest tightening for a moment and then releasing. The past was the past, and she couldn't do anything about the summer her mother had spent here on Nantucket, seemingly with many boyfriends. She did wonder if Mom had continued to see Ryan Harper after she'd been married, what with that house on Southampton nor far from his...

She hadn't brought it up to Julia yet, and right now, she wasn't even considering doing so. "Are you feeling better?" she asked Maddy.

"Much," she said, her gracious smile making an appearance. "I just had a headache. My knee hurt too, but I'm fine."

"I'm glad."

"You really didn't need to bring dinner," Maddy said.

"I need the practice making recipes. Julia and I are working on a menu."

"Oh?"

"Yes," Maddy said, coming more alive now. "I have a culinary certificate. It was something that helped me get the job. We're not just an inn; we provide breakfast and dinner for our guests."

"Kind of," Julia said, exchanging another look with Maddy, this one somewhat nervous. Tessa had the distinct impression that these two women were still learning how to work together, and how to get along. She admired that, because it was never easy to start a new job, let alone with someone else brand-new too.

"We're going to do breakfast every day," Julia explained. "But dinner only Thursday through Sunday."

"We're going to do our community things on the other nights," Maddy said. "Clam bakes and beach picnics and whatnot. Like they used to do decades ago." She offered up a smile, and Tessa took it and then returned it.

"I remember coming to things like that hosted by the inn," she said. "We came to Nantucket every summer, and I loved the bike parade, the craft classes here on the beach, and the fishing day."

"Fishing day," Julia said, snapping her fingers. "That's a good one." She seemed so much more animated when talking about the inn, and she reached for her phone and started typing. "We've got the dock, and perhaps that's what all those old poles were for in the upstairs closet."

"Perhaps," Maddy murmured, and she took another bite of cake.

"The inn did children's game night," Tessa said, her memories flowing thick now. "They hosted a dance every summer. They had lookout days, where you could go up onto the tower and look through the old telescopes, just like they did a hundred years ago."

"Seems like a lot of stuff for kids," Julia said.

"It was," Tessa said. "Locals could attend, or anyone not staying at the inn. If they weren't a guest, there was a fee. I think it was another way for them to make money. Oh." She reached for the knife to cut herself a piece of cake, though she'd already had two of the chocolate chip one back at the cottage. "They always did a hot dog feast on Halloween. That was mostly geared toward locals, and I never attended it, though I begged my mother to bring us back to Nantucket specifically for it."

"Did they charge for that?"

"I don't think so," she said. "Margo Michaels had a killer chili recipe, and she'd make a huge pot of that. Phil would grill hot dogs. As kids came to the inn for trick-or-treating, they and their families could eat too. It was just something they did for the community."

"Community outreach," Maddy said, her left eyebrow cocking up.

"I know," Julia said, still tapping away on her phone. She looked up several moments later. "Got it." She met Maddy's eye. "Can you make chili?"

"We don't have to do everything they did. We can put our own spin on it."

"I'm going to take that as a no." Julia smiled as she said it, and Tessa volleyed her gaze back to Maddy to watch her reaction. Her smile came much slower, with a hint of surprise riding in those blue eyes to accompany it.

"I can make the best clam chowder in the state of Massachusetts," Maddy said, tossing her hair over her shoulder.

"Oh, wow," Julia said, half a laugh popping out of her mouth. "That is a huge statement."

"Hello?" Janey called from the front of the inn, and Tessa's attention got diverted there. At the same time, Maddy's phone rang, and she looked down at it.

"Private number?" she asked as Tessa rose to her feet.

"I'll get Janey," she said while Maddy's phone continued to shriek out a shrill ringtone that drove Tessa toward insanity on the second ring. Why would anyone pick such an abrasive ringtone?

Maddy said, "I'm not answering it," as Tessa went by, and Julia argued with her about it being someone they needed to talk to. "I gave them the number for the inn. They wouldn't have my private cellphone number."

"I still think you should answer it," Julia said.

"You answer it then," Maddy said, plenty of disdain in her voice. Tessa wanted to stay and figure out their relationship, because it was obviously nuanced and filled with history, but she left the dining room and went down the few feet of hallway to the lobby to greet her own sister.

They too had a nuanced, somewhat precarious relationship, and she took in Janey's unwashed hair and the fact that she only carried one bag of food. "Hey," she said. "I was thinking you'd need help carrying the food."

"I just got crab cakes and corn salad."

"There's four of us."

"Helen's coming too," Janey said. "She said she'd bring the wine. Apparently, she got some amazing cabernet at the Wine Festival earlier this year, and she's been dying for a 'special occasion' to drink it." She smiled and handed Tessa the single bag with three Styrofoam containers in it.

Tessa peered first at it and then her sister. "You have a date with Sean tonight, don't you?"

Janey blinked and fiddled with the ends of her flowing, silk cardigan. "Yes."

Irritation filled Tessa, and she turned away before it would bleed onto her face too much. "Are you going to come sit down for a few minutes?"

"Yes," Janey said again, more bite in the word this time. She followed Tessa back into the dining room, where Julia stood with a phone pressed to her ear, a look of pure delight on her face.

Maddy had also stood, and she was trying to get the phone away from Julia, who kept dodging her. It looked like they'd been transported back to junior high, when one friend had called a boy the other one liked.

"Of *course* I'll let her know," Julia said, her voice halfway between sarcastic and playful. "Yes, yes, she's doing well. She's just trying out a new...cake recipe."

Maddy made another attempt to get Julia to hang up, this time making a slashing motion across her throat. If anything, Julia's face brightened. "Yes, Captain, I'm sure she'll be thrilled to hear from you."

With that, the call ended, and Julia filled the room with her laughter while Maddy practically ripped the phone from her hand.

Tessa watched as she un-bagged the containers, and Julia's laughter died quite suddenly as Janey entered the room. "Who was that?" Tessa asked, because she'd always been fairly good at smoothing over awkward situations.

Julia whipped her head back toward Tessa, who said, "Janey brought crab cakes and corn salad." She opened the first container to find four cakes inside, as well as a round container that must have the salad in it. Three of these. Twelve cakes. For five women.

Four, Tessa told herself, as Janey wouldn't eat a whole lot if she was planning to go out with Sean too.

"It was Captain Benjamin Downs of the Coast Guard," Julia said, the sing-song quality of her voice making a reappearance. "He wanted to check on Maddy." She fluttered her eyelashes at the blonde woman. "Check her *out*, more like."

"Stop it," Maddy said, no power behind the words at all.

"How do you think he got your number?" Julia asked, not stopping at all.

"I'm asking him right now." She kept her gaze on her phone, her fingers flying. She tapped one last time and looked up. "I'm sure he's just doing his civic duty."

"I think the doctor would follow up with his patient," Julia said. "Not the *gorgeous* captain."

"Gorgeous captain?" Janey repeated.

"He wasn't that good-looking," Maddy said quickly, while Julia said. "Drop-dead gorgeous. And—" She hit the word after Maddy had finished speaking. "You should've seen the way he looked at Maddy. He's definitely interested."

Maddy threw her a look that could've seared a person from the inside out. "No, he's not."

Julia shrugged, her smile going nowhere. "Whatever. I'm starving." She reached for a container of crab cakes at the same time another voice called into the inn.

"That must be Helen," Janey said. "I'll go help her with the wine."

"How many people are coming tonight?" Maddy asked, and Tessa didn't think she was super happy to be entertaining so many guests.

"Just Helen," Tessa assured her. "She's bringing some cabernet she got at the Wine Festival this year."

"I've heard that's really good," Julia said. "We should have something going on that weekend too."

"When is it?" Maddy asked, sitting back down in her

seat, her eyes glued to her phone. Tessa hadn't heard it make a sound, but she'd obviously gotten a message from someone, because she pulled in a tight breath. Others may not have seen it, but Tessa had exceptional observation skills, and she sure did.

"Usually in May, I believe," Tessa said, hoping to give Maddy a few moments to herself.

But Julia said, "What did he say, Maddy?"

Maddy looked up, and she may as well have been stunned for how wide her eyes stretched. "Who?"

"Captain Gorgeous," Julia teased.

Maddy's shoulders strengthened, and Tessa had seen this tactic in her own husband. She was steeling herself to say something she didn't quite believe but wanted to. "He said he works for the military, and they have many and varied ways to find a phone number."

Julia giggled, and even Tessa smiled. "Sounds scandalous," she said.

"What does?" Helen Ivy asked as she entered the dining room, Janey right behind her with a case of wine. A *case.* Tessa had been working on her drinking issues, and she told herself right then and there she'd have one glass, no more. No matter what.

"I love a good scandal." Helen's blue eyes twinkled like stars, and that got everyone in the room laughing, even Maddy. She glanced down at her phone again, this time gasping and throwing it a few inches. It landed on the table with a *bang!* and slid toward the middle before coming to a stop.

Tessa reached for it as the laughter died, and she picked up Maddy's device. It was already open to Captain Gorgeous's messages, so it wasn't hard to find what had caused the other woman's reaction.

"What does it say?" Julia asked, coming around the table to where Tessa stood. She crowded in close, her own gasp filling the room a moment later. She whirled toward Maddy. "What are you going to say?"

I was thinking we could go to dinner some time, the Coast Guard captain had said. *That's why I wanted your number.*

Bold, this Captain Benjamin Downs. Tessa supposed he hadn't become a captain in the Coast Guard without such a quality, and she didn't entirely hate it. She'd like a man who didn't beat around the bush, that much was certain. At this moment, she'd like a man who didn't lie to her, cheat on her, and then act like their separation and impending divorce was her fault—or even her choice.

Silently, she handed the phone back to Maddy, whose eyes had actually filled with tears. She shook her head, pocketed her phone, and sat down. "He's far too young for me."

"You don't know that," Julia said, her voice much quieter now, all traces of teasing gone.

"You saw him," Maddy said. "He's obviously only in his mid-thirties. I'm almost fifty."

"You're forty-six," Julia argued. "That is *not* almost fifty."

"If you round up, it's fifty." Maddy gave her a piercing look that said, *drop this now*.

Julia snapped her mouth closed and went back to her seat on the other side of the table. "Thank you for bringing dinner, Janey."

"Of course." She took a seat, and Helen came out of the kitchen with a corkscrew and a single bottle of wine.

"I'll help with the glasses," Tessa said, going into the kitchen to get them. Her heart pounded in her chest, and she wasn't sure why. She didn't know Julia or Maddy that well, but something inside her said she wanted to.

Jealousy nipped at her too, because she hadn't had a man interested in her for a very long time, despite her marriage to Ron. "Your crumbling marriage," she reminded herself in a mutter. She picked up the wine glasses and returned to the dining room, her resolve to have a single serving of wine wavering.

One look at Janey, and she firmed it up again. She wasn't going to drink herself into a stupor. Not over Ron. Not over anything.

After Helen gave them a little speech about the cabernet and poured the wine, Tessa sat down with two crab cakes and a spoonful of corn salad. "I was thinking," she said. "You two seem pretty swamped over here, and I don't work that much. I would love to come help." She looked back and forth between Maddy and Julia, who now wore identical expressions of surprise.

"We get paid," Maddy said.

"I don't need the money," Tessa said coolly.

"I do nothing either," Helen said. "I'd love to come chit-chat while I put up some drapes."

"The drapes are a long ways off," Maddy said. "We're mostly painting and hauling out trash still. Working on programs, meals, ordering supplies. That kind of thing." She kept her gaze on Julia, obviously begging her to jump in too.

"I'll be a taste-tester then," Tessa said. "You can serve me the meals you're thinking of for the guests."

"I'm in on that," Janey said quickly, and Helen wasn't far behind her. The five of them looked at one another, and Tessa's smile crept across her face with every passing second.

"It would be nice to run things by other people," Julia said, almost like she didn't want to say yes, but she clearly didn't want to say no either.

Maddy held all the power there, and Tessa wondered what had transpired between these two women to create that unbalance between them. Finally, Maddy's boxy shoulders relaxed, and she stabbed at her crab cake. "Fine," she said. "But we're not talking about Captain Gorgeous. Ever."

Tessa nodded somberly, and Janey agreed. Julia's smile

widened and widened, the tension in the room doubling. "Okay," she said, the laughter following immediately.

"Julia," Maddy warned.

"What? I just think it's funny *you* called him Captain Gorgeous too. It's okay to admit the man is good-looking. A little barky and brusque for my taste, but you always did like an in-charge man."

Maddy looked horrified for one, two, three beats, and then her smile crowded out the other emotions. She admitted to nothing, however, and simply shook her head before taking a bite of her crab cake.

CHAPTER FIFTEEN

"It's no wonder she was upset," Sean said, and that only frustrated Janey further. "We didn't have to go to dinner tonight. There are plenty of other times to get together."

Janey said nothing, the warmth of Sean's hand in hers all she wanted right now. Sean had come to The Lighthouse Inn to pick her up for dinner, and she'd introduced him around to Julia and Maddy. They'd seemed delighted to meet him, and Janey had been glad to leave.

Tessa hadn't been super happy about her departure, and she'd been annoyed about the food too. Janey had mentioned it to Sean, expecting him to back her up. Instead, he'd agreed with Tessa.

"There was enough food," she finally said. "I barely ate anything."

"Something I'm sure they noticed," he said.

"I doubt it," she fired back. "They were all talking about the accident on the yacht today, and then the Coast Guard Captain that came to the rescue." No one noticed that Janey had eaten a single crab cake and nothing more. She'd sipped her wine, participated in the conversation, and left after an hour. What did Tessa expect? That she'd stay all night, volunteer all of her free time to work on the inn when she wasn't getting paid, and become BFFs with her half-sister?

She shook her head. "Everything is so complicated."

Sean gave her space to expand on that thought, which Janey appreciated. Though he was a lawyer, and her experience with them was that they liked to hear themselves talk, Sean didn't do that.

"It's like...she wants me to be friends with Julia so badly. What she doesn't get is that she *forced* me to talk to her again when she had that little intervention on the porch."

"Mm."

"She didn't give me a choice in the matter. Maybe I just needed more time to figure out what *I* wanted." She shook her head and looked at the masts in the harbor. "With Tessa, it's always about what *she* wants."

Janey hadn't told her sister about how she'd gone into The Lighthouse Inn and met Julia Harper, realized who she was, and then panicked. She hadn't told her for a reason. Tessa always took over once she got something in her mind, and Janey needed something Tessa wasn't good at giving—time.

"Are you any closer to knowing what you want to do?"

"About Julia?"

"About your father," Sean said, looking up at the waitress as she arrived with their meals. He always chose the best restaurants for dinner, and tonight's was no exception. Right on the water, with amazing views of the harbor, the lighthouse at Brant Point, and Nantucket Sound beyond. The weather had cooled, and the sun went down so much earlier than it had in the summer.

But the lights reflecting off the water created their own kind of magic, and Janey allowed some of the tension in her muscles to seep away.

"We've got the butternut ravioli with lobster," the waitress said, putting the dish in front of Sean. "And the seafood salad, extra mushrooms."

"Thank you," Janey murmured, looking down at all the clams and shrimp in her own bowl. Sean had already eaten mussels and calamari, his two favorite seafood appetizers, and he'd already picked up his fork to dig into his pasta. Janey's stomach roared at her too, because one crab cake was not enough food.

"Anything else?" the waitress asked. "I'll have those two to-go meals ready at the end."

"Perfect," Janey said, giving the woman a smile. "I think that's all for now."

"I'll check back." She walked away, and Janey watched her for a moment, wondering what burdens she carried. She wasn't young, but she wasn't as old as Janey. Probably in her thirties, and working at a restaurant on Nantucket. There had to be a need there, and Janey wanted to leave her a big tip.

She picked up her blue cheese dressing and poured it over the salad. "I don't know what I want to do about my father," she said. "I'm thinking I'll start with something non-evasive. An email, I think." She met Sean's eyes, and he looked encouraging and kind at the same time. She appreciated that, and she appreciated that he'd given her some time and space to work through some things on her own. "See what he does with that. If he doesn't respond... then that's that. If he does, then maybe we'll work up to meeting."

She stirred her salad around. "Something."

"It's a good plan," he said. "Do you have his email address?"

"He's a partner in a huge firm in New York City," she said. "I have his work email address from the website."

Sean took a bite of his ravioli and swallowed before he said, "I could probably find a personal one. That might be better."

"Through that PI?"

"Yes."

Janey's stomach squirmed. She wasn't sure how much she wanted to involve other people. Viola had a private investigator she knew and trusted too, and she'd offered to put Janey in touch with him to learn more about her biological father before she reached out to him.

"You decide," Sean said. "It's just an idea."

Janey nodded and focused on her food again. "I'll think about it." They ate in silence for a couple of minutes, and then she said, "Have you heard anything about Riggs —or Rick Fry?" She'd immediately told Sean about the pictures and Internet articles, as well as Riggs's real name, last weekend. He'd said he'd have his PI look into it, and the man could work fast.

"He found the same articles," Sean said. "There's not much else to go on. He was working on getting the police interviews with the mother and Riggs, because they did speak to him a couple of times about the disappearance of his sister."

Janey nodded, though that wasn't really the answer she wanted. She'd like it much more if Sean would tell her that Riggs had been found in the Canadian Rockies somewhere, with overgrown hair and trying to hike into Alaska as a way to escape to Russia. Anything that would indicate he was as far from Nantucket as a person could get.

"Tessa wants to help at The Lighthouse Inn," she said next. "Do you think I should go on the weekends?"

Surprise colored Sean's expression. "Help doing what?"

"Hanging wallpaper and painting." She waved her fork. "I don't know. They're remodeling the place, getting it up to snuff to reopen before the holidays."

"Do you want to go help?"

Janey thought of the women she'd left in the dining room. She'd left her professional support system when she'd quit her job. She'd left her daughter and her boyfriend in New Jersey. All of her friends. Her motorcycle club of women. She had Viola and Miles, who she lived with in the big mansion on the south side of the island. She had Tessa. She had Sean, and the few people who came into his office, though she'd only worked there for a couple of weeks and hardly knew everyone yet.

"I think I'd like some friends here," she said slowly. "Julia and Maddy seem like nice women. They're both divorced." She didn't have to add, "like me," though it hung in the air. They were all roughly the same age too, with Tessa being the youngest. "Helen said she needs something to keep her busy, and I like talking to her."

She smiled at the thought of the older woman she'd met only a couple of weeks ago. She reminded Janey so much of her mother, and she needed that influence in her life right now. She took another bite of salad, her fingers moving to the necklace she only took off to sleep and shower. The starfish reminded her that she could constantly regrow and renew. It had been a gift she'd given her mother, and Mom had given it back to her after she'd died.

Janey felt grounded when she felt the weight of it against her collarbone, and she made her decision. "I can at least go for a few hours on the weekends."

"Sure," Sean said with one of his beaming smiles. "Whatever makes you happy, sweetheart."

INHALING THE SCENT OF FRESH PAINT MINGLING with chocolate did not make Janey happy, but she kept the roller moving. Once she finished with this wall, she was done for the day. She'd only been at the inn since two o'clock, because that was morning to her. When she'd walked in, Tessa had cocked her eyebrows and handed her a cup of tea.

The eyebrows meant, *Morning, Janey? It's two p.m.*, and the tea meant, *Roll up your sleeves, sister. We have work to do.*

Janey knew how to work; that wasn't the problem. The real issue existed inside her own mind. The idea of having friends here on the island sounded intriguing and fun. Actually having to talk to them gave her anxiety. She constantly battled with herself, pulling first on one end of a rope and then running around to the other side and tugging on that end too. After she'd done that for a couple of hours, she'd gone through her meditative yoga routine and finally been able to get herself out of the mansion and onto the shuttle that came to the Point every thirty minutes.

It had been a boring week in the law office, with no news from Sean's PI about Riggs. She hadn't told Sean to get her father's personal email, and she hadn't sent the email to his work address either.

She felt like so many things hung in the balance, and she needed to make some decisions and take the first step.

"You okay in here?" Maddy asked, poking her head into the bedroom on the second floor where Janey worked.

She lowered the roller and looked at the blonde woman. She didn't have a barrel-shaped midsection, though she likely had things about herself she didn't like. "Yes," she said, offering the other woman a smile. "Hey, can I ask you a question?"

"Sure." Maddy entered the room, pulling her jacket tighter around her. Rain had come to Nantucket, and that had driven everyone off the beaches and inside. The drizzle had been steady for a day or two now, and combined with the sea breezes, it had been downright cold. "Is it freezing in here?"

"I'm working, so I'm okay," Janey said, glancing around at the sheets of plastic on the floor. "But yes, you guys might want to have the furnace serviced, or at least offer space heaters for these upper floors." She looked back at Maddy, who nodded. "You two live in the basement, right? You must be icy down there too."

"I bought a space heater yesterday," Maddy admitted, tucking her hair with long, slender fingers. "I'll talk to Julia about it."

"I wonder about you and Julia," Janey said, speaking slowly as she tried to arrange her thoughts. "Have you two known each other for long? Sometimes I get the feeling that you have, and then other times, it seems like you hardly know each other."

Maddy let out a sigh, her eyes roaming the walls Janey had already painted. Someone else had done the ceiling at another time, and she'd been relieved to find the room empty, taped, and simply waiting for paint. Moving furniture wasn't exactly her strong suit.

"Both are true," Maddy finally said. "She and I were college roommates, in another life." She offered a strained smile that held painful memories. Janey knew, because she'd seen smiles like that before. Sometimes on her own face. They could hold up around the edges, but in the middle, the hurt and disappointment weighed them down.

"Fell out of touch," Janey said, going back to her paint tray and reloading the roller. "Perhaps have just been reunited?"

"Something like that," Maddy said.

Janey nodded, not needing to know too many details, at least right now. She slicked the soft blue paint onto the walls and said, "I like this color."

"This room is going to be named the Eastern Escape," Maddy said. "We want them all to be beachy and tranquil and romantic."

"I think this color does the trick." Janey kept working, and Maddy didn't leave.

"You're divorced, right?" Maddy asked as Janey reloaded the roller with more paint. She'd probably only need to do it two more times to finish the wall, and thus the room.

"Yes," Janey said. "Twice, actually." She flashed Maddy a smile that wasn't truly made of happiness. "It's easier the second time, believe it or not." She didn't want to repeat it a third time, that was for sure. Janey knew that was why she dated around, why she didn't allow herself or the men she saw to think they were exclusive. At the same time, she craved a monogamous relationship, and she wasn't opposed to getting married again. She just had to make sure it was to the right person, so there'd be no third divorce.

Maddy's mouth moved too, the tightness of it not allowing her lips to curl too far. She ground her voice through her throat. "How did you...I mean, did it take you long to start dating again?"

Janey stalled in her movement to get back to work. Her mind blitzed through answers for the question, knowing exactly why Maddy had asked. She gave her another smile, this one much more brilliant and from the heart. "Not too long," she said. "My first husband was a real jerk, so literally every man I met after him seemed like Prince Charming."

She focused on the wall again, knowing that sometimes it was easier to talk about delicate, humiliating things if one didn't have to look someone in the eye. "Are you thinking about going out with the captain?" The paint made squishing, squelching noises as it rolled onto the wall. "Sorry, I can't remember his name."

"Ben Downs," she said. "And yes, I'm considering it."

"You've been texting him." Janey wasn't asking this time, and she didn't need to see Maddy's face for it to be confirmed.

She didn't need the "Yes, I'm texting him," Maddy said either. It was exactly what Janey would've done, and it was probably terribly exciting and awfully confusing at the same time.

"And? He's nice? Julia made him sound a little grumpy."

"Oh, he ordered her around while I was unconscious," Maddy said dismissively. "She freezes sometimes, so she probably deserved it."

Janey nodded, covering up the last of the horrid taupe paint in the bedroom. Whoever had thought this color would work had obviously been blind. With the light coming in the window, even now as the sun went down on the other side of the building, the blue made everything seem bigger and brighter.

The bright white ceiling helped that, and when Maddy and Julia put in the accent art, bedding, curtains, and rugs, Janey could envision how inviting and nice this room would be.

"He seems nice." Maddy's tone couldn't have scared a mouse.

Janey slicked the paint over itself a few more times,

making sure she got it into every crevice and crack. "Then go out with him."

"I think I might," Maddy said. "Don't you dare say anything to Julia."

"My lips are sealed," Janey promised. She lowered the roller and exhaled heavily. "Okay, I'm done in here. You better have something phenomenal for dinner. Like lobster-mac-and-cheese-phenomenal." She faced the other woman, who folded her arms and cocked a hip. Janey liked her instantly, and they grinned at one another.

"Come see what I made, Picky Pants." She laughed, and the sound actually contained rust. "I used to call my daughter that." The smile slipped, showing the pain behind it, and Janey wanted to gather Madelynne Lancaster into a tight embrace and hold her together until she could do it herself.

She did, saying, "I'm so sorry about what you've lost."

Maddy said nothing, the vibration in her chest and the way she clung to Janey speaking volumes without making a single sound.

CHAPTER SIXTEEN

Maddy pulled up to The Lighthouse Inn, the last of the daylight fading. Dinner would be late tonight, but she'd texted Julia to say so. She hadn't been able to get away from her father's place as early as she'd have liked, mostly because his neighbors had kept dropping by, asking her questions while she tried to get his yard ready for the winter.

She'd fed him quickly, texted Julia, and made the drive back to the Point and The Lighthouse Inn. Julia had turned on the floodlights above the upper balcony, and the rays spilled out over the sand and the parking lot in every direction. That was how the shadowy figure against the east side of the lighthouse caught Maddy's attention.

She tensed, so many things running through her mind. She had mace in her purse; should she get it out now? She could hold her keys between her fingers like claws. She wasn't wearing heels, but she knew where to stomp to get someone to let go of her. Chris had insisted she and Chelsea take the self-defense courses, especially once the press started hounding their whole family and not just him.

The shadow shifted, along with Maddy's memories, and disappeared. She wasn't sure she'd even seen it, as she'd questioned so much recently. Deciding she could take another minute, she dialed her daughter, hoping and praying she wasn't with her father.

"Mom," Chelsea said, her voice as bright as sunrise in July. "What's up?"

Maddy sighed and closed her eyes, letting her head rest on the seat behind her. "Nothing," she said. "Just wanted to chat for a few minutes. Tell me what you did this weekend with Ethan."

Ever since Maddy had heard Chelsea tell Kyle to "let her come" to his wedding, she'd been texting her and calling her. Her daughter had answered too, and Maddy's heart had started to heal and beat more normally in the past couple of weeks.

"He took me whale-watching," Chelsea said.

Maddy opened her eyes, the conversation on now. "Uh oh."

"Right?" Chelsea giggled, and Maddy imagined her shaking her head as she stirred her tea, something she'd seen her daughter do many times. "I told him I don't really like boats, and he was *convinced* he could change my mind."

Maddy smiled at the strength in Chelsea's voice. "Did he?"

"Of course not," Chelsea said at the same time Maddy thought it. Her daughter had been headstrong the moment she'd come out of the womb. "Needless to say, I won't be seeing him again."

"Over whale-watching?"

"It was more than just the whale-watching," Chelsea said. "It was the theatrics of trying to get me to like boats. I don't have to like what he does. It's okay to not like boats."

"Yes, it is," Maddy said. Chelsea had spent her life campaigning—not really, but it felt that way sometimes—that individual differences should be celebrated. She could be friends with someone who didn't think or believe the same way she did. She didn't have to like what they did; they didn't have to like what she did.

Everyone could still be treated with mutual respect and dignity. Maddy had supported her daughter and let her think for herself, and if she didn't want to go out with a guy who'd tried to sell her on liking boats, that was fine with Maddy.

"Anyway," Chelsea said with a sigh. "You'll be happy to know I got registered for winter semester at BU."

Maddy opened her mouth to respond, but no sound

came out. She still checked her children's social media accounts every day, and she'd seen no indication of this. "I didn't even know you'd applied."

"Yes, you did," Chelsea said. "It was one of the requirements for me to go to Chile."

"That was over a year ago."

"Right," Chelsea said. "I got in. I just deferred until January."

"That's great," Maddy said, her heartbeat settling into normalcy again. The shadows around the inn took on natural shapes, without anyone hiding along the sides of the building. "What are you taking?"

"English—gag me. Some entry-level math I'll probably fail. Cross-country, which will probably be the only class I'll like. And art history."

"You might like that."

"You never know, do you?" Chelsea asked, that same mega-watt tone attached to her voice. "I don't know, Mom. How did you know what you wanted to be when you grew up?"

"I didn't," Maddy said. "I took a lot of classes, trying to find something I liked. I finally got a culinary certificate, but I didn't graduate from NYU."

Chelsea hummed, and then fell silent. After a few seconds, she said, "Dad told Kyle he better invite you to the wedding."

Maddy bolted upright again, her pulse pouncing right

against her tongue. "He did?" For some reason, in her head, Chris had been the one to approach every single person in Maddy's life and say, "Choose. Her or me. Choose now, and stick with it forever."

"Did you tell him we've been talking?" Maddy didn't want to cause a problem between Chelsea and her father. She'd left Boston and stayed with her brother, then come to Nantucket, just to give Chris the room he needed. Sometimes, in her quietest moments, she couldn't believe she'd done that. It was almost like she was still serving him, still making things as easy and as out-of-the-spotlight for him as possible.

She loathed herself if she thought too much about it. If he wanted to leave, *he* should've left. Not her.

"I haven't yet," Chelsea said. "But I think I will. I don't care what he thinks, Mom."

"He pays your bills," Maddy said. "He's your boss."

"So I'll get another job. Whatever." Chelsea had never worried about things like that, and Maddy envied her for that. At the same time, *she'd* provided a life for Chelsea where she'd never *had* to worry about money, jobs, or burning bridges.

"Kyle said he'd send an invitation to the inn, because that was the address you put in the form."

Maddy nodded before she realized she had to talk. "Okay, great."

"You really can slip in the back and up the steps. They

booked the Pilgrim Cathedral, and the steps are right by the front door. I'll come sit by you."

"You don't need to do that," Maddy said, clearing her throat. "We don't need to divide the family, and besides, Bea will want you in the wedding party."

"Oh, my word," Chelsea gushed, her voice growing more animated. "You should see these bridesmaids' dresses, Mom. You would *die*." She went on to detail the "horrible fashion faux pas" that was a dusty blue dress, the "abhorrent" string of pearls they were gluing—"gluing, Mom!"—to the waistband, and the "hideous" heels that would make her taller than her date.

Maddy basked in the sound of her daughter's voice, because it was her only connection to her family right now. A seed had been planted when Chelsea had started responding and they'd begun talking, and it sure felt like Chris had just poured a little bit of water onto her heart by telling Kyle he better invite her to the wedding.

By saying their divorce needed to happen for Chris to maintain his power, he'd indicated that Maddy was weak. Ever since the night she'd seen Julia and Alan in that diner, she'd felt some measure of weakness. She hated it, and while she hadn't fallen as far this time as she had then, she definitely still felt like she was clawing her way back to the surface of the Earth. Once there, she could exert her muscles and show her strength. Somehow.

"Anyway, I have to jet, Mom. I'm meeting a guy for coffee."

"You be careful meeting men," Maddy said.

Chelsea only giggled. "I will, Mom. It's in the shop right here in my building, and James is on tonight."

"Good," Maddy said. "Text me how it went once you get home."

"I will. Love you."

"Love you too."

With that, her daughter was gone, and Maddy's heart continued to pulse in her chest in strange and wondrous ways. "Please protect her, James," she whispered, hoping the man that Chelsea had befriended in high school and who now ran the coffee shop in her building could do such a thing. Maddy had met James plenty of times, and he did seem to have quite the protective streak when it came to Chelsea.

Her daughter was charismatic and beautiful, so she had no trouble getting dates or boyfriends. That only made Maddy worry about her more, and she tucked her phone into her purse and got out of the car, another prayer in her heart, this one aimed at God instead of a twenty-two-year-old named James.

She forgot about the mace, splaying the keys between her fingers, and stomping on someone's instep—until a man emerged from the shadows on the *west* side of The Lighthouse Inn, his jacket flipped all the way up to his chin.

Maddy froze, her mind barreling forward at a mile a

minute. "I have mace," she warned, her voice steady and strong.

"Not necessary," the man said, and Maddy recognized his voice. It was the same rich, deep tone that had followed her into unconsciousness on the yacht, and brought her back from it once they'd reached land.

"Ben?"

He stepped into the light pouring out of the double-doors of the inn, a smile touching that handsome face. "Guilty."

"Have you been skulking around back there?" She looked to her right, to where she'd first seen the shadowy figure.

"I'm assuming you forgot about our date tonight," he said. "I inquired inside, where Julia was *quite* excited to let you know I'd stopped by." He nodded to the glass on his left.

Maddy looked that way too. "No, I didn't forget. We're going out tomorrow night." And no, she hadn't told anyone, least of all Julia. At the same time, she couldn't tell her daughter, and she didn't really have any other friends to speak of. Perhaps Janey Forsythe, who'd come to help paint guest rooms yesterday. Or Tessa Simmons, who'd come *every* day last week to lend a hand around the inn.

"Are you sure?" Ben asked, and Maddy pulled her phone from her purse.

"Quite sure," she said, sliding to get her device unlocked. "You said, and I quote, 'Dinner on the eighteenth, six o'clock, I'll take you somewhere you've never been before.'" She looked up, wondering if her tone had sounded flirty. When she'd read that text, she'd imagined the captain saying it in a flirty, throaty voice—just like the one he laughed in right now.

"I'm sure I didn't say that."

Maddy turned her phone toward him. "You did, Mister. It was like a checklist. I'm surprised you didn't say fourteen hundred hours."

He peered at the phone with those gloriously blue eyes. "First off, that would be two o'clock in the afternoon. Hardly dinnertime." He grinned at her out of the corner of his eyes and read the text. "Huh, I did say that."

"Yes," Maddy said, enjoying that she'd been right. "And today is very clearly the seventeenth." She navigated to her calendar and showed him the phone again.

He didn't even look at it. He stared straight at her. "Maybe I just wanted to see you."

She laughed and shook her head. "You made a mistake. Just admit it."

"I made a mistake," he said, grinning like it was the best one he'd made in his lifetime. "So...can I take you to dinner tonight and tomorrow?"

"Oh, you shouldn't commit to tomorrow so soon," she said.

"Why not?"

"What if tonight goes badly?"

"It won't."

"You sound so sure of that." She grinned up at him from beneath her eyelashes, a tactic that had worked on the men in college. It worked now too, if the electric charge in Ben's eyes meant anything about his attraction to her.

"I am," he said. "I like talking to you, Maddy."

She stepped slightly closer to him, wishing she wasn't wearing a paint-splattered T-shirt with the outline of the earth on it. "How old are you, Ben?"

"How old am I?"

"Yes." She reached out and smoothed that collar down, her fingertips brushing the skin along his neck. Fire licked through her, and she didn't try to quench it. "How old do you think I am?"

"I don't really know," he said. "Haven't thought about it."

Maddy's eyebrows went up. "I have."

"Why?"

"I suspect I'm much older than you, that's why." Maddy wasn't purposefully trying to ruin the relationship. But she knew better than most to be realistic about things. "I can't give you kids, for example."

"Wow, Maddy," he said, looking away. "We haven't even gone out yet, and you're talking about kids?" His gaze came back to hers, and he was a little rough around the edges. She hadn't seen a single female among the Coast Guard members on the boat or at the station, and perhaps Ben was severely out of practice.

Hiding in the shadows would suggest such a thing too.

She glanced to the parking lot and didn't see a car. "How did you get here?"

"I have a bike," he said.

She searched for a bicycle and didn't see one. "Where?"

"Right there." He pointed to a motorcycle, not a bicycle, parked down on the end of the sidewalk, and Maddy's pulse flopped, flipped, and floundered in her chest.

Looking back at him, she saw Captain Benjamin Downs for what he was. An extremely handsome man in his mid-thirties if she was a day. A renegade. The bad boy. The very sexy, renegade, bad boy. He was someone who played with fire, and where there was fire, there were flames.

And flames burned.

She suddenly *wanted* to get burned by this man.

"I'm not talking about kids," Maddy said. "Though I have two. Kyle is twenty-two, and Chelsea is nineteen, about to be twenty. How much older are you than them, Ben?"

He sighed in a slightly exaggerated way and said, "Fourteen years older than your oldest."

Maddy hadn't excelled in math, but she knew what twenty-two plus fourteen was, and that only added up to thirty-six.

She'd be forty-seven just after the New Year. He was

going to be very glad he hadn't committed to *any* dates once she told him.

She looked back to the motorcycle. "I told Julia I'd make the Sunday feast tonight. It's something we want to put on the menu for when the inn reopens. You could stay for that, if you'd like."

"I'd like that," he said, the words almost a growl in his throat.

With her attention back on those beautiful eyes, she asked, "What are the chances that motorcycle seats two?"

"High," he said, swallowing. His eyes dropped to her mouth, and Maddy curved it into a smile.

"Maybe our second date then." She stepped back, realizing how far forward he'd been leaning. The magnetism between them snapped, leaving Ben blinking and Maddy moving toward the entrance to the inn already.

He scrambled to follow her. "How many years older than me are you?"

"Almost eleven," she said over her shoulder, expecting him to stutter-step, stall, and slink home under the stars on that sporty cycle.

Instead, his footsteps kept pace with hers, and they reached the steps at the back of the lobby at the same time. He looked at her and took her hand in his almost simultaneously. "That's not too many," he said.

"No?"

"I see what you mean about the kids, but no. It's not too many for me. Is it too many for you?"

Maddy honestly didn't know. When she reached the top of the steps and saw Julia fill the doorway, she released Ben's hand and said, "Jury's still out," to him, and "I'm so sorry I'm so late. My daughter called, and she can *talk* and *talk*," to Julia.

Julia looked past her to Ben. "Is he staying for dinner?"

Maddy paused in front of her. "Is that okay? I can send him away if you'd like."

"It's fine," Julia said without hesitation, and she brought her eyes back to Maddy's. They'd once been able to communicate without saying much, and the moment between them deepened and lengthened as the same thing happened now.

Julia's dark eyes danced with mischief, and Maddy shook her head slightly. "Ben got the date of our first dinner mixed up," she said, turning back to him. "I hope he doesn't mind waiting about an hour to eat what could be potentially disgusting."

"I'm fine," he assured her.

"It won't be disgusting, besides," Julia said, grinning at him for all she was worth. "Maddy is the best cook on the island of Nantucket right now."

"Oh, ho, that is not true," Maddy said, the pressure on her shoulders intensifying.

"Come with me," Julia said, ignoring her as she went past. "We can hang your jacket in the lobby, and then I want to get your opinion on some bedding."

"Bedding?" Ben looked at Maddy blankly, and while

Julia's back was turned, she held up two fingers. Ben cocked his head, clearly puzzled, and Maddy hurried to drop her hand when Julia spun back to them.

"Yes, bedding. Now, come *on*, Captain. We have a few minutes before dinner."

CHAPTER SEVENTEEN

Julia just *knew* Maddy had somehow influenced Ben to choose all the same bedding she had. She didn't know how, but as he picked yet another sheet set that Maddy had insisted on, Julia decided to put them away.

"Thank you for your help," she said.

"They'd all be nice," he said, his eyes so bright.

Julia gave him the best smile she could muster. It stretched her face oddly, but she didn't know how to make it sit right. She didn't want to tell him she was going for so much more than *nice*. She and Maddy wanted words like *upscale*, *inviting*, and *luxurious* to show up in their reviews.

The scent of something turning brown and delicious rose from the kitchen below, and Julia turned to leave the linens behind in the closet. They'd ordered far more than one sheet set per room, of course. They needed at least three to be able to make up the rooms in their themes, keep up with the laundry, and provide fresh sheets every day should a guest desire it.

Sometimes Julia wondered what she was doing. Running an inn wasn't a walk in the park, and she felt like that was what she should be doing with her life right now. Taking her phone, tucking it in her pocket, and finding a bench. Then she could watch families play with their dogs and children, check her messages, and enjoy the New York City skyline all around her.

Here, there were big buildings, especially in the downtown area. Out on the Point, though, the view was more ocean and sand for miles, which she also liked. It calmed her in a different way than the vibrant city atmosphere, and as she led Captain Ben back downstairs, she asked, "Have you been stationed in Nantucket long?"

"About a year, ma'am."

"How long do your appointments usually last?"

"I requested Nantucket, after having served in various other places. Unless I mess up, I think I'll get to stay here as long as I want."

"They let you do that?" She reached the bottom of the steps and looked back up to him. He was extremely good-looking, for a woman who liked that corn-fed, blue-eyed type of look. Maddy always had, while Julia usually preferred a darker-haired, more brooding, mysterious kind of man.

Ben didn't mince words, that was for sure, and he didn't look like the type to play games in his relationships.

"The Coast Guard is pretty good about that, yes," he said, smiling as he took the last few steps. He sighed and looked around. "I was expecting this place to be a bit more shambly."

"You were?"

"Maddy made it sound like you two existed in chaos nearly all the time." His gaze met hers for half a second and flitted away. "But the office is nice. The lobby is ready. Even that room just needed to be loaded with furniture."

Julia looked around, trying to see things the way he did. Vivian from the Historical Society would be dropping by next week to get an update on their progress. At that point, they'd be in their fourth full week of renovations, with only five more until the Society would like the inn to be open for the holiday season.

"The structure of the inn wasn't in question," she said slowly. "But we'll take down all the curtains in here and put up new ones to match the new aesthetic. New rugs. New blinds. Even the displays will all be updated and new." Julia had taken the old album to a historical documents restorer in one of the oldest buildings on Nantucket. The scent of ancient things still stuck in her nose.

"We need to hire people," she said. "Maids and hotel staff. We need booking software. The only thing the previous caretakers were using was the phone. People had to call and make a reservation, which they kept in a book."

"You're kidding."

The weight on Julia's shoulders testified that she wasn't. She shook her head, because Ben probably couldn't see how much the tasks to be done weighed her down. "I'm not. So we need a website too. Everyone does everything online. We need to assign prices to the rooms. Learn the taxes. Come up with programming. We'll have boat tours, island tours, family activities, and canoe rentals. Maddy has to perfect all the menus."

She drew in a deep breath. "And things take time, because she and I are not the same, and we sometimes don't agree on which bedding will look the best in each room." She flashed him a smile. "You picked all the same things she did."

"I did?"

"I suppose you two are compatible," Julia said, deciding to cut off her teasing there. Maddy wouldn't appreciate it, and Julia didn't want to do anything to upset her delicate relationship with her once-best friend. In fact, she was doing all she could to rebuild that relationship, and that included knowing when to stop talking.

"Let's go see how Maddy's doing in the kitchen."

Ben led the way this time, going around the staircase and into the dining room. This room hadn't been painted yet, though Julia could've sworn all they'd been doing for days was painting. Not just her and Maddy either, but

Janey and Tessa too. Helen brought pastries and a Bluetooth speaker to play her oldies throughout the house. Julia could admit that the work had been easier and faster with more hands and the hope of real friends here on the island.

Her thoughts moved to Tessa, and as she took a seat at the far end of the huge dining room table while Ben went into the kitchen, she removed her phone from the pocket of her shorts. *Anything from your PI on Rick Fry?*

Tessa had been keeping Julia in-the-know with regards to the man they claimed had kidnapped and drugged her just this very summer. Julia's stomach swooped just recalling the story she'd heard second-hand. She'd looked up the incident, and there had been several articles about it, including one where Tessa—an "unknown woman"—had washed up on the shore in mainland Massachusetts.

Fear gripped her lungs now as it had then. Rick or Riggs or whatever name he went by, wasn't to be trifled with. She knew that very strongly.

When Tessa had mentioned that she'd hired an old friend from the town in Pennsylvania where she'd used to live to look into Julia's father, Julia had suggested they switch the focus of that PI to Rick Fry. Tessa had made the call instantly.

Julia had been telling Tessa anything she wanted to know about her dad. Familiar heaviness settled in her gut at the thought of her father. She'd had no idea of his indiscretions, and she supposed she should be grateful for that. She wasn't sure if she should allow them to color her opinion of him now. He'd been a kind, loving, doting father. He'd worked a lot to provide a good life for her, her mom, and her siblings.

Nothing substantial, Tessa said. *I'm hoping to talk to him tomorrow. We have a call set up.*

Perfect, Julia sent back, and then she tapped back to her main list, scrolled to her sister's name, and called Annie. Her sister had endured a divorce about three years ago, and Julia had connected with her on a completely new level this past spring and summer as her own separation and divorce had happened.

"Jules," Annie said, her voice bright enough to erase the frown from Julia's face. "What's new in Nantucket?"

"Sheet sets," Julia said with a sigh. "Paint color. Cold weather. What's new in Chatham?"

"Medical bills," she said. "A bacon-maple cheeseburger at the pub down the street. My daughter's attitude."

Julia laughed, glad when Annie started hers out with a scoff and then joined her. "Teenagers are the worst."

"Right? And I have two of them at the same time."

"Both girls." Julia had never raised teen girls, but her youngest sibling, Eric, had twin girls, and they'd been handful since babyhood. He claimed they only got harder and harder until about sixteen, which was the age of Annie's oldest. She had a fourteen-year-old too, the same age as Eric's twins, and Annie worked full-time as a nurse to support her girls.

Her husband of fifteen years had come out as a gay man, and he wanted to be involved in his girls' life, but he didn't want to be married to a woman anymore. Donovan still lived in Chatham, and as far as Julia knew, he did all the things a good father would do for his kids. He had a new boyfriend the last Julia had heard, but she didn't ask about that this time.

Instead, she said, "You and the girls should come to Nantucket," she said. "Fall break."

"That's in three weeks."

"Yes," Julia said, a new excitement growing inside her. "You can be mock guests, and we'll see how everything runs. We'll have a couple of rooms done by them, I'm sure." She actually wasn't sure if that was true, but she'd give up sleep to make it so. She suddenly missed her sister so, so much.

"I'll talk to Paige about it. She hates leaving during breaks, because she gets left out of friend stuff."

"Leave her with Don, then."

"She likes that even less," Annie said under her breath. "She can drive now, which is great for me, and horrible for me. She'll want to stay alone, but she's sort of dating this new boy... I can't leave her here alone."

"Sort of dating a new boy?"

"That's what she said."

"How do you sort of date someone?"

"You know, you like, hang out and stuff." Annie spoke in a super flippant, almost sarcastic, tone, and laughed immediately afterward. "Those were the notes I got. They hold hands, but they haven't kissed. He's absolutely *not* her boyfriend, because she doesn't want one of those, but he's already asked her to the Christmas Ball..." Annie sighed. "I have no idea how to talk Teen."

"It's September. Isn't it Homecoming before the Christmas Ball?"

"Oh, yes," Annie said, her voice pitching up. "They're going to that too. I told her if going to every dance with him is implied, then he's her boyfriend. She disagreed —vehemently."

"Wow." Julia had loved raising her boys, but dating for a boy was much easier. If her sons wanted to go to the prom, they went. There was no crying if they didn't get asked. No dress shopping. Shoes, makeup, body shapers, nope, nope, nope. Nothing terribly hard.

"Then she went to 'hang out' with Jackson, as if I don't know there's a difference between this Logan guy and the boy who's been her best friend since first grade."

"See? You know something about dating and teens," Julia said, hearing laughter coming from the kitchen. She got to her feet and wandered that way, taking in the dark landscape illuminated by street lamps and the distant restaurant across the parking lot.

"Sure," Annie said dryly. "Anyway, I'll talk to her. I could use the break, and I did take three days off from work already."

"No plans? I don't want to disrupt your plans."

"No plans, other than sleeping in."

Julia smiled, imagining her younger sister here with her. Annie had always been her best friend, as she was only three years younger than Julia. They'd been close, even as teens, and she folded one arm across herself and rested her arm holding the phone against her opposite hand. "I miss you. I miss the city."

Annie didn't immediately try to tell her New York City was dirty, loud, or not to be missed. *It's just a city*, ran through her head, but Julia had always loved the city.

"Are you going to Mom and Dad's for Thanksgiving?" she asked instead.

"I don't know. Are they hosting this year?"

"I think so," she said. "I'm not sure what rotation Eric is on. I'll call Mom and talk to her about it."

"Mm." Julia didn't want to commit, because she wasn't sure how she'd react when she came face-to-face with her father. "Annie, I have something to tell you. Something I learned a couple of weeks ago, here on Nantucket. Something I'm still grappling with; that's why I haven't said anything yet."

"Okay," her sister said slowly.

Julia had gone down the length of the table and now looked out the front of the lighthouse, which overlooked the dock and then the water beyond. She glanced toward the door that led into the kitchen, catching only a flash of movement as Maddy moved from one side to the other.

"I met a woman here," Julia said, turning and going

back the way she'd come. Maddy knew about Janey, but Ben didn't. She didn't need to air her dirty laundry to near-strangers. "Her name is Janey Forsythe. She's only six months younger than I am." Julia cleared her throat, appreciating that her sister didn't immediately jump in with questions.

"She's our half-sister. We have the same father."

Annie could be heard breathing on the other end of the line. "Are you serious?" she finally asked.

"Yes." Julia didn't want to get into all the details, the pictures, the meetings. "Do you think Mom knows?"

"No, I don't think Mom knows," Annie practically spat. "Are you *sure*? How do you know?"

"There are pictures. Janey tracked down a friend of Dad's, and he said they all had relationships with her mother that summer." Julia sighed. "She did a paternity test on two of the men. It wasn't either of them, and Dad was the other one."

"I—" Annie didn't continue. She cleared her throat. "I see why you've been grappling."

"It's a great word, right?" Julia smiled, the action once again pulling wrong.

"Almost ready," Maddy said behind her, and Julia turned toward her and lifted her free hand to say she'd heard.

"I'll let you go," Annie said. "Real quick: how are things going with Maddy?"

"Good," Julia said, and she realized that she meant it. "Really good."

"Wow, it doesn't sound like you're lying."

"I'm not."

"You sound really good," Annie said. "I'm glad, Jules."

"I am too," she said. "I love you, Annie."

"Love you too, sis." The call ended, and Julia stretched her neck forward and back as she replaced her phone in her pocket.

"All right," Maddy said. "I've got the Sunday feast ready."

Julia turned and watched her bring out a bowl of shrimp salad in one hand and a bowl of steaming mashed potatoes in another. "Ben is bringing out the chicken, and I'll grab the pot roast, and then we'll sample." She beamed in Julia's direction, and when Julia smiled back, the gesture finally felt like it fit on her face the right way, despite still having so many things up in the air.

It's fine, she told herself. *Tessa will talk to her PI tomorrow, and there will be some new information.*

There had to be. If not, Julia felt sure her patience would snap, and she'd have even more work to do around The Lighthouse Inn as she cleaned up from the aftermath of that.

CHAPTER EIGHTEEN

Tessa hung up and stared straight ahead, her thoughts bouncing around inside her head. The one at the forefront of her mind screamed that she should've recorded the call with Terry Pratt, the private investigator she'd hired.

She'd originally asked him to look into Ryan Harper, so Tessa would be armed with all the information she needed to help Janey make a decision about how or when or even if she should approach him.

She hadn't taken that from Terry's plate, but she'd also forwarded him all of the articles Julia had found about Rick Fry, as well as the pictures from the summer of 1974, and she'd asked him to find everything he could about the case, about Rick, about Riggs Friedman, and about little missing Louisa.

He'd given Tessa a fairly substantial background on

Ryan Harper last week, all done through email and encrypted zip files. There hadn't been anything too surprising or hair-raising in the files. His degree from NYU in English, and then a law degree from Harvard. His employment history, his public assets, his home address. The names of his wife and children, as well as the fact that he was a law-abiding, tax-paying citizen. He'd never been arrested. Always filed his taxes on time. Owned three cars and a boat. Standard stuff.

By all accounts, and with all of Terry's digging, Ryan Harper appeared to be a normal man. Maybe one who cheated on his wife, but Tessa had decided that such behavior was more normal than she'd like to admit. After all, she would've never thought Ron would do that to her, and he had.

She hadn't told Julia or Janey about her secret investigation into Ryan, and she didn't plan to. To her knowledge, Janey hadn't contacted him, and Julia seemed to answer questions about her father freely. If she needed to disclose that she knew a few things about him, including where he banked, she would. Right now, she didn't need to.

She looked down at the notebook resting on her lap. She'd started scrawling notes as fast as she could once Terry had started talking about Rick Fry. Phrases stuck out at her, and she clicked to open the pen and start to add some of the things she hadn't had time to get down in ink.

Got ahold of the police interviews stared up at her, and

she wrote Rick's name next to that, as well as his parents'. They'd all been interviewed when Louisa went missing. She added, "He'll send" next to that, and she got up to retrieve her laptop. Terry was nothing if not prompt, and she wanted to see the interviews.

He'd said they contained some really interesting information, and since Louisa had come to Nantucket Point with her family, but she hadn't left, he actually believed she was still somewhere on the island.

"Alive?" Tessa had asked.

"I don't know," Terry said. "Rick went back to New Jersey to his boat repair shop. He fled when the police showed up. That's what we know."

"Do you think he's Riggs Friedman?"

"Honestly? Yes."

Honestly? Yes.

The words haunted Tessa as she continued to add notes to the scribbles in the notebook. She didn't want to forget anything, and while she might not read it again, the act of writing something down helped her to remember things easier.

She paused again, trying to think through everything else he'd said. Rick's social security number hadn't been used in almost four decades. His father had died three years ago, and his mother lived in a memory care facility in a quiet suburb in New Jersey, not far from where she'd lived since the disappearance of her daughter.

The case had gone cold, though police departments in

both states—Massachusetts and New Jersey—had tried to reconstruct it.

Tessa had no idea how two people could simply disappear off the face of the planet without a trace, though she supposed it would've been easier years ago, when people weren't so easily tracked through devices and credit cards.

She opened the laptop and clicked over to her email. Terry had indeed already sent the police interviews, and Tessa started reading. Her life used to include shelving books and weeding her garden. She'd go for a walk each morning and look forward to seeing her husband on the weekends.

In the past few months, she'd learned she had no full-blood siblings, she'd been drugged and kidnapped, and she'd become a millionaire. She could read a police interview too.

The pages that Terry had scanned were clearly old, typed up on a typewriter, and included who was speaking in all caps.

Detective Lind identified himself, and said who he was interviewing: Jack Fry. The man told how he'd brought Rick to his marriage with Paula Davis, and then they'd had Louisa together. She was quite a bit younger than Rick—fifteen years younger—but he'd adored her from the moment she was born.

The detective asked questions about the family's vacation in Nantucket Point. Jack gave answers in a fairly detailed way. The four of them had come and they'd booked two rooms at The Lighthouse Inn. They'd stayed for a week. They'd returned to their home in New Jersey.

Detective Lind: Why didn't you notify the police of your daughter's disappearance while in Nantucket?

Jack: My wife didn't want to.

Detective Lind: Why not?

Jack: She thought Rick had taken her with him.

Detective Lind: What do you mean?

Jack: Rick left with Louisa before we did. We stayed for an extra night by ourselves, and we didn't realize Louisa wasn't at home until we got here.

Detective Lind: Where did Rick say she was?

Jack: He said she'd been taken from the beach.

Detective Lind: And you just accepted that?

Jack: Of course not. We called the police instantly.

Detective Lind: And you have no idea where your daughter is now?

Jack: If I knew where my daughter was, why would I be here?

Detective Lind: Maybe you want to protect your son. Maybe you want to stall so he can do something with the body. Maybe—

Jack: Stop it. Don't say body.

Detective Lind: So you think your daughter is alive?

Jack: Of course she's alive. A father knows when his child isn't alive.

Tessa sat back from the transcript, her heart breaking for Jack Fry. She'd been doing plenty of her own research while waiting for Terry's report, and she knew that people not found within twenty-four hours of their abduction had a very high chance of never being found, or at least not being found alive.

Louisa Fry had been missing for forty-five years.

Paula Fry's report matched her husband's almost exactly. They'd had a nice vacation in Nantucket. They loved going there as a family. Rick had taken Louisa and returned to New Jersey, so they could have a couple of days to themselves. When they returned to New Jersey, they learned that Louisa wasn't there. They'd called the police.

"It doesn't make sense," Tessa said, getting up from the computer. Rick had reported that Louisa had been taken from the beaches *here*, not the beaches in New Jersey. He'd said he thought she was still here.

"Could the whole story be fabricated?"

Terry had said it wasn't his job to make a judgment on the things he found. He dug them up; he gave them to his paying clients. What they did from there was up to them.

She opened the front door and greeted the morning breeze. The extra oxygen cleared her head and filled her lungs, making breathing easier. She went around and opened all the blinds and windows, needing to infuse some of this life into the cottage.

She and Janey had cleaned out all of the old and bad memories, leaving room for the good things to grow. Tessa had worked on the yard and it sat ready for the fall and winter. The garage had been cleaned, and all of the money had been moved and put in safe accounts belonging to her, or Janey, or the two of them jointly.

Back inside, she set the electric kettle to heat and went down the hall to change into her docent polo, as she had to work that afternoon at the Nautical Museum. She'd just started the job, and she'd managed to fit in a lot of painting at The Lighthouse Inn around her few part-time shifts each week.

With a fresh cup of tea and ready for work in a few hours, Tessa resumed her position in front of the laptop. She only had one more interview to read, and she double-clicked to get the one Rick Fry had given to the police before he'd fled and never been heard from again.

Two detectives had conducted his interview together, and in their opening statement, Detective Carrole made sure to mention that this was an interview, not an interrogation, though Tessa wasn't really sure what the difference was.

Detective Lind: State your name.

Rick: Rick Fry.

Detective Lind: Just Rick? Not Richard?

Rick: Just Rick.

A handwritten note sat out to the side that read: *It really is just Rick. Checked birth certificate.*

Detective Lind: Tell us what happened, Rick.

Rick: Louisa loves the beach, so on the morning we were set to leave and come back to Jersey—

Detective Carrole: And when was that?

Rick: July 16th.

Detective Carrole: 1974.

Rick: Yes, the summer of 1974.

Detective Carrole: Go on.

Rick: She begged to go out and build one more sandcastle. I said she could, and she went out with the caretaker while I started packing up. My step-mom went out a few minutes later. The plan was that I would get our bags ready to go, then get Louisa when we had to head to the ferry station.

Detective Lind: Who was the caretaker?

Rick: Farrah Garland? Garfield? Something like that. She was an older woman, and she was going out to get some activity set up that would happen after we left. She said she'd take Louisa.

Another handwritten note out to the side said: *Caretakers—Farrah and Ralph Garry.* Tessa had never known the Garrys. In her memory, the Michaels had always tended to The Lighthouse Inn, but this was about a year before she'd even been born.

Detective Lind: When did you realize Louisa was gone?

Rick: When I went to find her about an hour later. She wasn't with Farrah, who was setting up rings on the beach. My parents weren't around. I went back to the inn to ask about them, but no one had seen them.

Detective Lind: And you just left Nantucket? You didn't wait to tell your parents?

Rick: No, I did. I missed the ferry and the flight back to Jersey, waiting for them. When they finally returned, they said to go ahead. I had to get back to Jersey to work. They'd find Louisa and she could stay with them. I even went up onto the upper balcony, because it looks out over the whole beach, east and west. I remember, Louisa loved that spot, and while it was busy on the beach that day, I couldn't see her.

I did see Farrah running the games for the kids, and I searched the line for her. She wasn't there. We always went west on the beach, and I spotted a sandcastle down the beach a little bit. A little girl ran over to it, and she had on Louisa's pink swimsuit. It was her. I even yelled to her from the balcony.

In that moment, someone came out of the crowd and scooped her up. They disappeared among the bodies and beach umbrellas. That was the last time I saw her.

Detective Carrole: Your parents said they sent her ahead to New Jersey with you.

Rick: That's not true.

Detective Lind: What happened after she disappeared into the crowd? Did you see who it was?

Rick: I couldn't tell from so far away. They wore a pair of blue trunks. It was a man.

Detective Lind: What color was his hair?

Rick: I don't know.

Detective Lind: How tall would you say he was?

Rick: I don't know.

Detective Carrole: Come on, Rick. You expect us to believe this?

Rick: Yes. I'm telling the truth.

Detective Lind: Did anyone hear you yell for her?

Rick: I don't know. Farrah was right there.

Detective Lind: Did you go down to the beach?

Rick: Yes, I ran down there as quickly as I could, but the sandcastle was gone. No one knew where she was. No one had seen her.

Detective Lind: So you then left Nantucket?

Rick: Yes. My parents said they'd take care of it.

Detective Carrole: I'm confused. Did you see Louisa from the upper balcony before or after you told your parents she was missing?

Rick: Before.

Detective Carrole: In the time between when you couldn't find her, and they showed up. Sometime in there? While you were missing your flight?

Rick: Yes.

Detective Carrole: They didn't find that odd?

Rick: Mom said she knew a lot of people in the cottages along the beach there, and Louisa had probably gone home with one of them for lunch. She didn't seem worried.

Detective Lind: When did you know you should worry?

Rick: When they got back to Jersey and said they

couldn't find her. They said there had been an accident, and that we needed to call the police.

Detective Lind: Who called the police?

Rick: My dad.

Detective Lind: And you have no idea where Louisa is?

Rick: No. None.

The transcript ended, and Tessa leaned away from the computer screen, her heart thumping in the back of her throat. "The stories don't match up. The parents said they didn't know she was missing until they returned home. Rick says he didn't take her from Nantucket."

She got to her feet and left everything right where it was. Outside, she headed across the sand toward the beautiful, creamy lighthouse that had always been such a beacon to her. It lit the path for plenty of others too, and Tessa had such a fascination with lighthouses. What they symbolized meant a great deal to her, and she'd enjoyed her childhood playing in the shade of this one, and seeing the light calling to sailors from the operational one further down the beach.

She had to get to work soon, but she entered The Lighthouse Inn and headed for the steps at the back of the lobby. Neither Maddy or Julia stopped her, and she supposed they were either in one of the second-floor bedrooms, working, or out running errands.

No one intercepted her as she reached the roof above the second floor, and no one told her she shouldn't scale the ladder going to the upper balcony. She arrived out of breath, with her heartbeat sprinting laps around her ribs.

She stood there, the wind whipping her hair this way and that, looking west over the beach. She tried to imagine it as Rick would've seen it. Golden July sunshine. Scads of people. Brightly colored umbrellas, chairs, and suits.

A caretaker setting up games below. The crash of the waves against the dock directly in front of and below her. She closed her eyes and tried to hear his voice reading the transcript. Giving the interview.

Had he been scared? Nervous? Did he know he'd have to run then? Had he suspected his parents?

What happened to Louisa? Was Rick Fry really Riggs Friedman?

Tessa sat down, her back against the round column that continued up to a point, and looked out over the water, letting her thoughts and questions crash inside her mind, the same way the waves did on the shore below.

She didn't have any answers, but Julia had said there was a logbook. Perhaps she needed to get her hands on that and see who'd really come and gone from the inn that summer.

CHAPTER NINETEEN

Maddy took the last slice of lemon zucchini bread Tessa had brought from the bakery over on the aptly named Bakery Avenue. "I missed something." She looked back and forth between Tessa and Julia. The two of them had been whispering for days, always clamming up the moment Maddy or Helen walked into the room. If it wasn't that behavior, she'd found the two of them staring at their phones and then exchanging meaningful glances.

"Not much," Julia said, reaching for her drink.

Maddy huffed as she sat down. "Look, I'm just going to be blunt."

Julia started to blink with the speed of hummingbird wings, and Tessa didn't bother to tear her gaze from the Sound she faced. They sat outside on the outdoor dining patio, which they'd just finished sweeping and power-washing that morning.

"I know you two are conspiring about something. It's annoying, walking in on a conversation that abruptly stops." She narrowed her eyes at Tessa, the brunette who'd somehow come to be one of Maddy's closest friends over the past month. "I've told you all about Kyle's wedding, and my dates with Captain Gorgeous. I want to know what you're talking about."

"Nothing," Julia said, but she didn't possess the willpower not to look at Tessa.

Tessa definitely held everything closer, and she appeared calm as the most tranquil morning known to man. Maddy folded her arms and scoffed again.

"Rick Fry," Tessa said. "Well, really his sister, Louisa. She disappeared right here on Nantucket Point, and we've been gossiping about where she might be."

Maddy's eyes widened, and she volleyed her gaze back and forth between Tessa and Julia. "That little girl you mentioned from years ago?"

"Yes," Julia said, likewise folding her arms. "We've gone over the police interviews, the logbook from here at the inn, and as many newspaper articles as we can find. It's like she and her brother just disappeared without a trace."

Maddy sat back in her chair when she realized she'd started to lean forward. "Why do you care?"

"I knew Rick Fry," Tessa said. "Well, a man I thought was someone else, but who's actually Rick Fry."

"You know that for certain?" Maddy asked. She had heard this part of the story.

"Not definitively, no." Tessa became the third woman there to cross her arms, and Maddy forced herself to undo hers and relax. "I simply suspect. It's a strong suspicion."

"Helen says it's not him," Maddy said, because the older woman didn't keep anything a secret.

"She also called Janey by her daughter's name the other day," Tessa said quietly, refocusing back on the water beyond the railing surrounding the patio.

Maddy looked back and forth between the two women she'd just eaten lunch with. She and Julia had been making great progress on the inn, and they had no problem speaking and existing with each other now. Tessa came to the inn almost every day, and Maddy really liked her too. She was soft-spoken but a really hard worker, and she had a brain she used. Janey came less often, but when she did, she showed up with pastries and a smile, so Maddy hadn't been turning her away.

It had been wonderful to start fresh, something she'd wanted to do but had dreaded at the same time. Making friends could certainly be a chore, but Tessa and Janey had almost fallen into her lap, and she did like them.

"So you're looking into Louisa's disappearance?" she asked.

"Just trying to get the facts," Tessa said. "Riggs

Friedman—who I think is Rick Fry—kidnapped me a couple of months ago."

Maddy sucked in a breath, her mind whirring the way her computer did when it got too hot. "I had no idea."

Tessa simply nodded and watched the water, and Maddy wondered what she was reliving inside her memory box.

"Here you are," Helen said as she slid open the door and stepped onto the patio. "Did you not hear me calling you?"

Maddy jumped to her feet. "No, Helen, sorry." She offered her chair to the older woman, who took it.

"I even went up to the roof and yelled." She glanced around, a heavy frown weighing down her eyelids. "You didn't hear me? I would've been right there." She pointed up to her right, toward the second-floor rooftop. Maddy hadn't been up there since she and Julia had done their initial walk-through, as she didn't anticipate guests needing to access that area of the inn.

Now, though, she wondered if they should put some chaises up there and offer a drink service. With every corner she turned, Maddy could think of something else the inn could offer for guests. She needed to rein in her thoughts, or Julia was going to kill her.

Vivian was scheduled to come to the inn tomorrow for a walk-through and update, and instead of taking another seat, Maddy said, "We need to get that last room done up today. Vivian's coming tomorrow."

Julia sighed, but she got to her feet too. "You're right. Let's go get it done." She stepped over to Helen and leaned down to give her a kiss on the forehead. "Sorry we didn't hear you, Helen. The inn has a reinforced cement roof over the second level. They added it after the New England hurricane ripped across the island in 1938."

Maddy stilled, her turn to blink rapidly as she looked at Julia. "Since when do you know that?"

"Since I started studying Nantucket history for the island tours," she said, raising her chin a little. "There's a fascinating little volume on this building, and how it was rebuilt after a couple of bad storms, the worst of which was the New England hurricane of 1938."

"Is that when they sealed off the upper balcony?" Tessa got to her feet too, collecting her glass that still held half of its lemonade.

"What?" Julia asked, and all eyes flew to her and then Tessa.

"I was up there a few days ago," she said. "It's solid, though I swear the other lighthouses I've toured have their electrical components in the center shaft like that. It goes up to the lantern." She turned toward the door, and then spun back to the table. "Wait." The fire in her eyes suggested the inner workings of her mind as the wheels turned furiously.

"When did they shut down the lighthouse here?" Maddy asked. "Like, when did it stop being a lighthouse and start being an inn?"

Julia's eyes rounded now too, and true fear sat in them. "The lighthouse was still operational," Julia said slowly. "Until 1974—even after it had become the inn."

Silence rained down on the patio, and while Maddy didn't know all of the same information Julia and Tessa did, she didn't dare move. She'd heard plenty of their early musings, but she hadn't known Tessa had been up on the balcony a few days ago. She hadn't known they were looking into the disappearance of Louisa as more than casual bystanders. She still didn't know if they'd done that, but she had an inkling they had. Could the public just get police interviews, for example?

Maddy certainly didn't know how, and she gave a quick prayer of gratitude that she'd never had the occasion to know things like that.

"When did the inn open?" Maddy asked, looking to Julia-the-Nantucket-encyclopedia for the answer.

"1972," she said. "The first caretakers only lasted a couple of years. Then a new couple came in for about fifteen, but the inn almost went out of business. The newspaper article had a quote that said people liked staying in an *operational* lighthouse, but it wasn't operational anymore. Then the Michaels showed up, and they turned everything around."

Maddy nodded, her throat so dry though she'd drunk so much while snacking on coffee cake for the past half-hour.

"So the lighthouse was an operational lighthouse until

the summer of 1974," Tessa said, her throat working hard as she swallowed. "But the inn opened in 1972."

"Yes," Julia said. "That's what the book said."

"The caretakers were only here a couple of years."

"They left after the disappearance of Louisa Fry." Julia's voice barely disturbed the still-as-death air, and a chill ran down Maddy's arms despite the sweater she wore.

Seconds ticked by, and no one said anything. Maddy finally exhaled and said, "I don't think it was the fact that the lighthouse wasn't operational anymore that almost drove the inn out of business. I think people must've been afraid to stay here. Maybe they thought their children would disappear too."

Tessa turned and opened the door. "I'm going to go look in the upper balcony."

"Wait," Julia said, scrambling after her.

It took several seconds for Maddy's brain to process what she'd said—and what she meant by it. "Look *in* the upper balcony?" Her eyes felt as round and as big as the moon, and she took off after Tessa and Julia.

"No," she said under her breath as she moved as quickly as she could. Every time her foot hit the floor, she said the word again. "No, no, no." She made it to the second-floor rooftop just as Julia disappeared up the ladder to the balcony.

"Julia." Maddy shaded her eyes and looked up, trying to see whatever she could. "Tessa." The wind up here whipped through her very soul, and Maddy's labored breathing chilled her to the bone. Perhaps that was caused by the very thought of what they might find concealed in the upper balcony.

Something drove her up the ladder too, and when she arrived, she found Tessa down on her knees, rearing back with a hammer in one hand. The sound of splintering wood rent the air, cleaving through Maddy as if the clawed end of the tool had hit her straight in the chest.

"In the interview, he said the upper balcony was her favorite place," Tessa said, panting and sobbing at the same time. Maddy wanted to tell her to stop. She didn't need to do this. She hadn't even known Louisa.

The anguish of the other woman filled the air, and Maddy didn't understand it. "Tessa," she said, dropping to her knees too. Julia just stood out of the way, her arms cinched around her middle as if she needed them there to hold herself together.

Tessa drove the claw into the wood again, and then again.

"Stop it," Maddy commanded, her voice back to that Mom-tone no one would dare to defy. It at least brought up Tessa's head. "Give me the hammer." She held out her hand, as surprised as anyone when Tessa did what she said.

"We're going downstairs," Maddy said. "We're going to call the police. We're not going to do this. Not us." She looked from Tessa's shock-filled expression to Julia's terrified one. "Go now, Julia. Right now."

She nodded and went back down the ladder while Maddy helped Tessa to her feet. "You're next," she said to the other woman. She shook as if someone had stuffed her full of batteries and then wound her up to go, go, go. "Careful on that last step. It's pretty far."

Maddy hurried down after Tessa, who hadn't moved more than a couple of feet from the ladder. Maddy put her arm around the other woman's shoulders and said, "Come on, Tess. Let's go make tea." She'd call the police, and then Ben. She'd make sure everyone got something hot to eat and drink, and no matter what they found beneath the floorboards in the upper balcony, Maddy would deal with it.

That was what Maddy had been doing for the past twenty-five years, and all of that scandal prep and *I-know-how-to-handle-this* might as well pay off now.

She herded everyone into the kitchen and started brewing the tea before she pulled out her phone. "Okay." She let out a long breath. "I'm going to call the police. Any objections?"

Julia and Tessa shook their heads in such a similar manner, Maddy might have suspected they were partially related, though they weren't.

"Helen?"

"Do you really think she's up there? All this time?"

"We have no way of knowing," Maddy said. "The

police will come, and they'll sort it all out." She turned her back on the other three women and stepped over to the list of numbers taped to the wall. She had no idea who'd written this list or how old it was. It was one thing she hadn't pulled down yet, because it had the number for Poison Control and the fire department, both of which she might need to call in lieu of nine-one-one.

This wasn't an emergency—not at true one, though Maddy's heart beat like someone had only one more wire to snip and then her whole life would blow up—and when a recording said, "The Nantucket Sheriff's Department is open seven days a week..." she hit the zero and closed her eyes to pray.

A few moments later, a woman said, "Operator, where may I direct your call?"

"Hello," Maddy said as if discussing her lunch reservations with an upscale restaurant in the city. "My name is Madelynne Lancaster, and I'm one of the caretakers at The Lighthouse Inn. We need a couple of officers—detectives—someone to come...see if there's a body buried in one of our balconies."

CHAPTER TWENTY

Janey sucked back the tears as Sean made the turn and The Lighthouse Inn came into view. No less than six police vehicles barred the entrance to the parking lot, and when she blinked, all she could see was the street where she'd been staying with her sister. It had been nighttime when she'd finally made it back to Nantucket Point after Tessa's kidnapping, but all of the same feelings came at her, assaulting her and washing over her with the power of a tidal wave as tall as the Statue of Liberty.

"My goodness," Sean murmured, and Janey let a sob burst from her mouth.

"Just park here," she said, already reaching for the door handle. His luxury sedan wouldn't let anyone open the door if the car wasn't in park, so she couldn't get out until he did that. Then she spilled from the vehicle, already running toward the inn. "Do you see her?"

"Janey," Sean said. "She called you. She's okay." He caught her by the hand and pulled her back to him. "You need to calm down."

A wildness Janey hadn't felt in many years squirreled through her, and she wanted to shove Sean away from her. The care and concern in his eyes couldn't be for her. She didn't deserve it, and she'd only end up hurting him anyway.

Instead, she crumpled into his arms and cried into his chest. He simply held her until the storm had blown through her, and then they faced The Lighthouse Inn again. "Let's go see if we can find her," he said. "She did say they might be at the cottage." He took the first step, and Janey went with him.

They reached the outer ring of police vehicles, all of which had the lights flashing and rotating, somehow painting the sun-filled sky with red and blue when it didn't need to be.

"Oh, no. No," she moaned. "Is that a body bag?"

Two men exited The Lighthouse Inn with a black bag between them, and they passed it to someone inside an ambulance. "It didn't look like it had a body in it," she whispered.

Neither of them said anything, but a single word hung in Janey's head. *Bones.*

Bones, bones, bones.

After all these years, all that would be left of Louisa Fry would be bones.

"There's Tessa," Sean said, and he took her around the back of the police vehicles, sticking outside of the semicircle they'd created around the inn, and toward a cluster of women standing together.

Tessa held Julia's hand, and Maddy had her arm around Tessa's shoulders. Helen gripped Maddy's other hand, and when they heard footsteps, all four of them turned toward Sean and Janey as a single unit.

"Janey." Tessa's voice held pure relief, and she ran to Janey and hugged her tight. "She was up there, Janey. They found her."

Janey didn't know what to say, and she thought if she let go of her sister, they might both stumble to their knees and never get up again.

"Are you sure it's her?" Sean asked.

"No," Maddy said, and she alone had dry eyes. Janey pulled away from her sister and joined the other women. "They don't know. They found some bones, and they kicked us all out at that point. They just brought a bag out, but we don't know what's in it."

Sean faced the inn, and Janey kept her hand in Tessa's, quietly slipping one into Sean's too. She watched a hive of worker ants go in and out of the inn, each of them uniformed in black and wearing very somber expressions.

Janey felt like she existed on the other side of an invisible barrier. No sound reached the group of women where they stood, but everything played out in living color in front of them. The wind seemed to bring with it the scent of death, and her stomach churned though she and Sean hadn't taken their lunch before Tessa had called.

Thankfully, he'd been at her desk when her phone had rung, and because Janey had been transcribing a client call for him, she swiped on her speaker phone. Sean had heard Tessa's panic, and Janey was so glad she hadn't had to repeat it. She was glad she hadn't had to drive over here. She was glad she didn't have to be standing here alone.

"Madelynne Lancaster?" a woman asked, her voice of the no-nonsense variety. It also tickled all the wrong vibes in Janey's memory.

"Sheriff Cochran?" She stepped out of line and grabbed onto the Sheriff. Probably not the most professional thing to do, but Janey's emotions had been tied into a knot. A tight knot.

"Janey," the Sheriff said. "I didn't see you."

"I just got here." She stepped back and wrung her hands together. "Tell us what's going on."

"I'm afraid I can't tell you much of anything," she said, wearing a sympathetic look that extended all the way to the downturn in her mouth. "I also can't let anyone back into the inn until our officers have gone through it."

"What about to get clothes or anything?" Maddy asked.

"I can have an officer escort you inside," Sheriff Cochran said. "I understand there's two of you working on this place?"

"Yes," Maddy said, and she was definitely the one in charge. "I am, and Julia too. We'd love to go inside and grab a few things. Then the inn is all yours."

"Where will you go?" Tessa asked. "You can stay at the cottage with me. Both of you."

"I have room too," Helen said.

"Thank you," Maddy said. "I'm sure we'd love either spot." She stepped forward, taking Julia with her. "We're ready to get out of your hair."

"Follow me." The Sheriff nodded at Janey and Tessa and walked away.

"Sheriff," Janey called after her. "You're going to find him, right?"

Sheriff Cochran put her hand on Maddy's arm and stepped past her. "Who, Janey?"

"Janey," Tessa said.

But Janey knew what Tessa had been doing. Her sister was terrible at hiding her notebooks, and she really needed a password on her computer. At least the report about Ryan Harper had only contained good things. In fact, the file she'd read on him had been one reason she still hadn't emailed him, despite the fact that Sean had gotten his personal email address for her.

The seven-page document hadn't revealed any skeletons in the man's closet, and Janey didn't want to cause any issues in his seemingly problem-free life. She hadn't known about him for the first forty-seven years of her life, and she wasn't sure she needed him to know about her now.

"Riggs Friedman," she blurted out. "He's the one who did this. His real name is Rick Fry."

Sheriff Cochran tilted her head the way dogs did when they heard the word *park*. "Riggs Friedman? You think Riggs Friedman is responsible for...what we just pulled out of that balcony?"

"Yes," Tessa said, stepping forward and joining Janey as a united front. "She's right, Sheriff. His legal name is Rick Fry. Remember how we knew he wasn't Riggs? It was just a nickname from college."

"I remember," the Sheriff said slowly. She looked between Janey and Tessa. "Don't you ladies go too far, okay? I can find you at the cottage when I'm ready to ask a few questions?"

"Yes," Janey said quickly, nodding for emphasis.

Sheriff Cochran turned and looked at Maddy and Julia. "That goes for you two as well. We're going to have a lot of questions for all of you."

Hours later, Janey watched the lights reflect off the water as Sean drove back toward downtown

Nantucket. He owned a house on the outskirts of that, off the water, and Janey had been there several times in the past.

He pulled into his garage and killed the engine. They sat in the silence, because there had been plenty of talking throughout the afternoon and evening, but the Sheriff had never come to the cottage. They'd answered no questions, and Janey had heard the story from beginning to end in Tessa's voice.

She had indeed hired a private investigator, and that man had looked into Ryan Harper—Janey had not been the only one unhappy about that little tidbit—and then Rick Fry, the disappearance of Louisa Fry, and the Fry parents.

He'd found news articles they didn't have, the official police interviews, and his mother. No one had gone to talk to her, because Tessa had called, and she was in the advanced stages of dementia. Though Janey had read it all already, on the sly, she'd looked through all of it again with Tessa, Julia, Maddy, and Helen.

She wanted to believe Riggs hadn't been the one to hurt his younger sister all those years ago. She found it very hard to believe that he could come back to the Point only a couple of years later and no one would recognize him.

Nothing really made sense in Janey's head, other than one thing: She didn't want to be alone anymore. She'd told

Sean she didn't want to go back to the dark mansion where Viola and Miles would be asleep. Nothing else had been said, and he finally sighed and looked at her. "Let's go in."

"Yes," she said, and she dragged her weary body out of the passenger seat. He waited for her at the front of the car, lacing his fingers through hers. "Sean?"

"Yeah?" He led her inside while Janey's mind whirred and whirred.

"Can I borrow your computer?" she asked.

"Sure," he said, nodding toward where a desktop computer sat dark on the built-in desk. "It's right there. I can unlock it for you." He stepped over to the machine to do just that, and when it brightened and woke, he indicated it. "I'll go change."

"I'm going to email him," Janey said, and that got Sean to turn back to her.

"You are?"

She nodded, her long hair in front brushing her chin. "It's time, and I'm ready."

"You don't have to do this," he said. "If it upsets you, you don't have to do this."

"I think I'm prepared for anything," Janey said. "He can choose what he wants to do with the information." She nodded like that was that, and Sean gave her a single head nod in return. He continued down the hall, leaving Janey in his immaculately clean kitchen, staring at the computer monitor.

Before she could lose her nerve, she pulled out the chair and sat down. Using someone else's computer always unsettled her, but she managed to get the browser open and logged into her email. She looked at her phone, where Sean had texted her the email address several days ago.

She simply searched for "Ryan" and the text came up. She typed the email address into the To: field and stalled at the subject line.

How did one tell a man that he was her father, especially if he might not know about her?

Janey's fingers flew across the keyboard and the message took surprisingly few seconds to type out. Before she sent it, she stood from the computer and backed up. Her fingers felt like ice cubes grafted to bone, and she pressed the tips of them together.

Sean came back down the hall, wearing a pair of joggers and a T-shirt the color of dark chocolate.

"Will you proofread it for me?" Her voice only shook slightly, but she was glad more of the quaking happening inside her hadn't come out.

Sean gave another nod and sat down in front of the computer.

Hello Ryan, Janey read over his shoulder, edging closer and closer to him. She wanted to be close to him, feel his body heat, and experience a human connection.

This email might come as a shock to you. It might not. I'm not really sure what my mother told you and what she didn't. My name is Janey Forsythe, and my mother was Lydia Lyons. You knew her in 1974, on the island of Nantucket. She owned a blue beach cottage there, and she brought me and my sister there many times growing up.

After Lydia died, my sister and I went through her estate, and as part of that, I discovered that Gregory Clarke was not my biological father. You are.

This is the best email to contact me should you wish to do so.

She'd also left her cellphone number, and then told him he didn't need to respond if he didn't want to, if it would cause problems in his life, and that she really was okay with whatever he decided to do.

"It's perfect," Sean said, not changing a single thing.

"Yeah?"

"Yeah." He stood and took her into his arms. "You're very brave for doing this." He bent and touched his lips to her neck, sliding them up to her ear, and then the corner of her eye. She melted into the warmth and security of his touch, but he pulled away only a moment later. "I'm going to order sandwiches from Bayside. Do you want the clam chowder? Garlic cheese bread?"

"Yes." Janey slid into the seat he'd just vacated, her heart banging with the intensity of gunshots. *He has a choice*, she told herself, and she quickly hit *SEND* before jumping to her feet. "I want the clam chowder, garlic cheese bread, *and* the black tie cheesecake."

She ran her hands up Sean's chest while he tapped on his phone. "You got it, sweetheart," he said, and the moment he had the food ordered, Janey pressed into him and kissed him properly.

CHAPTER TWENTY-ONE

Maddy waited until Janey and Sean had left, smiling and waving them out of the cottage where she and Julia had decided to stay while Tessa walked them out.

"I'm going to bed," Julia said, and Maddy put the coffee mugs in the kitchen sink and turned toward her. She wiped her hands down the front of her shirt and over her hips.

"Okay," she said. Her nerves fired at her like cannons, and Maddy wasn't sure why. She stepped forward awkwardly and grabbed onto Julia. "It's going to be okay."

Julia held her back, her grip almost painful as their shoulder bones pressed into one another. "I just can't believe this."

Maddy nodded, because her life in the past month had morphed into one she hardly recognized too. She cleared her throat and stepped back. "We'll be all right. Vivian's texted a few times tonight, and we'll explain everything to her tomorrow. The police too. It's okay."

Julia wiped her hand through her hair, which just flopped right back where it had been. "Do you think the inn will close now?"

"I don't know," Maddy said, glancing toward the door as Tessa closed it. She wanted to talk to her alone, because she seemed stronger than her sister, and Maddy didn't want to alarm Julia needlessly. "We'll figure it out."

If there was anything she'd learned from her divorce, it was that she could figure things out on her own. She didn't need her husband to tell her what to do, nor did she need a man to guide her at all. She thought of Ben, who'd texted and called once he'd heard about the bones in the balcony. Maddy had told him to stay at the station; there was nothing he could do anyway.

I can be there for you, he'd said, and Maddy had left the conversation on that. She'd get back to it once she figured out what to say.

"See you in the morning."

"Mm." Maddy hugged herself as Julia went down the hall and up the stairs to the second floor. The cottage had plenty of bedrooms, and Tessa had bustled around for the first several minutes, pulling out extra blankets, fresh towels, and fancy soaps.

Maddy's world spun as Julia's footsteps receded. She had to go see her father soon, as the news would reach him by morning. She wanted Ben to hold her while she wept and tell her what she'd just told Julia—that everything really would be okay. They really would figure it out.

You don't have to figure it out, she told herself. *You're not the Sheriff.*

Not only that, but she hadn't done anything wrong. As she turned back to Tessa, who sighed and opened the fridge, Maddy had a suspicion that Rick Fry hadn't done anything wrong either.

She cleared her throat, which drew Tessa's attention. "I wanted to show you something."

Tessa straightened from the fridge and closed the door. "What kind of something?"

"I found it in my room when I moved into The Lighthouse Inn," she said, her nerves and fear combining into a block and scraping her throat. She once again tried to clear it all away. "The caretaker's room is on the bottom level. Usually, it's a couple—historically, it always has been—but there's two bedrooms down there. The Michaels used the blue room, as it's called, as extra storage or an office from time to time. That's where I actually live."

Tessa folded her arms and nodded for Maddy to go on.

"The place was empty when we arrived." Maddy turned and took a couple of steps. "I mean, mostly empty. There was an old photo album, where Julia found those pictures. All the business stuff. The furniture. But someone had obviously gone through the inn and cleaned it out."

"Okay."

"I'll be right back." Maddy hurried toward the staircase and up it, following in Julia's footsteps. The difference was, she felt like her night was only beginning, while Julia stood in the bathroom, brushing her teeth.

Maddy said nothing to her as she went by, and she went into the bedroom she'd been given and closed the door. A uniformed officer had accompanied her to the blue room so she could pack a bag, and Maddy had brought the essentials: clothing, toiletries—and the recipe box she'd found in the top of the closet in the blue room. She'd thrown in the family photo albums too, and her explanation to the cop that she didn't want to lose her priceless and irreplaceable family heirlooms had gotten a nod.

There were no recipes inside the box, however. She tucked it under her arm and flew back downstairs. Tessa waited at the kitchen table, a cup of tea in front of her. In the second spot across from her, another cup waited, empty, with a bag on the saucer.

"Tea?" she asked, and Maddy nodded.

While Tessa got up to collect the water, Maddy sat down and put the recipe box in front of her. The orange lid could be described as peach now, and the flowery bottom did make her smile.

"What's that?" Tessa asked as steaming water got poured into Maddy's teacup.

"I found this in the closet in the blue room," Maddy said, swallowing. "It meant nothing to me. It seemed meaningless and like it should've been thrown away. Nothing really seemed to go together."

She slid it across the table as Tessa sat back down, not bothering to replace the electric kettle on the burner across the room. Maddy drew in a deep breath while Tessa studied the box, nowhere near moving to touch it. Their eyes met, and an arcing, electric charge of fear flowed between them.

"I don't think Rick Fry—or Riggs Friedman—killed his sister." The words ground against the tender flesh in her throat. "I think he tried to protect her, and I think he came back to the inn every year to honor her memory."

The movement in Tessa's throat suggested she had a lump there, but she nodded.

"I haven't read them all," Maddy said. "Like I said, they didn't make much sense. But when you showed us the police interviews tonight, I noticed the date. I'd seen it on everything I'd read in this box."

"July sixteenth," Tessa whispered.

Maddy nodded, and that got Tessa to reach for the lid on the recipe box. It lifted up, staying connected along the back, and Tessa peered into it. She meticulously pulled things from it, starting in the front the way Maddy would have.

The bright blue card that reminded Maddy of the circus came first, and Tessa laid it out on the far left edge of the table. "Welcome to the blue room. There's only one rule here: Don't try to change the paint color. She doesn't like it," she read.

Tessa looked up again, alarm in her eyes. "She doesn't like it? Do you think...is The Lighthouse Inn haunted?"

Maddy shook her head. "No."

Tessa's eyes widened, and she flinched as if Maddy had flicked water in her face. "You sound so sure."

"I think Rick was simply trying to make...something for his sister. I couldn't pull the old logbooks out of the storage room in front of the cops, obviously, but I'm willing to bet that when we can look at them, we'll find that he stayed there—in the blue room—every July sixteenth. There's a new letter for years following her death."

Tessa removed the first folded, lined paper and opened it. "This one is from the very next year."

Maddy nodded. "He says he stood on the upper balcony and looked out over the beach, just the way Louisa liked to do."

Tessa's eyes ran left to right, down, and left to right again. "He doesn't name her. He didn't sign it."

"All of the handwriting on all of the letters—at least the ones I've read—is the same. It looks like that old-fashioned, male writing, don't you think?" Maddy could close her eyes and see the shape of the letters. Half-cursive, with square tops on the capital A's—and he'd always used a capital A, even in the middle of a word.

"Yes," Tessa murmured, pulling out another letter. She

read it, and tucked it beneath the first one. "When did you stop reading?"

"I think the last one I read was 1990," Maddy said. After that, the only sound in the kitchen was the scuffling of paper, the clinking of a teacup when one of them took a sip and replaced it on the saucer, and an errant, audible gasp from one of them.

The letters ended in 2011, with Rick saying *I've done the best I can. I have my suspicions about who's responsible for your death, but I can't prove it. I don't know where you are. I miss you. I love you. I can't help but think about what you'd look like, and what you'd be doing with your life now, but it's time for me to let you go.*

Tears pricked Maddy's eyes, and she looked up from the short letter Tessa had finished reading a minute ago. "This is so sad."

"I can't believe he left all of that in the inn," Tessa said. "Seems a little foolish."

"If it's the man you knew as Riggs..." Maddy didn't know how to finish. "Maybe he couldn't keep it at home? Maybe his wife didn't know?"

"If he was staying in the inn every July sixteenth, Bobbie would've known," Tessa said, exhaling heavily as she got up and collected their teacups. "They had a house right here." She nodded toward the hallway that ran down to the bedrooms. "They lived right next door."

"Who owns the house now?" Maddy asked, watching Tessa as she put the dishes in the sink.

She turned back and leaned against the counter. "I suppose they still do. Bobbie is in jail right now, right here on Nantucket."

Maddy had the thought that they should go talk to her, precisely at the same time Tessa obviously did. Her dark eyes lit from within, and she said, "I bet I could get in to see her."

"Didn't she kidnap you?" Maddy asked. "You really think you can face her?" She leaned against the wall, having turned sideways in her chair. "Not only that, but face her *and* ask her about her husband's real identity, *and* his missing and presumed dead sister?" The words sounded harsh coming out of her mouth, and Maddy wished she could recall them.

They did the job though, because Tessa's face paled. "Probably not."

Maddy got to her feet, her muscles tired but her brain buzzing with adrenaline. "I could go."

"She won't tell us anything," Tessa said. "I know Bobbie Friedman, and she's only motivated by one thing. Money."

"I have plenty of money," Maddy said.

Tessa's eyes widened again, but she quickly shook her head. "She's in jail. Money isn't going to help her now."

Maddy's high started to wane. "You're right. I still think it might be worth trying."

"The Sheriff will definitely go talk to her," Tessa said. "We don't want to get in their way."

"You're right," Maddy said. "I know you are. What am I going to do? Bake her some cookies and win her over?" She smiled, though she didn't mind that her skills lay in baking, cooking, and piloting a boat.

"I could catalog something for her," Tessa said. "I used to work at a library. Or lead her on a tour of the nautical history of Nantucket." She grinned, and the tense moment between the two of them broke.

Maddy laughed first, but Tessa wasn't far behind her. Maddy started to refile all of the old letters, being careful to put them back where they'd been in the box. She wasn't sure why, but she wanted to respect the man who'd written them, and respect the person he missed. She believed that to be Rick Fry and his sister Louisa, though there were no names on them.

"Should I give these to the Sheriff?" she asked Tessa.

"I think we should," Tessa said. "We can take pictures of them if you think we want to have them."

"Oh, that's a good idea," Maddy said. "I have a scanner on my phone." She meticulously pulled out all of the pages again, scanned them all into one document by taking individual pictures of them and saving them into one document. "Okay."

Tessa helped her tuck them back where they belonged, and Maddy closed the faded, orange lid. They looked at one another, and Maddy quickly drew Tessa into a hug too, this one far less awkward than the one with Julia an hour ago. "I'm sorry for all you've been through this past summer."

"We all have something we're dealing with," Tessa said, but her voice sounded like she'd swallowed nails and was trying to speak past them. She stepped back and swiped at her eyes. "Once the divorce is final, I might be able to think about the future. Or at least something besides finding the biggest bottle of wine and drinking it all."

Her eyes flitted around the room, her pain streaming from her in great waves that pulsed, pulsed, pulsed against Maddy's breastbone. She knew pain like this, and it tore a person in two, then four, then eight. The divide continued endlessly, until a heart was left shredded and a life felt tattered beyond recognition or repair.

Maddy wished she could tell Tessa things would get better. Intellectually, she knew they did. She also knew Tessa didn't want to hear it. So she grabbed onto her again and whispered, "I'd be in to share that bottle with you any time you need me to."

The next morning, Maddy pulled up to her father's house before the sun had made its full appearance for the day. He sat in the rocking chair on the porch, as if he was expecting her before dawn. She smiled as she got out of the car, because her dad had always been there for her. Even when he and her mother had divorced. Even when Maddy had gone to her mother's second marriage and supported her in that new relationship. Even when he'd moved to Nantucket and she hadn't been able to come visit him as often.

"Morning, Dad," she called up to the porch before ducking back into the car to get the cream cheese Danishes she'd bought at the bakery that morning. She'd been the first one through the door the moment they'd opened, and she'd wanted to buy one of everything.

She went up the steps and bent down to kiss her father's forehead. "I brought your favorite."

"The coffee's probably done," he said in his gravelly voice. "And something came for you." He barely moved his head toward the small table beside him, and Maddy dropped her eyes to it.

An envelope sat there. A very fancy, very expensive envelope. Her breath died in her lungs, and her fingers dropped the box with the Danishes as she reached for the velvety envelope.

She flipped it over and saw her name on the front of it, with Kyle and Bea's names in the top left corner, where the return address should be. "Oh." She flipped it back over and opened the envelope, the texture of it thick and porous while somehow remaining silky smooth. This was definitely not a recyclable paper, and she wouldn't expect anything less from Chris's son.

Kyle and Bea smiled out at her, both of them sitting on

a set of steps somewhere in the city. They looked absolutely smashing together, and the joy radiating from the picture gave her hope that their marriage would last longer than hers had. She wanted them to spend their lives together and find a way to make things work, even when they went bad.

Her eyes filled with tears, and she pressed the invitation to her heartbeat and let the tears roll down her face. "Thank you, Lord," she whispered.

Her dad got to his feet, and while it took a few extra seconds, his embrace was just as tight and just as comforting as it always had been. "Thank you, Daddy."

"He's a good boy, Maddy. He'll come around." He released her and shuffled past her. "I'll go get the coffee."

Maddy collapsed into the second chair on the porch and looked through her tears to the date and time of the wedding. She saw Bea's due date, and she quickly entered it all into her phone so she wouldn't miss the things that meant so much to her.

CHAPTER TWENTY-TWO

Julia tugged on the bottom of her blouse, wishing she looked as sophisticated as effortlessly as Maddy did. She'd been gone that morning by the time Julia had finally stumbled her way into the kitchen to get caffeinated for the day. She'd returned with a brown bakery box, already dressed in her classy clothes and ready for this meeting with Vivian.

A sharp knock sounded on the front door, and Julia turned in that direction while Maddy got to her feet. Tessa had left ten minutes ago, claiming she needed a walk along the beach to iron her thoughts flat, and that she'd stop by Helen's afterward. Julia appreciated Tessa's willingness to stay out of the way during the meeting, and she was grateful for Tessa's hospitality and friendship.

Julia stepped over to the door and opened it. Vivian stood there, carrying a leather briefcase bag and wearing a flowing black-and-white striped skirt that fell to her mid-calf. She'd paired that with a burnt orange blouse with dark green and white flowers embroidered along the collar. She looked professional and put-together, even if Julia would've given the blouse to her mother for her birthday.

"Good morning," Julia said, stepping back. "Come in."

"Thanks for meeting us over here." Maddy came to Julia's side, and she felt stronger and less alone. "We obviously can't get into the inn right now."

"I got a brief from Sheriff Cochran last night," Vivian said as she crossed the threshold of the house. "I won't take much of your time."

"Coffee?" Julia asked, as she had entertained plenty of people in her home. Maddy probably had too, and with far more important people than Julia.

"Yes, please," Vivian said, and Julia scampered off to get the drink. When she returned to the living room and handed the mug to Vivian, she said, "Thank you. How are you feeling about the progress of the inn?"

Julia turned and looked at Maddy, who wore a confident expression on her face that gave nothing away. "Good," she said, hating how false the four-letter word sounded. "If we could keep going, I know we would've been able to open in time."

"We won't lose too much time," Maddy said, her smile one from her political days. "I can cook here and continue to develop our menu. We've been working on that the past week. Julia has been learning all of the history of

Nantucket and developing our tour programming. She can continue doing that here too. We don't need to be physically in the inn to accomplish those things, and everything has to get done."

Vivian nodded, and Julia found herself doing the same. "I have a couple of partnership businesses you might want to contact." She plucked a sheet of paper from her briefcase and leaned forward.

Julia did too, taking it from her. "I have talked to Arianna at The Glass Dolphin," she said. "She seemed excited to offer a ten-percent discount to our guests."

"Ari is a fantastic contact," Vivian said. "Do you have your budget sheet?"

"It's on the computer at the inn," Maddy said. "The moment we get back inside, I will email it to you." She glanced at Julia, and they said so much in that single breath of time. "Julia has not let us go a penny over." She smiled back at Vivian. "Even when I wanted to."

Vivian did not smile, and Julia hated the squirmy feeling in her stomach like she'd done something wrong when she hadn't. "That's great. I can's wait to see it. Sheriff Cochran made it sound like they'd just need a day or two to gather any other evidence, take pictures, and go through the inn. Then they'd release it all back to us."

"Great," Maddy said, and she made it sound like the cops would be doing improvements on the inn. Julia actually had no idea what shape it would be in by the time they all stopped tromping through their newly painted and furnished guest rooms. Would there be black scuffs all over the stairs? What would the upper balcony look like? Would they have to repair it?

Julia wasn't sure she'd even be able to go up there again. Ever. The thought of a little girl being put down beneath floorboards... She shivered, and Maddy reached over and took her hand. The touch calmed her and strengthened her, and she was able to look at Vivian with confidence.

"Okay, well, that's all." Vivian sighed and took a sip of her coffee. "Anything else you'd like to report?"

"Oh, the photo restoration is going well," Julia said. "I spoke to Ezra a couple of days ago, and he's making good progress on them."

"I'm planning to put up our first help wanted ads today or tomorrow," Maddy said. "We can do that without being physically in the inn as well, and we can conduct interviews from anywhere."

"Great idea," Vivian said. "How many people are you planning to hire?"

"With only five guest rooms, we're thinking two part-time maids," Julia said, because she'd made the list of personnel they needed. "One full-time maintenance person. Two people to work the desk in the lobby. Maddy and I will handle everything else."

Vivian nodded and said, "You'll be busy with tours, activities, and meals, that's for sure. Managing the books, the bookings, the software... How's that coming?"

"We've licensed it," Maddy said, giving Julia another glance.

"We're waiting for the website to be finished," Julia said. "Then we can integrate the two of them, and the marketing can start."

"Let me know when that's done," Vivian said. "I can put things out through the Society's social media, and I can submit to the Nantucket Town announcement board. They'll add the inn back to the tourism site. That always helps a lot."

"Perfect," Maddy said, and Vivian stood.

"I have another meeting," she said. "Thanks for sitting down with me, ladies." A rare smile touched her mouth, but it disappeared so fast Julia barely saw it. "I have full confidence in you, and you've been doing great work."

"Thank you," Maddy and Julia said together. They rose as a single unit too, and Julia took Vivian's half-drunk coffee while Maddy then escorted her to the door. Once she'd gone, the tension bled from the walls, and Julia's lungs managed to operate normally again.

She sent a text to Tessa to let them know they were done, and Tessa responded with, *I have the paper and a ton of doughnuts. I'm grabbing Helen and we're heading back now.*

The paper? Julia asked, but Tessa didn't respond again.

"I'm going to go change," Maddy said. "I don't need to wear slacks to post a job on the Internet."

"Tessa's bringing doughnuts," Julia said. "She said she

has a paper too. There must be an article in it about the discovery."

"I'm sure there is," Maddy said. "Nantucket isn't all that big, and there's no tourists here right now." She went down the hall, and Julia turned in a full circle, trying to find her bearings. She did have things she could work on that day, but her mind couldn't settle on any one thought long enough to make a plan.

Maddy returned, wearing a pair of cotton shorts and a tank top that would require a jacket should she choose to leave the cottage.

"Where did you go this morning?" Julia asked.

"To see my dad," Maddy said, and she sounded happier than she had over the past month. "I got the invitation and announcement for Kyle and Bea's wedding." The rays beaming from her contained pure joy. "I put it on the calendar, and I'll be gone for a few days in January."

"I'm sure it'll be okay." Julia didn't swipe to open her calendar. She just wanted to make it through today. January was months away, and Julia had no idea if the inn would even open at this point. "Vivian didn't act like the inn would close."

"No, she didn't." Maddy turned toward the front door as it opened. Shouts filled the air, causing alarm to tug through Julia too. "What is going on?"

Janey burst into the house and slammed the door, sealing out some of the noise. "Reporters," she said breathlessly. She raked her fingers through her hair and looked like she'd fought her way through a mob that morning.

Julia looked at her half-sister, so many pieces of herself in the other woman's face. She strode over to the front window and pulled down one slat in the blinds. "My goodness," she said, jumping back. "They're on the porch."

"I told them to get off the property or I'd call the cops!" Janey yelled the last few words, and Julia flinched away from her. Janey exhaled again, her chest rising, rising, rising as she drew in another breath.

"Where's Tessa?" she asked.

"She went for a walk while we met with our boss," Maddy said from the kitchen.

"She's bringing back doughnuts and Helen," Julia added.

Janey hadn't really met her eye yet, but she did now. Their gazes locked, and Janey looked like she'd rather be anywhere but here.

Julia dropped her gaze first. "Are you not working today?"

"No," Janey said. "Sean closed the office. It's a perk of owning your own firm." She flashed a tight smile and cut a glance at Maddy.

She seemed to get some unspoken message, because Maddy said, "I'm going to go...change my clothes."

She'd already done that, but she walked out of the kitchen without a hitch in her step. "What's going on?" Julia asked. She'd been friendly with Janey over the past few weeks, but all of her conversations and bonding had been happening with Tessa. Janey was the aloof sister. The one who showed up when it was convenient for her, who didn't say much to rock the boat, and who didn't seem all that interested in getting in the boat at all.

"I emailed our father last night," Janey said, her face turning even more pale. With the dark, dark hair, and the blue streak, she looked utterly gothic. "I said he could respond or not, and, well, he did." She thrust her phone toward Julia, who suddenly felt like it had turned into a rattlesnake. A scorpion. Something dangerous and deadly.

"It's not bad," Janey said, and the only thing alive in her face were her eyes. They glowed like someone had put fireflies in them, and Julia found herself relaxing and reaching for the phone.

She quickly read Janey's message to her dad, and right below that sat his response.

Janey, it's good to hear from you. I have to say I didn't know about you, though I suspected when I learned Lydia had married Greg and they'd had a daughter right away. I didn't see much of your mother after that summer, and no, I never told my wife about what happened in Nantucket that year.

I'm not opposed to meeting you, but I would like to have some time to tell my wife and family before that happens. I hope you understand.

Ryan

Julia went back up to the top of the email and re-read

everything, her pulse hammering at some parts and calming at others. She finally handed the phone back to Janey, the first words entering her mouth also streaming out of her mouth. "I don't want my mom to hurt."

"I don't want that either." Janey glanced at the phone and tucked it away, almost like it was a dangerous weapon she needed to conceal. "What do you think I should say to him?"

Julia's mind blanked, and to be honest, she wanted it to stay that way. Thinking about *so* much made her *so* tired. "I have no idea."

"You must have an opinion," Janey said, her voice somewhat gruff. "What will you tell him if or when he sits you down to tell you about me? We already know about each other." She gestured between the two of them, and Julia realized in that moment how tumultuous Janey's life had been in the past few months.

She couldn't imagine finding out the man she'd thought was her father, the man who'd raised her, the man she thought half of her DNA came from...wasn't really her father. There were so many meanings of that word, and Julia's eyes filled with tears.

"I'm sorry, Janey," she said, grabbing onto the other woman and holding her. "Everything must be so scary for you right now."

Janey didn't say anything, but she gripped Julia back with similar power in her hands and arms. She stepped back when Maddy's footsteps reached their ears, and Julia pushed her hair out of her face and then wiped her eyes before she faced the other woman she'd been reconciling with.

"Did I come back too soon?" Maddy asked. She wore the exact same thing she'd had on when she'd walked out. "Tessa said she's at the top of the block and might need help getting Helen though the mob of press."

Janey sniffled and straightened her shoulders. "Let's go get them." She faced the door but didn't open it. "Last time I had to deal with a crowd, Tessa and I linked arms. We managed to make it through easier, I think."

Julia stepped to her side and linked her elbow through Janey's. Maddy did the same, sandwiching the other woman between them. "Let's do this," Maddy said. "I'll yell at them. I'm good at that." She gave them a grin. "Just ask my kids." She reached for the doorknob, and while Julia had always remembered her as a strong, confident woman, she'd been so broken when she'd first come to The Lighthouse Inn. She'd hardly been the woman Julia remembered.

But now? Maddy's true personality—a huge, powerful spirit—shone through, and she stepped onto the porch first. "Do not touch us," she said as she led the way outside. "We're just going to get a couple of friends."

Questions got hurled at them, but Maddy simply kept saying, "We have no comment. Move. Step aside. No comment," until they left the crowd behind. Tessa and Helen appeared at the end of the road, and Maddy wiped her hair back and gathered it into a ponytail. Since she didn't have a holder, she released it and it fell back over her shoulders.

"I think we should go down the next street over and come in from the beach," she said.

"No," Tessa said. "You guys got through once. We'll do it again."

Julia exchanged a glance with Maddy, who looked exhausted already. She wondered what time she'd finally gone to bed, and how early she'd gotten up. "I raised three loud, obnoxious boys," she said. "I can yell this time."

CHAPTER TWENTY-THREE

Tessa straightened the pillows on the couch and reached for the handle on the vacuum cleaner. She'd missed a week of work. She'd sent Maddy and Julia back to The Lighthouse Inn three days ago. Janey had been staying in the cottage with her, and they'd been talking more and more about anything and everything.

"No more secrets," she murmured to herself as she switched on the vacuum and kept cleaning. She loved having everything in its place, and putting the cottage back together now that Janey had decided she could return to the mansion in Wainscott would allow her to think more clearly.

They'd made it through the couple of days the press had camped out on the road and beach across from the cottage. They'd all been interviewed singly by the police. Tessa had been present when Maddy had turned over the recipe box. One thing Tessa had learned under the spotlight since her mom's death was that life could change drastically for her while it marched on in normalcy for everyone else.

Chaos reared up, but life calmed again. The sun rose whether she felt unsettled and unsure or not. Things felt charged and electric, and then everyone packed up their cameras and headed home.

A new article had come out every day since Maddy had called the police about the possibility of bones being in the upper balcony. Today, Tessa hadn't seen one at the bakery. Life really did move on, and people got swept along with it.

Her phone buzzed in her pocket, and she finished vacuuming and tucked the machine back into the front closet. Standing in the doorway, she looked at her text.

Tessa, we're going to release the news to the public this afternoon, but I wanted you to know first, Sheriff Cochran had sent. *The medical examiner has done his tests on the bones, and he's concluded with near-one-hundred percent certainty that they belong to Louisa Fry.*

For some reason, a sense of relief filled Tessa. She tilted her head back and said, "Thank you, Lord," while dozens of other emotions streamed through her. It felt like closure, and while Tessa hadn't known about Louisa Fry for very long, knowing that the girl had been found made her heart glad.

Thank you, she sent to the Sheriff. It felt odd to do, but she took the broom out and went onto the front porch and started sweeping the debris from it. Did people sweep their porches after learning the identity of a person who'd been missing for over forty-five years?

Tessa was going to, and she felt a bit outside of her body as she did so. Autumn brought a lot of wind, and it was surprising what the weather could pull up from the beach. As the cottage was the first one touching that sand, sometimes the corners accumulated quite a bit of undesirable trash.

Tessa wanted to clean out the corners of her life, and she wished it was as easy as swish-swish-swishing a broom along wood. She thought about Ron as she made a pile in the far corner, and she sighed as she looked up. Facing down the street, she saw all the quaint cottages that usually bustled with activity and life in the summer months.

In the off-season, however, there wasn't much going on. So the movement in the house next door caught her eye and threw her heart up into her throat.

Bobbie and Riggs had lived next door.

Tessa stepped forward, bumping into the railing she strained so hard to see past the trees between the two houses. She tossed the broom, ignoring the clatter of the handle against the porch, as she ran toward the steps. She hadn't done as much running in her whole life as she had in the past few months, and her lungs protested the quick movement.

Her feet crunched over the gravel along the side of the road, and Tessa would've tripped and fallen had anything been in her path. She couldn't take her eyes from the house where her mom's best friends had lived, because if Riggs was there, she wanted to talk to him.

No, she *needed* to talk to him. He'd said so many confusing things the last time they'd talked, as well as right before Bobbie had drugged Tessa. She needed clarification on those things, and she couldn't really step into the future without them.

Her mind screamed warnings at her, and she realized she should've brought the broom with her. Stooping, she picked up one of the ugly garden gnomes lining the sidewalk that went to the Friedman's cottage.

"Hello?" she called, glancing down the street and trying to decide which houses might have someone in them. She had no idea; for all she knew, she was the only one on her street living there permanently.

She heard nothing; the very air held its breath.

Tessa reached out and banged against the door with the stone gnome. Perhaps it was one of the Friedman's children, come to check on the cottage and their mother. Maybe they'd been texted about the bones too, though Tessa wasn't sure why Sheriff Cochran would do that. Surely she'd have to positively identify Riggs

Friedman as Rick Fry first. Otherwise, they weren't related.

He'd said he'd lost his boat repair shop in "Hurricane Joan," and that Dale and Joan Harton had then sued him.

He'd said he hadn't explained everything.

He'd said he didn't want to hurt her.

"I'm coming in," Tessa said, and she reached for the doorknob. It turned easily, and the door settled open a few inches. Tessa tried to see through the gap, and she inhaled deeply, using all of her senses to assess the situation.

No movement. No sound. No smells, other than the usual stale air and forced heat scent of a furnace. She had the mental space to wonder who was paying that bill before she toed the door open a little further.

"I'm coming in. It's Tessa Simmons from next door. I'm alone and unarmed." She stepped into the house, glancing left and right, trying to take in everything at once. Human sight really was amazing, but no one could see in a three-hundred-and-sixty-degree circle all the time.

The living room stood empty, and this cottage didn't have the same open floor plan as hers. She'd been here enough to know the kitchen sat through the doorway on the right and opened up onto a beautiful garden and patio off the back of the house. The Friedman's yard butted up against hers, as she'd learned only a couple of months ago.

He'd always been more interested in Janey than Tessa, and she hoped she could use that to her advantage today. Janey had left that morning, but she'd said she'd bring

Sean—and plenty of steamed mussels from Tessa's favorite seafood restaurant—for lunch.

"Riggs?" she called, not daring to take another step. The doorway on the left went down the hall to the bedrooms and bathroom, and Tessa didn't want to commit to a spot where she didn't have a way out. If he was here, how could Tessa draw him out?

If he was here, what had drawn him back?

Louisa, ran through her mind. *Louisa, Louisa, Louisa.*

"I just got a text from the Sheriff," she said, calling into the rest of the house. "They identified the bones they found in The Lighthouse Inn as Louisa Fry's."

Quick as a breath, Riggs Friedman appeared in the doorway leading into the kitchen. He hadn't made a sound, and Tessa blinked at him, the gnome raised between them.

"You're lying," he said, his voice old and unused, as if he'd buried it when he'd run from Nantucket two months ago.

"I'm not," she said. "I have it in a text message." She cleared her throat, her heartbeat nearly deafening her. "They're going to release it in a public statement this afternoon."

"I didn't kill her," he said.

"I know," Tessa said, and that made him cock his head in confusion. His frown deepened, and Tessa took in the dirty, loose clothes he wore. "A friend of mine who's renovating the inn found your letters."

Horror washed across his face. "Margo told me she'd thrown them out."

"Margo Michaels? The former caretaker?"

He only nodded, and more questions joined the ones still sitting in Tessa's head. "You told me that Joan Harton sued you. I couldn't find that record."

"That was a lie."

"You did lose your boat shop."

"Yes."

"Are you Rick Fry?"

"Yes."

Tessa nodded, and she paused to search her feelings. She didn't fear him the way she once had. Janey had found him downright creepy over the summer, how he showed up out of nowhere all the time, but he didn't put out that air now at all.

He seemed...defeated. Downtrodden. A fugitive for the second time in his life.

"I didn't want to hurt you or Janey," he said. "That was...Bobbie was obsessed with finding that money."

"I understand." Tessa lowered the garden gnome. "Would you like to see your letters?"

"You have them?"

"I have a digital copy," she said. "We turned over the box to the police, and when they interviewed me, I told them I didn't think you were responsible for Louisa's death."

"I didn't kill her."

Tessa took another moment, forcing herself to inhale so she wouldn't fire question after question at him. "Who did? Do you know?"

"No," he said. "I don't know for certain." He looked away and ran his hand up the back of his head. "I think... Every time I tell someone what I think, they end up dead."

Tessa fell back a step, wanting him to keep talking while also wanting him to never speak to her again. "What do you mean?" she asked, her voice muted and hardly her own.

"I've only told two other people what I thought, and they both died shortly afterward."

"Who?" she asked.

"My dad," he said, bringing his eyes back to hers. "And yours."

Tessa's chest seized. "What?" Her father had died of a heart attack, decades ago. "My dad died in an accident."

"Maybe," Riggs said. "All I know is I told him, and then he died the next week. My dad too."

Tessa swallowed, her throat so dry. "Who do you think killed her?"

Riggs's bright green eyes flickered with something—malice or interest or just life, Tessa wasn't sure. "My step-mother," he said.

Tessa would need years to unravel how a mother—step or not—could hurt her child, and her mind spun and spun. It rotated so much, it took her a few moments for her to realize Riggs's gaze had left hers and looked to her right, toward the door.

"Don't move."

Tessa blinked at the voice, which was very familiar.

Her sister stood there, oh-so-familiar.

The gun in her hand was definitely *not* familiar.

CHAPTER TWENTY-FOUR

Janey had no idea how to fire a gun. She only had one, because her daughter's boyfriend had suggested she get one. She'd bought it, and Travis had video-called her to show her how to load it and use it.

She'd never actually done either. In fact, standing in the doorway with her feet shoulder-width apart, Janey wasn't even sure the gun held bullets. She didn't know if it had a safety, though she'd heard of such a thing. She had no idea how hard to tug on the trigger to get it to go off.

She knew she'd been driving by the house when she'd noticed the front door open. She knew the crashing of her heartbeat as it cymballed through her ears. She knew she was not letting Riggs out of her sight until he had handcuffs on.

"Janey," Tessa said, her voice made mostly of surprise. "What are you doing? Where did you get *that*?"

"Have you called the cops?" Janey asked out of the corner of her mouth. She wasn't sure why she needed to whisper to Tessa. Riggs knew they were there. He stood across the room, filling the doorway that went into the kitchen, every muscle in his body tense. Janey did not take her eyes from him.

"No, and I'm not going to," Tessa said. "Put the gun down."

"Why aren't you going to call the cops?" Janey realized she should've done that before grabbing the gun from her glove box. Somewhere in her mind, she'd assumed Tessa had done it. She'd heard them talking, and the conversation hadn't sounded out of control. Of course, with Riggs, things usually escalated very quickly, and Janey hadn't wanted to take any chances.

"He didn't do anything," Tessa said. "That's why."

"He's a fugitive twice over," Janey said.

"I should turn myself in," Riggs said. "Just answer all of their questions. Let them do whatever they want to do."

"There you go," Janey said. "That's the right thing to do."

"It was all Bobbie's idea," Tessa said. "The money stuff and everything that happened over the summer. She's the one who drugged me, not him."

"He was there!" Janey practically yelled. She would never understand Tessa. In so many ways, she admired her. She could forgive easily, which Janey definitely needed in her life. She operated like a duck—the showers of life just rolled off her back. Her husband had admitted to cheating on her? Okay, she'd file for divorce, pay the fee, and let him go. Easy peasy.

Janey hadn't even loved her first husband by the time they got divorced, and she'd still dissolved into a puddle of non-functional once everything was said and done. She had never been very good single.

"He didn't kill his sister."

"Again, he was probably there." She cut a look at Tessa, who wore wide eyes with desperation in them. "He knows what happened."

"I don't know what happened," he said. "The reason I ran when the police came to the boat shop in New Jersey was because I'd just gotten a call from my father. He said my step-mom had told the police more about the wrong timeline than what had actually happened here at the inn, and they wanted to talk to me. I'd already given them one interview where the detectives didn't believe me. He told me I should leave town. Just run, and never come back."

"Wait," Janey said. "Your dad?"

"He thinks his step-mother killed Louisa," Tessa said from her side, her voice low and hissing into Janey's ear. "Can you please put the gun down? You don't even know how to use that."

Janey's arms trembled, and she lowered the gun. Relief

ran through her muscles, but she remained tense. "Your step-mother?"

"I don't have any proof," Riggs said. "The timelines don't match up—what I know happened and when, and what my step-mom and dad told the police. We all did an interview with them when Louisa was first reported missing."

"I know," Janey said. "We read those."

"I did not take Louisa home to Nantucket early," he said. "I told my parents she'd been abducted before I left. They said they'd find her. They didn't, and they came home anyway. I was so angry." He looked it too, his eyes narrowing and his face growing ruddier. "It was me who said I'd call the cops if they didn't, and my dad was the one to do it. We did the interviews. I went back to work." He paced out of the doorway, and while Janey knew there was a door back there, she didn't think he'd flee again.

"He didn't do it," Tessa said, glaring at Janey. "When did you get that gun?"

"A few weeks ago, okay?" Janey snapped at her. "You're not my mother."

"You should at least take a firearm safety class," Tessa said, undeterred. "You're more dangerous with it than without it."

"Better than a garden gnome," Janey shot back.

Riggs reappeared in the doorway, anguish on his face. "My dad called me at work the day I ran. He said my step-mother had told the police more of the same lie, and it really sounded like I'd done something to her. He told me to run. I ran."

"But you came back to Nantucket only a few months later."

Confusion crossed his face. "I went to Europe for a year. I got cosmetic surgery. I worked on the docks. I came back to Nantucket on July sixteenth, because that was the last day I'd seen Louisa alive, and I happened to meet Bobbie that summer. We did get married fast, and yes, we bought a cottage here to raise our family."

"Because you thought you were my father," Janey said.

"That was definitely part of it for me," Riggs said. "As was being close to The Lighthouse Inn. The caretakers who'd been there when we visited were gone. No one seemed to talk about Louisa or the Frys, ever. Odd as it sounds, I felt safe here. No one recognized me, or if they did, they didn't say anything."

"You're not my father," Janey said, needing him to know that.

"I know," Riggs said, his gaze switching to Tessa's. "I tried to stop Bobbie. So many times, I tried. That woman is like a force of nature. She does what she wants, when she wants, and anyone and anything in her way just gets blown down."

"Have you seen her since...?" Tessa let the question hang there, and Janey found she wanted to know the answer too.

"No," he said. "I only returned to Nantucket now

when I saw the news about bones being discovered in an old inn."

"Did you ever confront your step-mother?" Tessa asked.

Riggs's face hardened, and he shook his head. "I haven't spoken to her since the day my dad called to tell me to run."

Sadness bled through Janey. She could not imagine blaming her son for something she'd done. Who did that? What kind of woman sacrificed her son to save herself?

Janey reminded herself that Rick had been a step-son for his mother. He wasn't hers biologically, but the way he'd been blamed—if that was true—was unfathomable. Having the knowledge that anyone had done that to her would wreck Janey in a way she'd never recover from.

How Riggs had carried that burden all this time astounded her.

"I've been considering going to the authorities," he said. "I could help them with Bobbie's case. Make sure she doesn't get out for a while." He wiped his hand through his hair, which hung down to his collar and seemed dirty and unkept.

"Maybe it's time," Tessa said, her voice kind and unassuming. She'd always been good at cheering someone on and making them feel important without pressing her will onto them. Everything about Janey was a hair harsher, and she wanted to be better about that.

"If you're innocent, you have nothing to fear," Janey said.

"That is so not true," Riggs said. "Do you know how many innocent people they have in jails?"

"We'll vouch for you," Tessa said, linking her arm through Janey's. "We'll tell them everything you told us. They've got all the letters. Maybe the bones will be able to tell them something about how your sister died."

"Maybe." Riggs's expression took on the look of someone who'd seen ghosts, and he shook his head. "Fear drives so much of what we do, you know?" He looked back and forth between the two sisters, and Janey found herself nodding.

She did operate from a place of fear quite often. She wished she had the same confidence Maddy seemed to, or the ability to compartmentalize the way her sister did. Instead, Janey allowed herself to feel everything, all the time, and that often left her exhausted and moody.

"I don't think I'm ready to turn myself in yet," he said. "I think I need to make a trip to the mainland and...speak to my step-mother."

Beside her, Tessa drew in a breath. "After all this time?"

"Maybe she'll have her guard down," Riggs said. "Though I doubt it. She was always a sharp tack, my step-mother."

"She has dementia," Janey said. "Did you know that?"

"I've kept tabs on her," he said. "My dad and I used to

talk all the time, and as I told Tessa before you got here, he died only a few days after I told him I thought Monica had killed Louisa."

"Do you think she did it?" Janey asked, another dose of horror hitting her right between the ribs.

"Honestly?" Riggs nodded, accusing her without using words. "I know she's not well. Perhaps now, her tongue will be loose."

"Perhaps now, she'll kill you too," Tessa said.

Janey couldn't believe she was even considering letting him walk out of here. Bobbie may have been the one to plunge the needle into Tessa's neck, but Riggs had surely carried her. He'd done anything and everything Bobbie had told him to do, and he shouldn't get off the hook just because it was her idea.

"I think you should go after you turn yourself in," she said. "The police can go visit her as easily as you can. She'll tell them, and everything will be over."

Over sounded so nice. Janey really wanted this nightmare to be over. She wanted to focus on building a relationship with Sean, and she wanted to enjoy her friendship with her sister, Viola, Miles, and the ladies at The Lighthouse Inn too.

The message from her biological father hadn't been precisely what she'd wanted to see, and Julia's reaction to it hadn't helped. Janey wanted to tell Ryan that she'd met Julia here on Nantucket, and she already knew about her.

Perhaps that would nudge him to tell everyone in the family, and then include Janey in his life.

On the other hand, she had no idea why she wanted to be included in the life of a stranger. She did not know Ryan Harper. She'd been raised by a good father. At her very core, Janey didn't want to be an orphan, and when her mother had passed earlier this spring, she had become one.

With the discovery that Ryan Harper was her biological father, Janey hadn't felt so alone in the world anymore. She'd had a new anchor thrown her way. But anchors sunk; they pulled people down with them unrelentingly, and she felt like she might drown at any moment from the way her father had said he was glad to have met her, but he needed more time to figure out if he really wanted her in his life.

"Things aren't usually that easy," Riggs said. "I just stopped by for something to eat. I've been starving, and I was hoping to read over a few things that have come out since I've been traveling here."

"Where have you been staying?" Tessa asked.

"I'm not going to answer that." Riggs gave her a crooked smile.

"I want you to turn yourself in," Janey said.

"I'm not going to do that," he said. "Right now."

Janey dug in her pocket for her phone. "I'm going to call the police."

"Janey," Tessa said. "Give him some time to talk to his step-mother."

"I can't believe you," Janey said. "Who do you think carried you onto that boat? Bobbie? She's half your size." She glared at her sister and then Riggs. "No. This ends today. He doesn't just get to run off again, do whatever he wants, and then retreat to whatever foxhole he's been living in."

Her chest stormed, and her fingers shook. One hand held her phone; the other still gripped the gun.

With her attention on her phone, she started to dial nine-one-one, but she tapped the nine twice on accident, trying to dial with one thumb as she was. She swore under her breath at the same time a familiar, aged voice said, "Janey, dear? What are you doing here?"

She turned toward Helen's question, her arm slipping away from Tessa's. She gave a startled yelp, and Janey spun back to her, instinctively raising the gun. So much was happening at the same time, and adrenaline licked through her system.

Tessa raised the garden gnome.

Janey dropped her phone, the crack of it against the wood floor somehow as loud as if she'd fired the gun.

Helen yelped.

Riggs barreled down on all of them, crashing through them as if he were a bowling ball and they the pins. Janey went flying into the wall behind her, her eyes squeezing shut.

She pulled the trigger.

The gun went off, and no, a phone hitting the floor was absolutely, in no way like a gunshot.

Pain ripped through her tailbone as she landed on it.

Her ears rang.

The world had gone mute.

The scent of gunpowder and hot metal filled the air, choking her.

Tessa said something Janey couldn't comprehend, and she was crouched low behind the loveseat, only a few feet from Janey. As Janey tried to get her bearings and figure out what had happened, Tessa scrambled forward and yanked the gun away from her.

She threw it out the front door and then dropped to her knees to help Helen.

Noise and movement rushed at Janey again, and she twisted in a circle, trying to see where she'd shot the bullet. There, in the ceiling, she found a hole. Relief burned through her veins, and she too turned toward Helen.

She'd been knocked down in Riggs's flight too, and Janey practically leapt over her and Tessa to see if she could find him. If she knew which way he was going, she could tell the police.

The street in front of her sat serenely in sunshine. No one cared that she'd shot a firearm. No one cared, because there was no one here to know.

"What were you thinking?" Tessa demanded, helping Helen to her feet. She got up too, and then she got right in

Janey's face. "You've blown things up—*again*. Literally and figuratively." She marched out of the house, her hand in Helen's tight.

"He's a fugitive," she called after them, but Tessa kept right on going. She stooped and picked up the gun, which only made Janey furious. "That's mine!"

"Not until you take a class," her sister yelled back at her. "You could've killed any one of us. You're so stupid. So hot-headed."

"And you're right all the time."

Tessa spun and marched back to her, her face one of pure danger. "How dare you? I never said I was right. I said he was innocent, and he is. I said you don't know how to use a gun, because you don't. You fired a weapon three feet from my face, with your eyes closed." Her chest heaved as she came right at Janey. "You're dangerous. I know you're dealing with a lot, but Janey, you need help. You need a good therapist and some strong medication. You need to talk to me, or Maddy, or Julia instead of keeping secrets and doing everything 'the Janey way'. You need to figure out how to trust *someone*. Maybe it's Sean. I don't know." Her eyes possessed a wild quality that Janey recognized, because it ran freely through her.

"What I do know is that you're not welcome in my house until you pull yourself together. You will *not* get this gun back, and you will *not* endanger anyone again." Tessa walked away for a second time, gathered Helen from where she'd left her near the road, and continued toward the blue cottage, which Janey technically owned too.

The moment the two of them were out of sight and the world had silenced again, Janey sank to her knees and sobbed. "She's right," she said. "I need so much help."

She cried and cried and cried, and when the tears were finally all gone, she crawled into the house and found her phone. Sitting there, her back against the couch in Bobbie and Riggs Friedman's house, she dialed Sean.

"Hey, sweetheart," he said. "My number just got called. I'll be there in twenty minutes."

"I need help," she said, a new round of tears starting. "Can you come get me and help me? Please?"

"Yes," he said. "You're scaring me. Are you okay?"

"I'm next door to the cottage," she said. "Where Riggs and Bobbie used to live. I think..." She gulped at the air, trying to find enough. "I think I need to see a therapist today."

Right now, she thought.

"I'll be there in twenty minutes," Sean promised, and Janey knew when Sean made promises, he kept them.

CHAPTER TWENTY-FIVE

Julia looked around as the door to the psychiatric unit opened. This place was not somewhere she'd ever want to be. Nothing hung on the walls; the furniture was all plastic. Two windows at the back of the room let in some light, and a few people milled about in a couple of molded chairs that were bolted to the floor.

No one had any phones, and Janey had told Tessa when she'd come to visit that there was a television they could watch, but Julia couldn't see it.

Janey appeared, and she wore a pair of flowing black pants, a plain white T-shirt, and one of her flowing caftans over that. No shoes, no shoelaces, no drawstrings in anything. Tessa had to remove them before they'd let her bring in the clothes. She'd brought a couple of books for

Janey, but hardcovers weren't allowed; only paperbacks. No devices whatsoever.

Julia swallowed and put a smile on her face. "Good morning."

"Good morning," Janey said. Her hair hung in strands, like it hadn't been washed in a couple of days. Tessa had said there were showers, but there was barely any privacy to use them. People came in and out of the rooms at will. Janey shared with another woman named Edith.

Janey hugged Julia, and she felt calmer than Julia had ever known her to be. She could still see the wild quality in Janey's eyes as she'd tried to run from the porch at the cottage, the first time Julia had shown up with pictures and printouts.

Julia clung to her, hoping she'd know how much she was loved. She cleared her throat and stepped back. "Tessa says you'll be here for a couple more days."

"Maybe tomorrow," Janey said. "It depends on what Doctor Robinson says today." She offered Julia a small smile and indicated a couple of the molded plastic chairs, the kind that looked like they belonged in a small airport that only flew to Siberia. "Do you want to sit?"

"Sure." Julia perched in one of the chairs. The attendants at the desk out front wouldn't let her bring anything in. Her purse and device sat in a locker out there, and she didn't know what to do with her hands. "I just wanted to see you." She reached up and tucked her hair. "I'm going to Southampton today."

Janey sat gracefully in the chair, her legs crossed. She seemed to be a completely different person now, and Julia supposed therapy and good medication could do that for a person. She seemed so much happier, and so much more in control. While Julia had doubted Tessa when she'd said the psychiatric unit was exactly where her sister needed to be, now that she'd come and seen Janey with her own eyes, she had to agree.

"That's great," Janey said, not a trace of anxiety in her expression. "What are you going to say?"

"Annie's meeting me there," Julia said. "We're going to tell our father that we know about you, so he doesn't need to keep it a secret."

"What about your mother?"

"He can decide what to tell her," Julia said. "Annie just wants to tell her; get everything out in the open. I keep telling her he should get to decide that." She shook her head. "Annie is a little bit more...fiery than me." She gave Janey a smile. "She'll be coming back to Nantucket with me, so you'll get to meet her."

That lit up Janey's face. "I'd like that."

"She's bringing her two daughters for a few days. Fall break." Julia swallowed. "She's been going through some rough times with them."

"Is she married?" Janey asked.

"No," Julia said. "Her husband left a few years ago. He has a boyfriend now."

Janey nodded, like such things were normal. Perhaps

they were. Julia knew Donovan's lifestyle changes had impacted her sister like a load of bricks being dropped on her head, but she did the best she could.

"I wouldn't force the news onto your mother," Janey said quietly. "You're right; your father should get to decide that."

Julia could only nod. "I can't really control Annie. She's this spitfire that runs on extra batteries all the time. She's used to dealing with difficult situations and people; I'm not. I can't predict what she'll do."

"I'm sure that's true," Janey said. "But you're her sister. Sisters influence in the subtlest of ways." She gave another small smile and looked across the room to a large clock encased in a plastic cage. Julia wondered why they needed to do that. Would someone really reach that high and pull down the clock? And then do what with it?

She couldn't even imagine, and she suddenly wanted to leave.

"I have therapy in ten minutes," Janey said. "I'll have to let you go."

"Oh, okay." Julia jumped to her feet and waited while Janey moved much slower, so much more deliberately. She thought she should probably learn to do the same—slow down, enjoy each moment with more deliberate thought.

She hugged Janey again, buzzed to be let out, and was escorted back to the desk to get her purse. The moments and all of her thoughts melded together while she drove to the ferry station, rode the triple-decker boat to 35th Street in New York, and then hailed a cab to take her to her hotel.

The ferry only ran between Nantucket and New York on Sundays and Fridays, and she'd arrived in the city at nine-thirty that evening. She didn't want to make an appearance on her parents' front porch so late at night. Annie would make the drive tomorrow from Chatham, and her parents were expecting the two of them for a few days at their home in Southampton.

By the next day, when Annie texted to say she'd arrived outside the hotel, Julia's nerves felt like she'd fed them to a tiger. She snatched up her purse and her carryon and headed out to the street. Being back in New York City churned up hundreds of memories for Julia, and she ducked into the passenger seat of her sister's SUV as quickly as possible.

The noise here reminded her of past years. The sights of the tall buildings, the smells of food carts and restaurants, even simply seeing men and women dressed in suits and skirts—all dark blue or black—making their way to work brought back a flood of memories from a life she'd left behind.

"Morning," Annie chirped, glancing over to her. "You look smashing."

"Are you British today?" Julia asked, leaning toward her sister to give her a hug. A side-squeeze was the best they could do in the car, but at least Annie grinned while she did it.

"Thinking about it," she said, hitting the T's really hard in an exaggerated English accent.

"How's Paige?" Julia asked. She used to hate it when her mom would ask how "the boys" were, as if the three of them were all the same person, experienced all the same things at the same time, and Julia could give a report on all three of them in a couple of sentences.

"She's good," Annie said, her voice pitching up. She turned to check her blind spot and pulled back into traffic. "She might be 'off' Logan now. I guess she's still deciding if him putting the spotlight on her in French class makes him more attractive or break-up-worthy." She shook her head, her lighter brown hair bouncing with the movement.

"Wow, okay," Julia said, smiling. "No spotlight on Paige. Even I knew that."

"Right?" Annie grinned. "Have you heard anything from Andrew about his internship?"

"He sends emails," Julia said, thinking of her youngest son. "He says it's too early to apply for new internships, but he'll go back to the FBI if he can."

"Good for him. I think working for the government in cyber security would be a great place for him."

"It'll keep him out of trouble, at the very least." Julia flashed a smile in her sister's direction. Andrew was her youngest son, and definitely the one who'd given her the biggest run for her money. He'd loved to party and smoke with his friends, but the FBI didn't allow any of that.

"Spencer's cut all of his hair. Shaved that beard. He's

going to the Central New York...Training...Apprentice... something. It's the best electrician training facility and school in New York."

"Did he get in then?" Annie kept both hands on the wheel but looked at Julia.

Pride filled her. "He did. He just called me yesterday. He starts in January, and it's five years, but he'll be working that whole time too. When he's done, he'll be one of the most highly certified electricians, part of the union, and able to work anywhere in the country."

"Good for him."

"Yeah." Julia had spent the bulk of her time on her knees praying for Spencer. The child had lost his way for a while there, and since he'd graduated from high school four years ago, he'd had at least eight jobs, a dozen others he swore up and down he was going to do, and no real drive or purpose to actually do anything.

Then he'd met Allison, and everything had changed. He wanted a real life with her, and she'd influenced him to clean up his act, make real adult decisions, and be the man a woman like her deserved.

"And Will?" Annie asked.

"Will's Will," Julia said. "Doing great." Her oldest had always led the boys toward greatness. He'd gone to college, graduated last year, and had a job clerking in the Supreme Court in Washington D.C. already. "What about Bri? How is she handling staying with Don this week?"

"She asked to stay with Margo," Annie said, her fingers tightening on the wheel. "I let her."

"You did?" Julia studied the side of her sister's face. Annie had always been fairer than Julia, and she'd gotten the most sunburns growing up. "What about Paige?"

"She's staying with Jackson," Annie mumbled, and Julia looked back out the windshield, blinking rapidly. "Look, you don't know what it's like to make them stay with their dad."

"I didn't say anything."

"You're doing that rapid-blink thing that means you're stunned and judging."

"I am *not* judging."

"You're blinking fifty miles a minute."

"I don't even know what that means." Julia forced herself not to blink again. When she had to—it was something the human body had to do—she turned toward the passenger window to do it.

"Peter moved in," Annie said. "The girls don't like going there anymore. Don said he understands, and he takes them to lunch or drives them home from school to see them. We're all doing the best we can."

"I'm sure you are." Julia looked at her sister again. "I was just surprised for like ten seconds. You told me once that you'd never let the girls stay with friends when their father was only a half-mile away."

Annie shifted in her seat. "Things change."

"Boy, do I know that." The two sisters looked at each

other, and no truer words had ever been spoken. "I'm sorry," Julia said. "I didn't mean to blink-judge."

Annie's hard features melted into a smile. "I'm sorry too. I shouldn't have assumed you were blink-judging. Or that you don't know what it's like to deal with hard situations with an ex-spouse."

The conversation moved into easier things, and before Julia knew it, Annie had arrived in the posh, quiet community where they'd grown up. She pulled into the driveway, and the two of them looked at the house.

"Ten bucks says Mom made lemon squares," Annie said.

"I'm not betting against that," Julia said. "I can smell the citrus from here." Their mother thought lemon squares could solve the world's problems, and she hated how her mom sugar-coated everything.

Before either of them could move, the garage door started to lift. Julia watched as her mother's shoes and legs came into view. She hefted a bag into the bag of her luxury electric car, and the door had risen fully by the time she faced Julia and Annie's father.

He looked out to the driveway where the two of them sat in Annie's SUV. Their mother turned toward them, didn't smile, didn't wave, didn't even seem to see them. Then she stepped past her husband and got behind the wheel of her car. She backed out, the scene moving in slow motion and striking Julia as absolutely surreal.

Annie rolled down her window when Mom paused

and did the same on her car. "Hello, girls," she said, her voice crisp and smooth at the same time. "I forgot about a trip with my mother and aunt. I'm afraid I won't see you this week."

"Which aunt?" Annie challenged, while Julia just wanted to say, *Okay, Mom. Sorry, Mom. I love you, Mom.*

"Aunt Brenda," their mother said without missing a beat. "I'll be up in Toronto through Sunday. Grandma wants to go see all the family graves before winter." She offered a tight smile Julia could only barely see due to where she sat in the car. "You girls have a lovely visit with your father."

With that, she rolled up her window and continued backing onto the street. Julia watched her dad step out of the garage, wearing a pair of navy slacks and a light green polo. He never dressed down, even when he didn't go into the office. He still had a head full of dark hair which had only just started turning silver, and his dark eyes watched the electric car go down the street until it disappeared.

Julia got out of the SUV first and said, "Morning, Dad."

He smiled at her and opened his arms. She hurried to him and hugged him, because he was her father, and he'd always been very, very good to her. "Hey, baby," he said, his voice half hurting and half joyous. "How was the trip from Nantucket?"

"It takes forever to get here," Julia said. "I had no idea."

"If you fly, it's faster," he said, stepping back. "Did you take the ferry out of Hyannis or New York?"

"New York," she said. "I got in last night."

He nodded, his smile real and genuine. Julia hadn't seen him in a few months, and she'd missed him. He turned toward Annie and hugged her too, saying, "How's my favorite second daughter?"

"Good, Dad," Annie said, squeezing her eyes shut as she squeezed her father hard. "How are you?"

"Oh, well, I'm surviving." They parted, and he looked between the two of them. "I told your mother about Lydia and Janey last night. She..." He glanced down the road, but it was empty now. "She didn't take it well. She was hoping to leave before you girls arrived, but we—we started talking, and she got delayed."

"Is she really going to Toronto?" Annie challenged, and Julia wanted to tell her to back off a little. So many things were new and changing, and while she'd had time to get used to it, her father hadn't, and Mom definitely had not.

"I honestly don't know," Dad said. "But come on. I've got coffee and those fruit tarts you girls always loved." He put a smile on his face and started for the door that led into the kitchen from the garage. "We can talk inside."

Julia followed him without a word, but Annie muttered, "Right. Wouldn't want the neighbors to know Mom just left and might not be coming back."

CHAPTER TWENTY-SIX

Maddy looked left and then right when she exited The Lighthouse Inn, the cool night air kissing her face in both directions. She'd just left Julia and her sister to get situated in the Ocean-side View room, and while she'd remembered meeting Annie years and years ago, somehow the air inside the inn with all three of them there didn't feel like enough. Like she'd somehow arrived on a space shuttle with only enough beds and oxygen for two, but there were now three of them trying to survive.

Outside, she could breathe. Outside, she could think. Outside, she could feel like herself again.

She didn't see Ben's motorcycle in the parking lot, but squishy, shifting footsteps met her ears to her right. She looked toward the beach to find the silhouette of a man coming toward her, and a moment later, Ben said, "Maddy, it's just me."

Just me. Like they were so familiar with one another, she'd know him from his gait and the sound of his voice. And they were; she did.

You're kissing him tonight, she told herself as she turned to meet him. She wasn't really sure if they were dating, though they'd gone to dinner four or five times. He'd sat with her on the dock overlooking the Sound once. He'd comforted her after the police had come and removed the bones from the upper balcony.

Ben had been the one to come rebuild the balcony too, as the police had definitely ripped it apart and then left everything gaping and splintered—which was how Maddy had felt since returning to the inn.

She hurried the last few steps to the edge of the sidewalk and threw her arms around Ben. "Hello," she said, a sigh accompanying the greeting.

"You okay tonight?" he asked, holding her right against his body. She adored the warmth he gave off, the strength in his arms and torso, and the delicious scent of sugar and spice that made up his cologne.

"Kind of?" she guessed, pulling away. She laced her fingers through his. "I don't know. Julia's here with her sister, and they obviously had a stressful week. I couldn't stay in the inn alone for some reason I still can't name, and the guest bed at Helen's messed up my back." She sighed as they started walking down the sidewalk in front of the inn. "It's fine. None of that matters."

"I think it matters," he said, his voice low and sexy. "It's real, Maddy. You can't just sweep it all under the rug."

"I know, but I don't want to dwell on it either." She smiled up at him. "Not tonight. You promised me chocolate and a good time."

His grin came out devilish. "Did I?"

On the next step, she nudged him with her hip. "Yes, you did." She drew in a deep breath of the night sky, the stars, and the half-moon. "Ben, I know you've been patient with me."

"I have not," he said.

"You have," she argued back. "You said you'd wait as long as I needed before kissing me. You said you were fine to keep seeing each other and holding hands." She adjusted hers in his, marveling at how good it felt to hold hands with someone other than Chris. "I just don't... I don't want to move too fast. I don't want to rebound. I don't want to hurt you—or myself."

"I know that, Maddy," he said. "You've said it all before, and I said I was fine with it. Your pace, remember?"

She did remember, but she didn't know how to increase the pace. She hadn't kissed a man in a very long time, and her stomach swooped and slid around inside her body. Near the end of the sidewalk, before the parking lot began for The Glass Dolphin, a small patch of cement sat in near-darkness, just outside the reach of the street lamp in the inn's lot and the one in the restaurant's lot.

Maddy paused there and looked up into the sky. "I love the stars here."

"Mm."

"Did you learn to navigate with the stars in the Coast Guard?" she asked.

"They have," he said. "Especially in the Navy. But when I went through training, no."

She moved her gaze to his face, and it was as brilliant as the vast universe above. He studied the sky for another moment before he felt the weight of her eyes. When his met hers, Maddy reached for his face, the moment so pure and so quiet between them. Nothing between her and Chris had ever been quiet.

The feel of his beard against her fingertips accelerated her pulse, and Maddy let her eyes drift closed. "I think I'm ready," she whispered. Her lips tingled, and the vibrations ran all the way down to her toes.

"Is that right?" Ben teased, though his hands both came to her face. He pushed her hair off her shoulder, one hand curling around the back of her neck, and the other sliding down to her hip. She sensed him drawing closer, and they somehow breathed in together only half a second before he touched his mouth to hers.

Maddy expected explosions and fireworks, heat and flame and fire.

She got quiet passion as Ben explored tentatively at first, only moving faster and deeper after several long seconds of pure bliss. He broke the kiss after only a few moments of that raw passion, and Maddy pulled in a deep breath.

"My word, woman," he murmured, cradling her face in both hands now. "That was worth every second of the wait." He kissed her again, and still there was nothing loud or obnoxious about it. He certainly knew how to kiss a woman, despite his claims that he hadn't done it for a while, and the excitement and steam moving through Maddy's body definitely testified of how much she enjoyed kissing him.

He was so completely opposite of Chris, and as Ben slid his lips down her neck and murmured how soft her skin was, Maddy felt the door on her twenty-four-year marriage truly close.

She was finally ready to move forward now, and she had a sexy Coast Guard Captain to take the first step with.

"Janey." Maddy ran up the last few steps at the blue cottage and hugged the woman. "You look great." She stepped back and held her at arm's length. Her hair had been washed, and her face practically glowed with life.

"Thank you," Janey said. "I feel so much better."

Julia had told Maddy about the psychiatric unit,

because Maddy had not gone to visit Janey there. Only Julia and Tessa had, and then Janey had requested that no one else come. *No one needs to see this place*, she'd said.

Julia had told Maddy the same thing. *Eerie* was the word she'd used.

Sean came out of the house as Ben arrived at the top of the steps, and Maddy stepped into his side and let him put his arm around her. "You remember Ben Downs," she said. "Sean, this is my boyfriend, Ben."

"Great to meet you," Sean said with a smile that could light up stadiums.

"Sean's Janey's boyfriend," Maddy said. "He runs a law firm downtown."

"Nice to meet you too," Ben said, and the two of them shook hands. "Do you two need help with anything?"

"I think Tessa is bringing out the sandwiches right now," Sean said, looking behind him. "We're eating in the backyard."

"This way," Janey said, and she stepped past Maddy and Ben and went down the steps. "We don't have a door that leads out back. I want to put one in, but Tessa says it's not necessary."

"It's not," Tessa said from the porch above Janey, who just continued around the side of the house. Maddy reached the bottom of the steps and looked back to Tessa. She wore a frown between her eyes that cleared the moment she caught Maddy looking.

"We have the money," Janey called from around the

corner, and Sean sighed audibly as he joined Ben and Maddy at the bottom of the steps.

"I'm sorry," Tessa said, coming down too. "I will not fight with her today."

"It's not your fault," Sean said. He looked at Maddy and then Ben. "She really is doing better, but it's a long road."

Janey appeared at the corner of the house. "Don't stand there and talk about me."

"I was just telling them that you have a long road in front of you," Sean said gently. "Because you do." He stepped out of the group and approached her. "It's nothing against you. No one's judging you or talking about you. We all just want you to heal the way you need to heal." He put his arm around her shoulders, and together, they started around the corner of the house again.

"He is a Godsend," Tessa murmured. "Honestly, I don't know that she'd still be alive today without him."

"Is there anything I can do to help?" Maddy asked.

"No," Tessa said with a sigh. "She's the one who has to do all the work."

"For you, though," Maddy said, stepping in front of Tessa, who carried a large, heavy tray of sandwiches. "Give me those." She took them, her arms shaking from the weight, and gave them to Ben. "Let Captain Muscles carry these." She grinned at him, and he seemed to get the message that he should take the sandwiches into the backyard and leave Maddy and Tessa alone for a minute.

The moment he rounded the corner of the house, Tessa broke down into tears. Maddy simply gathered her into her arms and let her cry. She knew how this kind of helpless pain felt, and she knew crying it out helped. At least it had for her.

"I feel like it's my fault," Tessa said. "When I'm not the one who fired the gun."

"I know," Maddy said. She'd felt the same way about the demise of her marriage. She wasn't the one who'd pulled that trigger. She wasn't the one who wanted the separation from her kids. She wasn't the one who'd forced everyone to choose. She'd had to deal with the fallout of all of it, though, and it wasn't fair.

Tessa reached up and wiped her eyes, drawing strength back into her chest and shoulders as she breathed in. "My divorce is going to be final next week. I feel...lost."

"You feel like it would be nice to have a sister to help you, for once." Maddy spoke in a voice barely above a whisper, so as to not be overheard.

Tessa met her eyes, the energy blazing in hers so strong and so dangerous. "Yes."

"Let me help you," Maddy said. "I've been where you are. I know what you're going through. Maybe the situations aren't the same, but I lost everyone in my life who was important to me." She swallowed, the lump there not quite as big as it usually was. "I was lost, for months. I had two things: my father, and this new job at The Lighthouse Inn. And even my father is going to leave soon enough."

Maddy yanked back on the emotion threatening to drown her.

Tessa touched her arm. "I'm sorry he's not doing better. Wasn't he going to come today?"

"He is," Maddy said, her voice only slightly pitched up. She blinked a couple of times to keep her tears dormant. "Miles is bringing him with Viola Martin. They're coming this way anyway, and Dad only lives a few blocks from them."

Tessa smiled, and kindness radiated from it. "That's great. I can't wait to meet him."

"Hello," Julia called, and Maddy twisted to see her and Annie coming across the street. They both carried a plate of goodies—the ones Maddy had made for this Sunday luncheon.

Tessa cleared the emotion from her face and turned to greet them. The ringing of a bicycle bell reached Maddy's ears, and she watched Helen ride her big beach cruiser up to the house, a smile filling her whole soul at the sight of the elderly woman on the bike.

"Look at you," Maddy said, steadying the bike while Helen dismounted. "I love this thing. Where did you get it?" She drank in the bright pink frame and the huge white basket on the front. A bakery box sat there, and Maddy's mouth watered.

"The bakery let me borrow it," she said. "One of the perks."

"The perks of what?" Tessa asked, but a sleek, black

Bentley turned the corner, drawing every eye in that direction.

"My word," Julia breathed.

"Who is that?" Annie asked.

Maddy simply watched as the car pulled into the driveway in front of her. A younger man got out of the driver's seat and smiled at the group of women. "Good morning, ladies," he said before stepping to the back door. He opened it and helped an aged woman stand.

Viola Martin. She wore a dress fit to meet a king, and she clung to Miles's arm like she'd fall without the support. Perhaps she would. "Good morning," she said in a kind voice that belied the permanent frown etched into her face.

"Viola Martin," Miles announced, as if she were the guest of honor at today's luncheon.

"Good morning," Maddy said as the others offered similar greetings. She leaned toward Julia and Annie. "That's Miles Greene. He lives with Viola and helps her. They live near my father."

"Viola," Janey said, running toward the older woman. She grabbed onto the woman, and they embraced. Maddy found it such an odd friendship, but one glance at Julia confirmed she had some of those in her life too.

"I'll get Dad," she said to Miles, who looked like he might fall down at any moment as he tried to steady Viola and now Janey too.

Maddy stepped to the other side of the car, her dad

having gotten the door open himself. "Let me help you, Dad." Maddy stepped into the space and offered her arm to her father. It took a couple of tries, but she finally managed to get him on his feet. He shuffled forward while she inched backward, and then he found his balance and could step with her at his side.

"We're just on the patio," Tessa said, leading the way. Maddy fell into step behind Julia and Annie, who went behind Viola and Janey and Miles. Helen brought up the rear with her pink pastry box in her hands.

The trees shaded the backyard, and Maddy sighed into the coolness of it. The sun shone today, but it certainly wasn't overly warm, as October had arrived for the weekend.

"How's the inn coming?" Dad asked as Maddy pulled out a chair for him.

"Great," Julia answered for her. "Annie's been staying in our Oceanside View room, and everything has been going perfectly." She beamed at her sister, and Maddy found she couldn't argue.

They'd tested a few recipes on Annie, and Maddy had perfected the timing on breakfast so it was ready at six-thirty and stayed warm through nine o'clock—the hours she and Julia had decided upon for their morning service. Julia had practiced two tours with her, and they'd taken the yacht out yesterday afternoon too.

Annie had given feedback, and Julia and Maddy had both made notes.

"You should come stay with us," Maddy said to her dad while he got settled. Julia left two spaces for her and Ben next to him, and she and Annie took the next available seats on the same side of the table. "Viola and Miles too. Just to test it out for us. We're still working on some things around the inn, obviously, and it's not open. But we have three rooms fully ready, and they come with bathrooms, and two meals a day."

"Free," Julia chimed in.

"Why would I want to stay at an inn when I have a home here?" Viola asked, her voice somewhat cross.

"To help them," Miles said diplomatically. He smiled at Maddy and then Julia. "I would love to come. I'm assuming you'd like feedback?"

"Of course," Maddy said, watching Julia wilt under the man's gaze. Stunned, she practically fell into her seat. Miles had to be far younger than Julia, though Maddy supposed her boyfriend wasn't exactly knocking on forty's door yet either.

"They'd like feedback," Miles said to Viola in a much louder voice. "You're very good at feedback." He gave them all another smile that said Viola was actually opinionated, and that could translate to "feedback."

Maddy and Julia could handle the old woman, and she grinned at Viola. Ben sat beside her, and Maddy slipped her hand into his for added comfort and a definite thrill.

"The elevator works," Annie said. "I think you'd love it, Miss Martin."

Viola lifted her chin and shook her shoulders. "Perhaps."

Helen put her box of pastries on the table. "House special," she said.

"How is the bakery doing?" Viola asked. "I'm so glad you didn't go out of business despite all the bad press last spring."

Maddy's gaze flew to Helen's, her surprise off the charts. Bad press last spring? Why hadn't Maddy heard about this? And why would that affect Helen?

Helen sat down at the end of the table, something guarded in her expression. "Online orders are all that saved us for a while," she said.

"And the Baking Society," Viola said, her voice full of self-importance.

"What's the Baking Society?" Tessa asked, the last to take her seat. She looked around at everyone at the table, and Maddy did the same. It seemed like only two people knew what was going on—Viola and Helen—and neither one of them spoke a word.

"What's the House Special?" Annie asked, breaking the silence. She reached for the pink pastry box. "Do you own the bakery, Helen?"

Every eye flew back to the bright-eyed woman, and Maddy marveled that she'd known her for five weeks and hadn't known anything about owning a bakery.

"Yes," Helen said, her eyes daring anyone to say a single negative thing about it. She switched her gaze back to Viola. "The Baking Society did not save my bakery, Viola, despite what you tell yourself. I know very well that it was you who turned that nasty reporter onto me in the first place."

"I did no such thing," Viola snapped back at her with a speed that belied her age.

"Okay, okay," Miles said, holding up one hand. "This is a wonderful lunch. Must we spoil it with things that are over and done with?"

Maddy very much wanted to hear the stories between these two. She also wanted to know what the Baking Society was, and if they were accepting members. Perhaps that was something that if she joined, could help bring people to the inn.

Silence filled the backyard, and then Ben reached for a sandwich. "I'm starving. What's in that pink box, Annie?"

"Almond macaroons," Helen said. "A three-generation Nantucket recipe, only found at my bakery, despite the attempts to steal the recipe from me." She glared at Viola, who simply opened her napkin and placed it on her lap. She clearly wasn't going anywhere, but neither was Helen.

"They look amazing," Julia said, reaching for one. "We can have dessert first, right? Maddy made her triple chocolate chunk cookies, and I'm *sure* they'll melt if we don't eat them first." She grinned and took one of those from the plate in front of her.

"Ooh, fudge," Ben said, and for some reason that struck Maddy's funny bone. She started to laugh while he collected three large squares of her dark chocolate Rocky Road fudge, complete with marshmallows and walnuts. He grinned at her and chuckled too, and before she knew it, the whole table had started to laugh, even Viola Martin.

Maddy wanted to bottle this moment and unstop it whenever she needed to remember that life was never all good or all bad. When she needed a moment of sunshine, a moment of cool shade, a moment of friendship, and plenty of chocolate, she could remember this. This moment would provide all of that, as well as the comforting feeling that she was in the right place, with the right people.

She looked around at the men and women at the table, finally feeling like her life held something for her she'd never dreamed of. Something simple and wonderful, and something kind and good. Something quiet, yet thrilling, and as she took an almond macaroon and bit into it, she couldn't wait for everything the future held for her.

CHAPTER TWENTY-SEVEN

Tessa made the short walk from her street over to Bakery Avenue, the morning sun barely warming the air. She kept her hands in her pockets and smiled when she saw the pink bicycle leaning up against the front of the bakery.

Finding out Helen Ivy actually owned the bakery had been a shock to her, because Helen had never said a single word about it. In fact, she'd told Janey that she "didn't do anything," and that she was "free almost all the time."

A bell tinkled as she went inside, and a young woman turned from the counter that ran along the back wall. A smile stretched across her face, and she said, "Good morning. What can I help you with?"

"I need a half-dozen box of your carrot cake bars," Tessa said, peering into the case.

"With raisins or without?"

"Without, please." As the girl got to work on those, Tessa checked out the éclairs down at the end of the case. "These are beautiful." Some of them held long, chocolate cigars that had been decorated like the stripes of a zebra, and others held fruit and flowers. "Simply stunning. Who makes these? Do you make these?"

"No," the young woman said. "But I'd like to learn. Our owner does classes for the éclairs. Aren't they beautiful?" She set the pink box of carrot cake bars on top of the case. "You have to work here for two years before you can apply to learn to make the éclairs. The owner is seventy-six, but she still does all the classes herself."

"It's Helen Ivy, right?" Tessa asked, reaching for her box.

"That's right." The younger woman smiled at her. "I've been here twenty months, and I can't wait to learn how to make those éclairs."

Tessa grinned at her enthusiasm and positivity. "I hope you get into the class quickly." She lifted the pink box. "Just these." She paid and took her treat down the street to the little house at the very top of it, where Helen lived.

She sat out front, in an old, wooden chair that faced the ocean, so she saw Tessa coming—probably the whole way from the bakery.

"Those better be carrot cake bars," she said once Tessa's foot touched the lawn. "And I'm not talking about the bakery."

"I wouldn't even *dream* of asking about the bakery you've owned for fifty years and never said a word about." Tessa gave her a smile and when she reached her, held out the box. "They are carrot cake bars. Your recipe?"

"My grandmother's," Helen grumbled, but she took the box.

Tessa looked around for another chair, spotted one in the shade, and went to drag it next to Helen's. She groaned and sighed as she sat down. She tilted her head back to absorb the weakening sunlight and the two of them sat in companionable silence for a few minutes before she asked, "Am I being too hard on Janey?"

Helen didn't immediately say yes or no. She ate through a second carrot cake bar and handed the box to Tessa. "I am so much like Janey," Helen said. "It's hard for me to answer."

"You shot a gun with your sister three feet away?"

"No." Helen smiled into the distance as a couple stepped off the beach and entered the bakery. "But I drove my sister absolutely insane with my antics."

"Describe 'antics'," Tessa said, sure they were little pranks Helen pulled in the kitchen, not dating three men at once, always finding a man to be with everywhere she went, joining female motorcycle clubs, and dying her hair odd colors.

"Oh, you know," Helen said, glancing to their right as a car made the turn and headed down toward the bakery. "Threatening to sell all the family recipes. Gloating when our mother signed the bakery over to me. Telling her she'd never be as good of a baker as I was. That kind of silly stuff." She sighed and closed her eyes. "I was cruel, to be honest. It's no wonder Prissy left Nantucket when I bought her out of the bakery. I haven't spoken to her much since."

"I'm sorry," Tessa said, remembering years where it was hard to talk to Janey too. "Did she give you advice all the time?"

"No, that's what I do to her." Helen glanced over at Tessa with a weak smile. "We older sisters tend to think we know better than everyone else. It's a curse that is actually our downfall." She reached over and patted Tessa's arm. "Be patient with her. My guess is she knows exactly what she's doing, and she hates it as much as you do. She wishes she could stop, but she's not sure how. It's like... being the older sister is hot-wired inside us, and we just can't flip it off."

Tessa nodded, trying to find an additional well of patience for her sister. "She could've killed you."

"I know that. I exchanged some words with her too."

"You did?" Tessa looked at Helen, who nodded and faced the sun again.

"I do think she's trying. She has therapy appointments every day. Sean is at her side to help her. She's not alone, as much as I'm not sure about Viola's role in her life. She will find her path back to full mental health...and you.

The important thing for you is to be there waiting for her, arms open, when she gets there."

"I wish it were as easy as you make that sound."

"Perhaps you'll get there at the same time as her," Helen said. "Have you considered therapy? The kind you don't find at the bottom of a wine bottle?"

Tessa flinched, but she couldn't necessarily argue with Helen. "Yes," she said honestly. "I've considered it. Right now, I'm getting by with pastries instead of alcohol, but that bakery down the street doesn't seem to have many new offerings, and I've tasted almost everything now."

Helen sat silently for a moment, and then she started to laugh. The sound grew and grew until it filled the sky, filled Tessa's soul, filled everything empty in her life. "You come by here tomorrow," Helen said. "I'll make my mother's chocolate-covered cranberry cookies. Then you'll think you've died and gone to heaven."

"Deal," Tessa said with a smile. The thought of making her own therapy appointment with a trained professional didn't go far from her mind. She'd been tossing it around casually from the left side to the right side of her brain, but now it took hold inside the stem. "Maybe I'll ask Janey for a referral to her counseling center."

"I can give you the name of who I see," Helen said, once again forcing Tessa's eyebrows to fly sky-high. "If you'd like."

"Yeah," Tessa said. "I'd like that."

"All right," Helen said. "Now, it's too early for this much talking. Don't you know the voice needs more time to wake up than the body?"

Tessa just smiled, leaned her head back, and closed both her eyes and her mouth. She did like the silence and the serenity of Nantucket on a fall morning, and she needed more things that brought her joy to crowd out the things she worried about, one of which was always Janey.

"I THINK IT LOOKS *AMAZING*," SHE SAID TO JULIA AND Maddy. The three of them stood just inside the Shipwreck Suite, which had just been put back together with all of the furniture, accent décor, and freshly laundered linens.

"If requested," Julia said. "We can remove the couch and bring in bunkbeds."

"Really?" Tessa looked at the sitting area almost behind the door. "That sounds like a lot of work. Where would you put the couch? Where are the bunkbeds hiding in this inn?"

"It's a foldable frame," Maddy said. "And look. Come see how we added an extra bed to the Beach Retreat room." She led the way down the hall to the room beside the Shipwreck Suite, which had been decorated with more yellows, whites, and teals than the one next door. It did look very beachy and very light, airy, and open.

"This looks like a cabinet, right?" Maddy said, placing

her hand on the credenza holding the television. "And it is. You can't store anything inside it though, and you don't have to move the television to make it a bed."

She pushed a button, and the front of the cabinet opened. She pulled out a drawer which ran the length of it, and then folded out a foam mattress that fit precisely in the new bed frame. "With the addition of sheets, a blanket, and pillows, this room now sleeps three."

"It's perfect for a young family with a couple of kids," she said. "Or even a couple vacationing with a teenager. They don't spend their time in the rooms when they come to Nantucket."

"No," Tessa said. "They don't."

Maddy started refolding the mattress and tucking it away inside the cabinet. It all slid together seamlessly, impressing Tessa further. "We only have two weeks until we open."

"You look nervous," Tessa said.

"We're launching the website tomorrow," Maddy said. "I hope we get people looking at it. We need to start getting rooms booked."

"Did you have a chance to go through it?" Julia asked, leading the way out of the room.

"Yes." Tessa followed her. "I made a couple of notes on my phone."

"Let's go down to the office and go through them," Maddy said. "My sister navigated around last night too, and she sent an email. Annie did too, right, Jules?"

"Yes," Julia said. "She even tried to book a room. I talked to her this morning and did the few things she found. Hopefully they're the same ones everyone else noticed."

Down in the office, Julia sat at the desk and started clicking on the big monitor. Maddy and Tessa sat opposite her, both of them ready with the notes from their phones. Tessa looked at these two women, neither of whom she was truly related to, and felt an outpouring of love overcome her.

"All right," Julia said, glancing at her. "What's wrong?"

"Nothing." Tessa reached up and brushed at her eyes. "Sorry, I'm fine."

Julia exchanged a glance with Maddy, and they both looked concerned.

"Really," Tessa said. "I'm just so proud of you two and how much you've done here at The Lighthouse Inn in what? Seven weeks? It's remarkable."

"You've helped a lot," Maddy said. "I'm fairly sure we'd still be painting without you." She gave her the brightest, friendliest smile imaginable. "And Janey."

Tessa wanted to tell her she didn't need to include Janey. Everyone sitting in the office knew Janey came by on her own schedule, and she hadn't come at all since getting released from the psychiatric unit. Tessa didn't blame her; she honestly didn't. She'd rather Janey took care of herself and didn't worry about the inn or the half-sister she had here. She knew seeing Julia was still hard for Janey.

"She's going to Southampton next week," Tessa said, looking at Julia.

"I heard," Julia said, her tone almost the same temperature as ice. "I'm okay with it. My dad has made his choices, and he invited her."

"I think it'll be good for her," Tessa admitted. "She needs some sort of...motion. Forward. Closure. Something. Not knowing drives Janey crazy."

"I understand that," Maddy said. "I think we all do, right?"

Julia nodded, and Tessa could agree. "Ron didn't contest the divorce or any of the things I asked for," she said. She'd gone to Pennsylvania, where she'd filed for divorce before making the move to Nantucket permanent.

"See?" Maddy said, no smile in sight. "Motion. Closure. Nothing left up in the air."

Tessa nodded, though the thought of thinking about Ron as her *ex*-husband still hadn't taken full root in her head. Saying it out loud hadn't happened either, and she didn't think of herself as divorced. She was simply...here cleaning out her mother's cottage after her death.

In that moment, Tessa realized she did have the closure she needed, and it was time to take a step forward. She didn't have to stay stalled in the past—or the summer—and she was strong enough and brave enough to take that step.

"Okay." She exhaled and then replaced all that air with a deep breath. "When I clicked on the RESERVE button at the top, I initially got an error. The second time I did it, it took me to the booking page."

"Yes," Julia said. "I fixed that, because for some reason, it had a loop on it."

"All right," Maddy said. "Brittany said she tapped on amenities, and nothing came up."

"Right," Julia said. "The page was unpublished for some reason. I hit publish a couple of hours ago, and it should be there..." She clicked and turned the screen. "Yep. There." She looked at Tessa, the hope in her dark eyes reminding her so much of a healthy Janey. The sister she'd seen for a week or two this past summer as they'd unearthed their mother's secrets and grown closer as friends and sisters.

"Thank you for including me on this," Tessa said, her emotion choking in the back of her throat. She shoved against it to keep it silent. "I've needed it these past couple of months."

"So have we," Maddy said simply. "I don't think we ever told you, but Julia and I...we didn't get along when we first started."

"Understatement of the century," Julia said with a laugh.

"You said you were college roommates." Tessa looked back and forth between the two of them. "I think that's what Janey told me."

"I stole her boyfriend and made him my husband," Julia said, just like that. Just blurted it out.

Tessa blinked and looked at Maddy. "Really?"

"I almost walked out when I saw her sitting in here the first day," Maddy said with a smile. "Look at us now."

"Forgiveness is a powerful thing," Julia said. "I'm not perfect at it, as my father will testify to, but we all have our own paths to walk."

"Helen told me something like that too," Tessa said. "Just a few days ago."

"Okay, can we pause and talk about Helen for two minutes?" Maddy asked, actually leaning forward now. "Did you know she owned the bakery?"

Tessa smiled and shook her head. "No, I did not."

"She's an enigma, that one," Maddy said. "I like her. She has spunk."

Tessa looked down at her phone and the notes she'd made about The Lighthouse Inn website. "She sure does."

"I just want that almond macaroon recipe," Maddy said.

"Oh!" Julia said. "I talked to her, and she agreed we can have three dozen of them every afternoon for check-in. Half-price."

"You're kidding," Maddy said, reaching for the paper Julia held up. She studied it for a moment and then giggled. "Jules, you're a genius."

"And don't you forget it," Julia said, and the three of them laughed together. Tessa so wanted Janey to be here and participate in these kinds of conversations, and as she laughed with her new friends, she prayed that Janey would know how loved she was, and how well she'd fit with them.

Right now, that was all she could do for her sister.

CHAPTER TWENTY-EIGHT

Janey walked along the boardwalk, all of the beachside restaurants and shops mostly closed in the off-season. She wore a jacket which hugged her hips, and she walked into the sunrise, breathing the same new-day-energy into her lungs.

She felt better today than she had yesterday, and yesterday had been her best day since being released from the psychiatric unit. Talking to her therapist helped. The breathing exercises she'd taught Janey helped. The journal-writing took so much from Janey's shoulders and gave it to lined paper and blue ink.

She'd learned how to relax her muscles. How to work through negative self-talk. The medication she took every single morning had been the single best help ever, and while Janey now viewed the world through a somewhat muted glass, it was better than holding a gun and pointing it at another human being.

She and Dr. Spendlove had been over and over the incident at the Friedman's cottage. Janey honestly couldn't remember what she'd been thinking, other than she'd been wildly out of control. She'd heard her sister's voice. She'd heard a man. She'd seen Riggs, and then nothing else mattered.

Dr. Spendlove had said that was one of their number one goals: Maintain control and memory and clarity at all times. Janey liked the sound of that, and she made a note at the top of every journal entry at the end of the day if she felt like she'd maintained her control and clarity that day.

She had sixteen days in a row now, and she thought she might be ready to return to Wainscott and Viola and Miles. She did like staying with Sean, who possessed more patience than any other man alive, and who lived close to downtown.

Janey did enjoy the thriving pulse of the downtown area of Nantucket, and she'd been walking the cobblestone streets and visiting her favorite shops. Dr. Spendlove did not approve of shopping therapy, and Janey had stuck to every single thing her therapist had suggested she do—and not do.

She wanted to get better this time. She really did. She'd done therapy in the past. She'd gone on juice diets, thinking that if she could get feeling better physically, the mental aspects of her life would follow. She'd always thrived with people around her, because she felt valued and appreciated. They laughed at what she said and found her witty and smart.

Here on Nantucket, Viola wasn't known for laughing, and she'd given up her friends and motorcycle club to... walk the beaches, spend time with her sister, and work in a law office with one other person.

So much had changed all at the same time, and Janey hadn't been able to find an equilibrium. That was Dr. Spendlove's word, not hers.

The sun inched up, and Janey breathed in through her nose, pulling the power from the sand and the shore. She loved Jetties Beach, and she walked here almost every morning. It was quiet this early, and she needed the time to think and center herself.

She did get to see people throughout the day in the office, and she did adore eating lunch with her boyfriend every single day. Previous to firing the gun, she wouldn't have called Sean her boyfriend. She might not have even used that label afterward, but Maddy had, and she and Sean had talked about it following the backyard luncheon.

"I'm only seeing you, Janey. We're exclusive, and if you don't want to be, you better tell me now. I have no problem being your boyfriend."

Janey hadn't known what to say. She always put men in boxes, and she made them work really hard to break free of them and move into a different one. None of them had ever complained too much—at least that she knew of.

"Sean's different, that's for sure." Janey often spoke to herself on her solitary walks, something Dr. Spendlove encouraged.

Don't let things fester inside, Janey. Talk. Talk to me. Talk to Sean. Talk to Tessa, the journal, or yourself. But talk it out.

Tessa had screamed something similar after she'd fired the gun. Janey did need to learn to trust someone, and she did need to confide in people. She needed to break down all of the box barriers, all the walls, and let people in.

Sean had kicked open the door, and Janey had tried to slam it in his face. After her initial resistance, she'd then held onto the doorframe for support, and she'd said, "I would like to introduce you as my boyfriend."

"It's not about the introduction," Sean had said. "It's about who I am to you. It's an emotional state, Janey."

"I want you to be my boyfriend," she'd told him.

Their relationship had grown leaps and bounds since then, and Janey smiled into the sunrise just thinking about him. She found the two rocks shaped a little bit like a throne, and she settled into the hard surface and listened to the waves gently lap at the beach.

She sighed, feeling so settled and so...comfortable in her own skin. She hadn't felt like this for a long while—years—and she hoped she could hold onto this feeling for as long as possible.

If she kept taking her medications, kept letting in the

right people, and kept doing what she'd learned to come this far, she felt certain she could.

A while later, an alarm went off on her phone, and that was her cue to get up and start walking home. Dr. Spendlove had encouraged the timer too. That way, Janey didn't have to hold so much in her brain. She could exist in the moment, and she didn't get bogged down in anxiety about what was coming later.

She made it to the parking lot and headed for Sean's car, which was running in the front space. The locks clicked a moment before she reached for the handle, and he said, "Morning, beautiful," as she slid into the passenger seat.

"Morning, handsome," she said, giving him a smile.

"How was the sunrise?"

"Amazing."

"I put your bag in the backseat." He eased out of the stall and started down the road that led away from the beach.

"Thank you," she said.

"You're sure you want to go alone?"

"You have a deposition tomorrow," Janey said.

"Depositions get rescheduled all the time."

"I'm okay, Sean. I want to go alone. I'm going to continue on to Jersey and see my daughter. I'm okay." She smiled at him and reached across the console to hold his hand. In the past, she usually made men come to her, and she liked showing affection to Sean.

He drove her the rest of the way to the airport, got her bag out of the back for her, and held her as he kissed her goodbye.

Janey enjoyed the sense of power she felt as she navigated her way to her gate. Even the simplest of things had become hard for her over the past few months, unanchored as she'd been. Losing her mother had been terribly difficult for her, and coupled with the discovery that Ryan Harper was her biological father, Janey had been spinning for a while.

She remained centered and in control on the flight to New York, and she remembered how much she enjoyed hailing a cab as she got one to take her to Southampton. They drove right by the mint green house that her mother owned, and Janey only recognized it by the pictures Tessa had shown her.

Her thoughts centered on Tessa for the rest of the ride, and Janey knew she needed to talk to her sister. Really talk to her. She'd already apologized, but the more whole Janey became, the more she realized she hadn't truly expressed her gratitude for her sister, nor had she honestly said how sorry she was for the things she'd put her sister through at the Friedman's cottage.

"Here you are, ma'am," the driver said, and Janey blinked her way out of her thoughts.

"Thank you." She swiped her credit card through the machine mounted in the back, hefted her bag out, and followed it. She faced the gorgeous house full of windows.

Someone took very good care of this house, and the bright red door opened and a tall, dark-haired man came out onto the porch.

Janey could only look at him—her father—and try to control her pulse. She'd felt so alone without any parents on earth, but now, looking at this man who was her biological father, she felt like she belonged.

You're being silly, she thought. She had two half-sisters on Nantucket she belonged to. Even as she thought that, she knew she was the one shoving against the door both Julia and Tessa had been trying to open.

"You must be Janey," Ryan Harper said, moving down the steps.

That launched her into motion, and Janey started down the sidewalk. "Yes," she said halfway there. "I'm Janey Forsythe."

Ryan smiled at her, his eyes exactly like hers. He bypassed the handshake and drew her right into a hug. "It's so great to meet you in person."

Janey relaxed into the embrace, feeling more and more of the trench inside her that had been open for years stitch back together. "It's great to meet you too."

He stepped back and studied her. "I didn't know about you. I swear I didn't."

"I don't doubt that," she said. "I didn't know about you until after a very long paper trail full of only clues." She shook her head. "My mother wasn't very forthcoming about her past."

Ryan grinned and indicated the stairs he'd come down. "Well, come in. I've got some lunch on the way."

Janey went with him up the steps and into the house. It was full of lights and brights, with billowy curtains and a pleasing gray, yellow, and light blue color scheme. It was an inviting atmosphere, with a woman's touch.

"Julia said your wife didn't take the news well." Janey wanted to confront all of the issues head-on, because the words had a way of piling up, and now that she'd learned to talk, she'd rather just get it all out.

"She didn't," Ryan said. "We're working through it."

"It was a very long time ago."

Ryan turned and gave her a smile. "Yes, forty-seven years. Unfortunately, Sandi thinks I've cheated on her for the duration of our marriage."

"Have you?" Janey asked.

"No," Ryan said quickly, with plenty of power behind the two-letter word. His dark eyes glinted with something dangerous. "Sandi and I got married very young. She actually got pregnant before the wedding, and I may have panicked that summer. Your mother was beautiful, and we only saw each other a few times."

Janey nodded, because she really didn't need the whole story. "She didn't put your name on the birth certificate."

"She didn't know it was me," he said. "That's the feeling I got when I talked to Dale Harton."

"You spoke to Dale?"

"I did," he said. "I looked up who Lydia had married. Gregory Clarke was best friends with Dale Harton, and he's still alive." He shrugged. "He said Lydia had been with several men that summer."

"She had," Janey said. "According to what my sister and I were able to determine."

"You mentioned your sister. Tessa, right?"

"Yes," Janey said, allowing a smile to touch her mouth. "I suppose she's as much my sister as Julia and Annie."

"No." Ryan shook his head and turned toward the front of the house as the doorbell rang. "No, Janey," he said as he moved away. "Tessa is your sister, through and through. You two grew up together under the same roof. It's not about blood."

She frowned at his back as he answered the door and took the bags of food from the delivery driver. "Thank you," Ryan said, and he turned back toward Janey.

"What do you mean, it's not about blood?" she asked.

Ryan set the white paper bags on the counter and looked at her. "Janey, you grew up with a mother and a father, whether biological or not. Tessa is your sister. Julia's not, though if you two are as friendly as she led me to believe when she came to see me, then sure, she could become your sister."

He pulled out a paper-wrapped sandwich and said, "This is the turkey, bacon, avocado. That's you." He grinned at her and placed the sandwich on a pristine, white plate.

"So you're not my father?"

"No," he said. "I am biologically." He looked up, his eyebrows high. "And I checked on that, Janey. Did the test. I am. But no, I'm not your father. There's so much that role means, and I haven't been a father to you." He cleared his throat and pulled out the second sandwich. "I'd like to get to know you. I'd love to see if I have it in me to take on that role, so I do truly become your father. To me, it's not about whose blood you have in your veins. It's about the part a person plays in your life. To me, Tessa is absolutely your sister, because she's the one fulfilling that role."

Janey nodded along with him, because the things he said made sense to her. "I'm not very good at relationships," she said. "Tessa's mad at me right now, and she has every right to be. I haven't spoken to Julia in a week or so."

Ryan started to unwrap his sandwich. "Why's that?"

"I made a mistake—a lot of them, actually, and I've been working on fixing myself before I try to fix things with them."

Ryan nodded and sat down at the bar. "Sit. Let's eat."

Janey sat beside him and unwrapped her sandwich too.

"You'll fix things with your sisters," Ryan said. "Don't be so hard on yourself."

"How do you know?" Janey asked, genuinely wanting to know. "You don't even know me."

"Sure, I do," he said with a smile. "We've been

emailing back and forth for a little bit, and now that I've met you, I can see how much like your mother you are. She had the biggest, kindest heart in the world, and so do you."

Janey shook her head, though she liked his assessment of her mom. "I really don't. If you asked Tessa, she'd say I'm so selfish."

"Maybe you've acted that way in the past," Ryan said. "That's part of what you're fixing, right?"

Janey nodded and took a bite of her sandwich so she wouldn't have to answer verbally.

"So you'll get yourself in the best place you can be, and then you'll go to Tessa and Julia. They'll keep, trust me. And they'll be waiting to hug you and accept you for the new woman you are." His smile was kind and oh-so-confident, as if he knew, simply *knew*, what he said would come true.

Janey liked the thought of it, and she held onto it and let it flow through her mind exactly as he'd said it would. Both Tessa and Julia would be at the cottage on the beach, and Janey would tell them how much she loved them, and how sorry she was that she'd messed up so badly these past few months.

They'd hug her, offer wine and coffee, and have desserts galore. She'd fit right in with Maddy, Helen, Tessa, and Julia, and the five of them would laugh and talk and start down a new path of friendship where they could all thrive.

She wanted the scenario in her imagination to come to fruition, and she smiled at Ryan. "Thank you," she said. "I hope you're right."

"I'm your father, Janey," he said with a grin. "With my other kids, I'm right eighty percent of the time. Trust me on this—it's part of my eighty percent." He chuckled, and Janey liked the sound of it.

"I was worried about coming," Janey admitted. "So thank you for making me feel comfortable."

"I was worried too," he said. "You put off an accepting air, Janey. *You* made it easy to make you feel comfortable."

Janey had often held back from showing too much emotion, but right now, she didn't. She didn't want to ever again. She slung her arm around her biological father and hugged him, feeling loved and comforted by a parent for the first time in far too long when he put his arm around her and squeezed her back.

Another broken piece inside her mended, and Janey beamed at Ryan, hoping he could see that he'd helped her take the next step in her healing. Now, she just needed to keep moving forward until she stood in front of Tessa and could make things right with her.

CHAPTER TWENTY-NINE

"Need some help?"

Julia turned from her trunk, where she'd just set a box at her feet and had been reaching for another. Janey stood there, and Julia's heartbeat stabbed at her as her eyes took in the woman before her.

She'd cut her hair into a deep, rich, black pixie style. She wore huge silver hoops in her ears and her signature flowing blouse in bright red, orange, yellow, and blue flowers. She'd paired that with a pair of black leggings, and she looked like a million bucks.

"Janey." Julia abandoned her task in the truck and practically dove at her half-sister. With the other woman held tightly in her arms, Julia said, "You look so good. How are you feeling?"

"Really good." Janey hugged her back, and her grip said more than words could.

"How's your daughter?"

"Engaged," Janey said, pulling back with a smile. "When Travis—that's her boyfriend—heard I was coming to visit, he planned this romantic dinner and asked her."

"That's wonderful," Julia said, her own eyes filling with tears. "I've missed you, Janey."

Janey smiled, and it was unlike any smile Julia had ever seen on her face before. It was soft, serene, and somewhat serious. "I've missed you so much, Julia." Janey hugged her again, something vibrating in her chest this time. "I want us to be great friends."

"I want that too," Julia whispered.

Janey drew a big breath and stepped back. "It looks like you're taking in some books." She stepped over to the box Julia had put on the ground.

"Sort of," Julia said, suddenly nervous. "They're the photo settings from the album we found. Past guests."

Janey crouched down in front of the box, which had an open top. She took out a photo and gazed at it. Julia joined her but stayed standing as she looked at the picture. This one featured The Lighthouse Inn and a group of children. The back of the photo had said "children's day 1982," and Julia had asked the documents restorer to put a plaque on it so anyone who came to the inn would see its history.

"We're putting them up in the lobby," she said.

Janey said nothing as she replaced the framed photo in

the box and straightened. She picked up the box from the ground and said, "I'll take this one."

Julia watched her go, feeling thrown back in the past just two months, when Janey had caught her taking boxes out of the trunk of her car in this very parking lot. She hadn't known who she was then, but as she watched Janey step up onto the curb and continue toward the entrance to the inn, she knew now.

Janey was a friend. She could be a sister.

After she retrieved the other box she'd picked up from the restoration shop that morning, Julia followed Janey into the inn. "Maddy," she called. "We have the pictures."

"Coming." Maddy's voice came from around the corner in the direction of the dining room, and Julia set her box on the check in desk and faced the wall running from the office to the stairs.

"Wow," Janey said, stepping to her side. "You guys have already planned it out."

"Have you not met Maddy?" Julia muttered, looking at the cardstock squares Maddy had painstakingly cut and hung last night. She'd made Julia stand back about a hundred times and tell her which shapes and sizes should go where. To her credit, Maddy had actually listened to Julia's opinion, and once the pictures took the place of the cardstock squares, The Lighthouse Inn would be ready for guests.

"You're opening on Thursday," Janey said.

"Yes," Julia said. "We're fully booked too. Vivian is coming tomorrow for the final walk-through, and she's bringing a photographer from the Historical Society and the Chronicles."

Janey must've been able to hear the tremor of nerves in Julia's voice, because she looked at her and said, "It's going to be amazing," she said. "You're ready, right? Tessa said you were ready."

"I don't see how we could be any more ready," Julia said. "We're completing the training of our staff tomorrow. I'm in charge of all their schedules, and I have it made for the first two weeks. I only have to submit their hours to the Historical Society, and they'll pay them."

"Not having to manage payroll is huge," Janey said. "I was a payroll manager years ago. It's a crazy job every two weeks."

Julia looked at her with wonder running through her. "I managed a diner for a few years. The payroll was definitely the hardest part."

A beam filled Janey's face. "I didn't know you managed a diner."

"When my husband and I were first married," she said with a nod. "Feels like another lifetime."

"Last week feels like another lifetime to me," Janey said, a giggle escaping her mouth a moment later.

Julia half-coughed and half-laughed, the sound morphing into a full laugh a moment later. Janey laughed with her, and she slipped her hand into Julia's.

"I met Ryan," she said. "He's very nice."

Julia sobered and studied Janey's face while she kept her gaze on the wall in front of her. "Did Annie go?"

"No."

"He thought he might ask her to be there. Sort of like a buffer."

Janey smiled, flashing a look toward Julia so fast their eyes couldn't even meet properly. "We didn't need a buffer."

"Dad is very good with people."

Janey nodded. "I would agree with that."

"I know he told Eric about you too."

"We talked a little about Eric," Janey said, turning toward the stairs as Maddy's footsteps sounded. "I'm sorry about your mom. I didn't mean to cause a problem there."

"Mom has always been a little dramatic," Julia said. "I think she'll come around, because my dad is trustworthy."

"Janey," Maddy said. "Look at you." She approached, throwing a look toward Julia before she stepped into Janey's personal space and hugged her quickly if a bit awkwardly. "I love your hair. It makes you look so sophisticated."

"I like it too." Janey reached up and touched the ends of her hair along her right ear. "Do you guys want some help putting these up?"

"Yes," Julia said quickly. "Maddy, why don't you hand out the pictures and tell Janey and I where you want them?"

Maddy readily agreed and stepped over to the check in desk still wearing her apron. She directed Janey and Julia to each cardstock piece, and then the three of them stood back and looked at the wall.

"I love how it's not chronological," Janey said. "It makes you want to go look and see what there is."

"It's less about the history and more about the people," Julia agreed.

"I think we're ready," Maddy said, her voice wavering in a way Julia had never heard before.

She glanced down past Janey to Maddy, who didn't try to hide her emotions. "Come on," she said. "Lunch is ready. When is Tessa coming?"

"I told them noon," Julia said, noting the way Janey tensed slightly.

"I'll take these outside," she said, moving to collect the empty boxes. Before she could get very far, the doors to the inn opened, and Helen walked in with Tessa not far behind. They spoke to one another, and the moment they saw Janey, everything stilled.

"Janey Forsythe," Helen said, a smile blooming across her entire being. "Look at you, child."

"Hello, Helen." Janey grinned and hugged the other woman. "Hi, Tess."

"I barely recognize you," Tessa said, and she easily embraced her sister too. Julia's heart expanded and grew, and she felt the love the two of them had for each other.

Sometimes the road between siblings was littered with potholes and nails and other hazards.

Julia couldn't pretend to know what they'd been through this summer, though Tessa had started to open up a little bit more about her mother and her own marriage. She just knew she was thrilled the two of them had become part of her life, and part of the restoration of The Lighthouse Inn.

"I'm an old woman," Helen said. "And Maddy promised me lunch, so I barely ate breakfast." She started for the dining room while Maddy linked her arm through hers.

"Sure," Tessa said almost under her breath but definitely loud enough for everyone to hear. "That means she only ate two doughnuts instead of three."

Janey snickered, and Julia couldn't contain her laugh either. They went into the dining room, where Julia's feet grew roots one more time. "Maddy," she breathed. "This is gorgeous."

The square table could seat twenty, five down each side. Today, Maddy had covered it with a soft beige cloth and put a four-foot vase in the middle of it. It ran straight up in a column, which she'd filled with sand and shells, and at the very top, blue sprigs of flowers and seaweed.

"This is what I think our celebration tables would look like," she said. "I'm going to leave it up for Vivian and the photographer tomorrow, but don't worry. We can replace the tablecloth if we spill on it."

Each setting held a large plate with delicate bumps around the outside edge. Another plate—this one in the precise color of blue as the seaweed—sat atop that, with blue napkins on the cloth, and sterling silver cutlery in a plain pattern. Glasses sat at each setting, and Julia hardly knew if she could sit at a table so luxurious.

"This is stunning," Janey said. "I'd get married here."

"The Lighthouse Inn doesn't do weddings," Julia said automatically. She'd already answered that question a half-dozen times, though it said so right on their website too.

"You should," Janey said. "Why can't you?"

"We'd need more chefs," Maddy said. "For one."

"Partner with The Glass Dolphin," Janey said. "They do excellent special occasion catering. A client of ours invited us to their anniversary party, and they had the Dolphin do the food."

"It's not a bad idea," Julia murmured.

"We don't have a ceremony space," Maddy said.

"You have the beach," Tessa said. "And at least part of it is private to the inn, isn't it?"

"I suppose," Maddy said. "But it's never been fenced off."

"Then you fence it off only for the weddings you book," Janey said, moving forward. "Something to think about. I know a bakery owner who could probably do the cakes." She smiled at Helen, who was hot on her heels.

"I'm terrible at wedding cakes," Helen said. "But I've got two pastry chefs who really know their stuff."

"There you go," Janey said, as if adding a wedding package to what the inn did would be just like blinking and making it so.

"We're not doing weddings," Maddy said. "At least not right now." She clapped her hands together. "Okay. Get ready for an amazing feast. I've made a roast chicken dinner, with fried potatoes, asparagus with hollandaise and flaked fish, and the most amazing brown butter layer cake for dessert."

"Can we have dessert first?" Tessa asked.

"No," Maddy said, throwing her a darted look. "So save room. I'll be right back."

"Hello!" a woman called, and Julia jumped to her feet.

"Annie," she said, hurrying toward the doorway. "We're in the dining room." She ran out into the lobby to find her sister and her two nieces standing in front of the pictures.

"These are great," Annie said. "He did a great job on them, Jules."

"He did, didn't he?" She stepped to Annie's side and put her arm around her. "Thank you for coming."

"Julia!" Maddy called.

"The chef does not like it when lunch is delayed," Annie said under her breath. "Come on, girls. Let's go see what Maddy made for lunch."

"Annie," Maddy said as she poked her head around

the corner. "You made it." She slipped into her perfect hostess persona. "Come on, guys. Leave your bags. The food is hot right now."

"I'm so excited you guys are here," Julia said to her nieces. "You'll get to meet Janey, and she is definitely going to be a cooler aunt than me."

CHAPTER THIRTY

Maddy woke in the blue room and took several long seconds to come to full consciousness. She had repainted the room, reasoning that they'd chosen a blue aesthetic for the inn, and that Louisa Fry would still love it.

Likewise, Julia had ripped out her floral wallpaper and made her room to match the rest of the inn. Now, should either of them leave at any point in the future, these two rooms on the basement level of The Lighthouse Inn could be used as guest rooms.

Maddy wasn't sure where she'd go, but she had been kissing Captain Ben Downs for a week or two now, and she didn't think she'd live in his bunk with him at the Coast Guard station. He could potentially move in here, but she wasn't sure if the Historical Society would then want the two of them to run the inn or not.

When she'd first seen Julia sitting in front of the desk as Vivian positioned herself between the two of them, Maddy had never dreamed that she'd see this day. "Opening day," she said to herself as she sat up, a smile accompanying the words and the movement. So many times over the past sixty days, her back had protested any movement. She'd had days where she just wanted to lay in bed and never get out.

The inn had given her a purpose, however, and she'd forced herself to get up and get in the shower, just like she did this morning. Today, she was excited to get in the kitchen and bake some oatmeal chocolate chip cookies to welcome their very first guests, who could start checking in at three p.m.

Before then, Vivian had arranged a ribbon-cutting ceremony to historically mark the official grand reopening of The Lighthouse Inn, and that celebration was set for noon. Fancy invitations had been sent around the island to all the wealthy locals, other business owners, and Maddy and Julia's friends.

Ben had confirmed that he'd be there in his uniform, and Maddy's heart thumped a little harder as she stepped into a professional pair of slacks that had been her go-to pants when entertaining with her ex-husband.

She picked up her phone and sent a text to her son and daughter. *Up and ready for today! Wish you could be here.*

Send us the video link, Mom, Kyle said. *It's going to be great.*

I will as soon as I have it, she promised, and she paused at the door and filled her lungs with oxygen. "Help Julia and I today, please," she whispered, and then she left her room. She left the inn completely and made the drive around to the south side of the island to pick up her father.

He once again waited on the front porch, but there was no fibrous, silky envelope next to him. "Morning, Dad."

"Morning, my baby," he said, though Maddy was the oldest of his children. Her heart swelled with love for him, and she helped him stand and steadied him as they went down the steps to the car.

Back at the inn, she put her dad in one of the recliners that looked like red denim had been salt-stained and told him she'd bring him an omelet in ten minutes. She'd find him asleep in the chair, she knew, so she didn't hurry to get his breakfast put together.

Julia entered the kitchen just as she slid the omelet from the pan, and she paused to take in the ingredients Maddy had gotten out. "Oatmeal is smart," she said. "It has that hint of cinnamon that guests will love but won't be able to identify."

"I can't wait until those candles get here," Maddy said, thinking of the cookie-scented candles they'd ordered. "I can't make cookies every day."

"You won't have to," Julia promised as she moved over to the coffee maker. Her hand trembled as she poured herself a cup. "I'm so nervous."

"Why?" Maddy asked. "We only had to impress Vivian, and she was blown out of the water, especially with the setback we had."

"Have you seen the paper this morning?" Julia stirred sugar into her coffee.

"No," Maddy said. "I went to get Dad so he could be here for the ribbon-cutting."

"The pictures are gorgeous," Julia said. "Like, I know what they're of, and I'm like, wow, this place looks like one of the poshest hotels in Nantucket."

"Really?"

"The light is fantastic," Julia said, setting her cup down and switching it out for her phone. "Look." She handed the phone to Maddy, who drank in the light, airy, almost pink pictures of the inn.

"We chose the best colors in the world for a seaside inn," she murmured.

"Look at that one of the sign for the Shipwreck Suite."

Maddy scrolled, ignoring the words in the article, though she did find things like, "Nantucket's old gem turned new again," and "Locals will want to book a room just to see the updates," along the way.

The sign met her eyes, and she smiled as widely as she ever had. The words had been hand-painted by Julia on a piece of driftwood they'd actually found in The Harbor House, an antiques shop just down the beach from the inn. "It looks just like it came from a ship."

"I checked our bookings this morning just before I

came upstairs," Julia said. "We're full through the New Year, suddenly."

Maddy lifted her eyes from the phone as they widened. "You're kidding. We only had two weeks full."

"The article came out an hour ago."

"I'm surprised we haven't crashed the website." Maddy didn't know what to do with her hands. Take her dad his food? Start the cookies? Call her mother and tell her to look at that article so she'd know that Maddy had done something amazing in the past two months, divorced and supposedly depressed as she was?

The bitter feelings about her mom surprised her, and Maddy pushed them right out of her head. Today was not a day for unpleasant things. "Was my dad awake?" she asked, glancing down at the omelet.

"I heard some snoring as I went by," Julia said with a smile.

Maddy's heartbeat crashed against her ribs once, realized it couldn't get away, and settled down. "I'm going to go wake him. Do you want an omelet?"

"No, Tessa is bringing the cream cheese Danish, and Janey said she'd stop by the organic market and bring that fruit bowl." She glanced at the clock. "I'll start creaming the butter and sugar while you sit with your dad. Then the cookies can bake while we eat breakfast." She offered Maddy a kind smile, and Maddy's emotions shook and erupted through her whole body.

She didn't pick up the plate, though her father's breakfast was growing cold. She stepped over to Julia and hugged her, saying, "Thank you, Julia." She had so much more to say to her once-again best friend, but the words piled on top of one another, tangled, and wouldn't come out of her mouth.

"We're a good team," Julia whispered. "Thank *you*, Maddy."

She stepped back and looked straight into Julia's eyes. "We *are* a good team, and this grand reopening is going to be so amazing."

"Mads?" Ben called, and Maddy turned toward the doorway and then back to the ingredients on the counter.

"Go," Julia said. "Go kiss your man and sit with your dad. There will be time for cookies later."

A giddiness rose up inside Maddy that made her feel in her mid-twenties again, and she nearly skipped as she left the kitchen and found Ben halfway across the dining room, obviously coming to find her. He scanned her from head to toe and whistled. "Who is this gorgeous woman?"

She laughed as she rolled her eyes. "Come on. You've seen this outfit before." She looked down at her ivory blouse with sailboats on it. Janey had told her of a shop in downtown Nantucket, and Maddy had found a day to steal away and get a new shirt a few weeks ago.

Ben grinned at her and received her into his arms. "Come on? I will not come on." He dropped his head to slide the tip of his nose down the side of her face. The way he breathed her in made her feel cherished and special, and he added, "You are a stunning woman, and I'm not going to keep that to myself when I think it."

He brought his lips to hers and kissed her slowly, sweetly, with sugar and spice and everything nice. "Mm." He pulled away. "I saw your dad out there."

"I'm taking him breakfast," Maddy said. "Then I need your help moving that dresser."

"Decided to go over the two feet?" He grinned at her, and he really shouldn't be allowed to do that to a woman.

"Yes," she said, swatting at his chest. "Now come sit with me and Dad for a few minutes." She scanned him down to his shoes. "You're not in uniform."

"I took the whole day off." He grinned at her and slung his arm around her shoulders. "So if you can sneak away after we move that dresser, I know a ride on the back of my motorcycle will clear your head."

Maddy giggled as they went into the kitchen to collect the omelet. "I'm not riding that motorcycle." She'd been *flirting* with him when she'd asked if it seated two. She didn't actually want to ride it with him.

"I think I'll get you on it," he said with a grin. "Morning, Julia."

"Good morning, Captain."

He chuckled and shook his head. "You don't have to call me Captain. I have a name."

Julia looked at Maddy, silently begging her to let her tell him what she called him when he wasn't around.

Maddy shook her head firmly and said, "Don't even think about it."

"Fine," Julia said. "I don't think you'll get her on that bike, Captain. When Maddy makes up her mind, she's quite hard to sway."

"I've encountered some more stubborn than her." He gave her that twinkling-eye smile that made Maddy's stomach lilt and light on fire.

"Stubborn?" she asked, picking up the plate. "I don't think there will be any time for anything but prep for the grand re-opening." She marched past him, giving him a look that said, *I can show you stubborn.*

"Mads," he said, turning to follow her. "You're not stubborn, okay?"

"Good luck," Julia called behind them, and Maddy marched on until she left the dining room. Then the mock anger left her body, and she let Ben catch up to her.

"Dad," she said as she arrived at the second recliner. "You can get the chair from the office."

Ben went to get that while Maddy got her father awakened. "I have your omelet."

He smiled at her and came right awake, reaching for the plate. "Oh, you're such a good girl, Britt."

"Dad," Maddy said, ice flowing through her chest now. "I'm Maddy." She touched his arm and ducked her head to look right into his eyes. Light shone there, and he flinched when he'd realized his mistake.

"Of course, Maddy. Sorry," he said.

Ben returned, and Maddy told her father about the re-opening ceremony that would be happening in a few hours. A vein of worry rode beneath her words, and she feared if she stopped talking, she'd burst into tears.

"All right," she said. "I have to make cookies. Are you two okay here?" She stood and gestured to the softer seat for Ben.

He took the recliner and sighed. "Yep. We're just going to take a nap, right, Brad?"

"I like how this one thinks." Her father handed Maddy his empty plate, and she took it back into the kitchen. Julia had vacated the area, and Maddy poured herself into the oatmeal chocolate chip cookies.

"Maddy, you need to step forward," Vivian said as she faced the group. "Just shift your weight on the other side of Julia there. Yes."

Maddy had spent plenty of time in front of a camera, and she knew how to make the shape of her body look more feminine. She knew how to push her hip away so she didn't look as heavy. She knew exactly how wide to make her smile to exude joy but not look like she was trying too hard.

The photographer took several pictures, the red ribbon draping nicely in front of them. The ends of the bow billowed in the breeze, and Maddy tucked her hair as it too tried to drift out of place.

"All right," Vivian said, joining the group. More pictures got clicked, and then Vivian stepped right up to the ribbon, which hung between two gold pillars that had been brought in just for the ceremony.

"I'm thrilled to have such a beautiful renovation to present to the people of Nantucket, as well as all of those who choose to come out to the Point—one of the most beautiful spots on the island—to experience a true beach vacation. Our new caretakers, Julia Harper and Madelynne Lancaster—" She indicated both women as she said their names, and Julia stepped to Vivian's right side and Maddy moved to her left.

"Have outdone themselves with the interior of the inn. They have exquisite menus prepared for the guests that will come, and they've achieved partnerships with local Nantucket businesses that will only bring tourists back to the island time and time again."

Maddy was impressed by the woman's level of professionalism and the steady clip of her delivery. "Their outreach programs for families include historical tours, yacht tours, and even a local bakery tour that will go with our children's beach activities that The Lighthouse Inn has always been known for."

She smiled at Julia and then Maddy, the camera clicking, clicking, clicking as she moved slowly and held their eyes deliberately. Vivian faced the crowd again and said, "Welcome to The Lighthouse Inn."

She waited while her assistant from the Historical Society brought her a giant pair of scissors that had surprised Maddy with their weight when they'd practiced this next moment.

Maddy looked out at the crowd, catching Ben's eyes. He grinned at her, looking so handsome and so normal in jeans and a polo the color of the summer sky right before darkness fell.

She saw Tessa Simmons, who had one hand pressed to her pulse and a smile of pure joy on her face.

She saw Janey Forsythe, with her new hairdo and her boyfriend at her side, already lifting her hands to clap.

She saw Helen Ivy's bright white hair and blazing blue eyes, her smile also broadcasting pure happiness toward Julia and Maddy.

Julia's sister Annie stood with her daughters, tears in her eyes. Dad sat in a chair next to her they'd brought out from the office. Others had gathered—business owners from the shops down the beach to the east. The chef at The Glass Dolphin. Their servers and busboys.

Viola Martin and Miles, who held a parasol—a legit parasol—over the older woman's face so she wouldn't be in the direct sunlight.

She looked right into the lens of the video camera which stood right in the middle of all of the people, hoping Kyle and Chelsea could see how happy their mother was, as well as how much she wished they were here for her to hug and tell them how much she loved them.

Maddy leaned forward as she lifted her left hand across her body and put it on the top handle of the scissors.

She met Julia's eyes, who had her right hand crossed over her body and held the bottom handle of the scissors still. Vivian had both hands on the scissors, one on top and one on bottom, and the three of them snapped the blades together, effectively cutting the red ribbon.

Cheers filled the air, and Maddy laughed as she looked at Vivian and then Julia. The three of them embraced, and when Vivian stepped forward to begin welcoming VIPs to the inn for their pre-check-in tour, Maddy embraced Julia again.

"We did it," she said into the chaos.

"We sure did." Julia pulled back and looked at Maddy and then out at the swelling crowd as they moved forward. "We sure did."

Tessa and Janey arrived almost simultaneously, and a group hug ensued, which included Annie, Helen, Sean, and Ben. With all of them offering congratulations and laughing, Maddy simply knew that she had made the right decision by coming to Nantucket for a job she wasn't even sure she could do.

She knew now she could. She had. Even when faced with someone and situations she'd never dreamed of, she'd done it.

"All right," she said once the group broke up. "Let me go grab the cookies."

Read on for the first chapter of ***The Seashell Promise***, the next book on Nantucket Point, featuring these new best friends, as well as Julia's sister Annie, as they continue to rebuild their lives.

SNEAK PEEK! THE SEASHELL PROMISE, CHAPTER ONE:

Annie Mason sighed over the side of the ferry, wishing she'd stayed in the car the way her daughter had. Paige was not happy to be coming to Nantucket for the holidays, and Annie hadn't the heart to tell her it was the Point and Aunt Julia's cooking, or an empty house with an empty fridge at her father's.

Donovan, her ex-husband, hadn't told anyone he and his partner had decided to leave Chatham. Annie had found out quite by mistake, when she'd called him on the way to his house with Brianne, and he'd blurted out that he lived in Vermont now.

An entirely different state.

"Guess he doesn't want to be as involved as he claimed," she said into the wind.

"What?" Bri asked, and Annie turned toward her, putting a false smile on her face.

"Nothing, dear." She lifted her arm and put it around her youngest daughter. Bri hadn't given her any trouble about coming to Nantucket for Thanksgiving, but she didn't have a boyfriend she had to leave for five whole days.

Five days. Annie rolled her eyes toward the sky, glad she stood taller than Bri so her daughter couldn't see. Annie herself, as a mother, had learned to see everything around her, and she knew Logan and Paige were *not* just friends.

Just like she'd known that Donovan had stopped loving her right about the time Bri turned ten years old. He'd stayed for a year or two, but in the end, he'd embraced a whole different part of himself, one he said had been suppressed for too long.

She didn't fault him for that. She wouldn't want to be untrue to who she really was. She simply wanted to be communicated with, and having the father of her children leave the state of Massachusetts without telling any of them had opened wounds she'd thought she'd stitched closed.

"Aunt Julia says Maddy is the best cook on the island, and she's already been baking for a week."

"Pumpkin pie?" Bri asked, a big smile on her face.

"And apple," Annie said, returning the smile. "Rolls, tarts, and I got a text this morning that she's even prepared the breakfast casserole already. Apparently, it has to sit overnight."

"I can't wait," Bri said.

Annie turned her face into the wind, because she was looking forward to five days where she didn't have to take care of things. Someone else could make breakfast, lunch, and dinner. Someone else would make her bed once she left. Life away from home, with someone who would tell her where to sit, what time to get up, all of it, was exactly what Annie needed right now.

Her stomach tightened at the thought of spending the holidays with a half-sister she barely knew. She'd met Janey a few times now, and they got along just fine. She didn't really know her, though, and something buzzed in Annie's blood.

She couldn't decide if she wanted to know her half-sister better or if she didn't.

What she wanted felt completely out of her control. She wanted the sense of stability she'd once had. She wanted to be able to talk to her daughters without it turning into an argument or hearing the words, "You just don't get it, Mom."

She wasn't so out of touch that she didn't know what the world was like for teenagers, though that was how Paige made her feel.

She wanted to feel happy again. Not just the brief kind of happiness she experienced when her daughters brought home good report cards or one of her patients got to check-out of the hospital early.

But true happiness. The kind that a person woke with deep down in their soul. The kind that made simple things like a child playing in a fountain bring a smile to her face and the general feeling that all was well in the world. The kind that told her she was good enough, just as she was.

Her phone rang, and she almost didn't want to check it. It would either be her shift boss, Ilysa, her mother, or Julia. At the moment, Annie didn't particularly want to speak to any of them.

She couldn't just ignore her phone, and she lifted it to check the screen. *Mom* sat there, and out of the three, she was the worst one.

"Don't answer it," Bri said. She even reached over and took the phone from Annie before she could even blink. "She'll just say something to make you mad or feel guilty." She silenced the phone and stuck it in her back pocket.

She glanced at Annie, who blinked at her in pure surprise. Her daughter looked out over the water too, and Annie took a few seconds of silence to figure out what to say.

"She's going through a hard time," she finally said.

"We all have things," Bri said without looking at her. "And I don't feel that bad for her."

"Bri," Annie chastised. "She..." She didn't have adequate words for her mother. A few months ago, they'd all found out about Janey Forsythe, a woman the same age as Julia, her oldest sister.

The only problem was, Janey wasn't Annie's full sibling. She only had her father's DNA running through her veins. Proven with a paternity test.

At some point in the past, he'd been unfaithful to her mother, and Annie didn't want to judge her mom's reaction and then subsequent actions.

She'd first gone to Toronto, where her family hailed from. She'd stayed there with her mother and sister for a few weeks before returning to the huge house in Southampton where Annie had grown up with her two siblings.

Then she'd asked Dad to move out, but he'd refused. They'd been living in the house, but barely speaking. Annie had witnessed it first-hand when she'd gone to visit in October. She'd never felt such tension in her life, not even when she and Donovan had sat down with the girls to lay things out for them.

Her mother was supposed to be hosting Thanksgiving dinner, but Annie had adequately warned Julia and Eric, her brother, and they'd all made alternate plans. Because of everything going on, Mom hadn't invited anyone until last week, and it had been easy to say they'd already made arrangements for the holidays.

"She's being childish," Bri said. "Grandpa has explained everything a thousand times over."

"It's hard to know what really goes on behind closed

doors, honey." She gave her daughter a closed-mouth smile.

"It's just...you've been through hard things." Bri met her eye, some measure of strength in hers. "I didn't see you shrink up and run away."

Annie's shock reverberated through her again. "What did you see?" she asked, wanting to see herself through her daughter's eyes.

"You told us the truth," Bri said. "And you didn't sit around feeling sorry for yourself. You went from part-time to full-time to support us, and you didn't even break stride with anything. I even saw you pack boxes for Dad, Mom."

Annie swallowed, her chest so tight. "We all handle things in different ways," she said. She had worked incredibly hard to maintain the sense of normalcy for her girls. She'd been working part-time as a nurse when she and Donovan had started the divorce process.

By the end of it, and through the grace of God, Annie had been able to move into a rare full-time position in the radiology department—a coveted job that didn't come up very often.

One layer of tension heating her muscles released, and Annie had the distinct thought that she needed to be better about acknowledging the things she'd been blessed with.

She also couldn't give up the job in Chatham. Julia had been needling her to come to Nantucket and work at the hospital there.

"Or any of the doctor's offices, Annie. They have a need here."

She'd been tempted by the job boards in Nantucket, Annie could admit that. It would be nice to be closer to Julia, who'd been going through her own divorce and major life changes. Now that Donovan was gone...

Annie cut the thoughts off and put her arm around her daughter. "I love you girls."

"I know." Bri leaned into her side, and Annie loved the weight of it.

Annie blew out her breath, letting more of her dread and tension go with it. "Now," she said. "What are we going to do about Paige this weekend?"

"There's a trick with Paige," Bri said.

"Oh, yeah? Do tell."

"Let her talk, and then agree with her before you try to give any opinion." Bri grinned up at her mom. "I think she just wants to feel heard, and with you especially, she doesn't."

Annie's first reaction was to say how unreasonable Paige could be. She held her tongue and let her younger daughter's words swirl through her mind. "That's why she gets so loud."

"Exactly," Bri said. "It would be great if we didn't have to scream at each other over Thanksgiving."

"It would be great," Annie agreed with a smile. "I'll work on that."

"Mom," Paige said from behind her. Annie turned that way and opened her other arm for her eldest.

"Hey, bug. You left the car."

"Grandma called," Paige said, stepping into her side. Annie took that as a major win, though her heart had dropped to the soles of her shoes.

"Why? What did she want?" Annie looked at Paige, and she really was a gorgeous girl. Nearly jet-black hair, with long eyelashes, and eyes the navy color of deep midnight. They could glint like the moon off still water when she was happy, and shine like gold in a dark cave when she had something up her sleeve.

Of course, Annie had also see the hard-as-nails flint in them when she wasn't pleased. She told herself to let Paige talk and to actually listen before she said anything.

"She wanted to know if Aunt Janey would be at the inn," Paige said. "I told her I assumed she'd be, yes. Isn't she bringing her kids?"

"Yes," Annie said with a sigh. "I've already told Grandma all of that."

"She asked if she and Grandpa could come. I had no idea what to say."

"What did you say?"

"I told her to call Aunt Julia. She's the one who knows how many people they have coming for Thanksgiving dinner."

Annie's pulse stormed through her veins, cracks of

lightning bolting out every few seconds, making her fingers twitch and her eyes blink rapidly.

"Can you imagine?" she asked, her voice barely louder than the wind. "Grandma and Grandpa...in the same room with Janey?"

"Janey's cool," Bri said.

Annie said nothing, because she knew more about Janey Forsythe than the girls. She knew the woman had been in a psychiatric unit and that she'd been to visit their father three times now. Dad had gone to Nantucket once, without Mom.

Why in the world would her mother even *want* to come to The Lighthouse Inn for Thanksgiving? It made no sense, and Annie fought the urge to drop her arms and demand Bri give back her phone. She needed to call Julia and warn her, then call her mother and tell her in no uncertain terms to stay home.

She didn't need to blow up this holiday for anyone, least of all Annie. If she wanted her family around, she should've planned better and sooner.

The ferry continued on toward Nantucket, completely unaware of the turmoil brewing inside Annie Mason. She didn't know how to exhale it out or release it into the atmosphere, and she didn't ask for her phone. It was as if someone had encased her in ice, and she was slowly going numb.

They reached the dock, and people began to move

toward the exits. They'd brought their car, so they had to return to it and wait their turn to depart.

"Let's go," she said quietly to the girls, and the three of them made their way toward the lower decks, where the cars drove on and off the ferry.

"Can I have my phone, Bri?" She held out her palm, and Bri gave her the device. Annie waited until she sat behind the steering wheel, seat-buckled in, waiting to get off the ferry, before she looked at it.

Julia had texted, and she went to that message string first. *Look what I found in the storage room at Maddy's father's house!*

She'd sent a picture with the words, and a book sat there. An old, tattered book with a pink, purple, and blue cover. Black lettering ran across the front of it that said *The Seashell Promise.*

No author name accompanied the title, and Annie frowned. Was she was supposed to know what this was?

Another message sat below the picture. *I wrote this in college, and Maddy and I want to do it while everyone is here.*

"Do what?" Annie asked as she typed out the letters. She sent the message, then started another one. *Did you talk to Mom?*

The ferry lurched, signaling they'd been tied and secured, and Annie looked up and out the windshield. They wouldn't be first to exit, as she'd barely made it onto this ferry. Everything seemed to take forever these days, including packing and getting the girls out the door for their vacation.

Her phone vibrated, and she looked at it. *I did,* Julia said. *I didn't know how to tell her no. They're only coming for dinner and one night.*

Oh boy, Annie said.

Yeah, Julia sent back. *Now I just have to figure out how to tell Janey...*

SNEAK PEEK! THE SEASHELL PROMISE, CHAPTER TWO:

Janey Forsythe stood on the dock, watching the ferry come toward her. Her anticipation climbed, and she'd been waiting for weeks for her children to arrive.

Both Rachel and Cole should be on this ferry, as they'd both texted on the family thread that they were. Her heartbeat pounded the same way the rain hit her heavy-duty umbrella, and she wished it wasn't raining so hard today.

A microburst had just arrived on the island of Nantucket, along with the ferry.

"Do you see them?" she asked Sean, who held the oversized umbrella above them.

"They don't even have it tied yet." He chuckled, but Janey pressed her fingertips together, trying to get her thoughts to align across her brainstem. Her therapist had taught her the exercise, and Janey often crossed sides of her body to try to quiet her thoughts.

She felt so much better than she had in months—probably since her mother had died last spring. She hadn't quite mastered everything at her job at the law firm where she worked, but she had a comfortable role there. It helped that her boyfriend was her boss and very forgiving. Sean had been willing to teach her any technical, lawyerly terms she'd needed to know, and Janey had enjoyed getting to know a lot of the permanent residents on Nantucket.

"Have you thought any more about moving in with me?" he asked now, startling Janey.

She dropped her hands and tucked them into the pockets of her windbreaker. "Of course I'm thinking about it, Sean," she said. "I don't think now is the best time to bring it up."

"Okay," he said. "It's just been a few weeks ,and I thought of it, because both of your kids live with their partners."

As if Janey didn't know. Rachel and Travis had gotten engaged a couple of months ago, and Janey had spent quite a bit of her off-the-clock time talking to her daughter about wedding plans.

Rachel wanted to get married in the tulips gardens at Holland Hollow, one of the largest flower fields and greenhouses in New Jersey. Janey hadn't been surprised by that in the least, because she'd taken her kids to Holland Hollow every year as they grew up.

She hadn't been a super-great mom, but she'd tried. Married and divorced twice, and then quite the stretch of being single now. She'd had boyfriends on and off, sometimes more than one at at time.

Those days were behind her, as she'd learned so many things in the past several months. About herself. About others. About how to have a healthy relationship.

Cole and his girlfriend, McKenna, had been together for years. Janey had no idea if they'd talked about marriage or not. They lived in Atlantic City, where Cole worked at a private marina, helping to guide the yachts and boats of the rich and famous into place.

He then detailed the vessels while their owners dined at the luxurious, seaside restaurants, or went to the nearby spas, or simply took their children to the private beach.

Her son made quite a bit of money with the work, and he'd said the tips were unbelievable. Janey knew he made enough to keep him in Atlantic City and at the job for the longest he'd ever kept the same one.

Her son hadn't excelled in high school, and college had intimidated him to no end. He'd entered the work force as an assistant to a chef, and he'd liked it. But something had happened that he still hadn't told her about entirely, and he'd left that job after only eight months.

Janey had a suspicion that he'd been fired, but he'd never admitted it.

"There she is," Janey said, almost darting out into the weather. The ferry station had a covered walkway from the watercraft to the building where one could buy tickets. She and Sean could've waited indoors, but she wanted to see her children the moment she could.

"Rachel," she called, lifting her hand high above her head. Her daughter shielded her face from the driving rain, the path soaking wet as the wind pushed it under the covering.

Behind her, her boyfriend, Travis, towed a rolling suitcase and wore a backpack. Janey's heart expanded at the sight of them, love thrumming through her with every step they took.

"Mom." Rachel ran the last few steps to her, and Janey flung her arms around her daughter. She was rail-thin, with long, almost white-blonde hair. She usually wore it in waves that spilled over her shoulders, but today, it had been pulled back into a messy ponytail.

They clung to one another, and Janey only released Rachel in order to hug Travis. "Can you believe your flight was delayed so much that you're on the same ferry as Cole?"

"We sat forever at the airport," Travis said, his hug strong and sure.

Janey stepped back, a sting pricking her stomach as the warmth of Sean's body reminded her that he hadn't met anyone yet. "Rachel, Travis." She cleared her throat. "This is my boyfriend, Sean Masterson. He owns the law firm where I work. Sean, my daughter Rachel and her boyfriend Travis."

"Fiancé, Mom." Rachel grinned.

Janey sucked in a breath. "I can't believe I didn't get that right." She shook her head, embarrassment streaming through her. "We've been talking about the wedding every day for two months."

She looked at Travis. "I'm sorry, Travis."

He chuckled and tugged his suitcase out of the way as people kept streaming by. "It's fine, Janey. You have a lot going on."

"Not that much," she said just as a man called her name. She turned back toward the ferry, spotting her tall, thin son easily.

Her mother-heart had never been so full of joy, and she took a few steps toward Cole. "My goodness," she said. "You cut your hair."

"He earns more in tips now," McKenna said, stepped into Janey at the same time Cole did. The trio embraced, and Janey held them so tight, one under each arm.

She breathed in and out, and said, "Oh, I missed you guys so much."

"Miss you too, Momma," Cole said, and McKenna echoed him.

She stepped back and looked at them both with adoration. McKenna had pulled her dark hair back on the sides, and her wide, brown eyes glinted with happiness. She wore a nose ring and false eyelashes, and Janey thought she was simply perfect for her free-spirited son.

"How's the jewelry-making?" she asked. "Did you sell out at the early holiday fair?"

"I have four pieces left," McKenna said. "It was unbelievable. I told Cole I'm doing that fair every single year." She glanced behind her, and Janey returned to Sean's side.

"Guys, this is Sean Masterson, my boyfriend. Sean, Cole and McKenna." This time, she didn't include any qualifiers. She didn't need to. She'd told Sean all about her kids.

Cole wore a wary look in his eye, and Janey didn't blame him. She'd put that anxiety in his attitude, and she hated herself for it. She hoped this holiday weekend would be good for all of them, and she hoped to be able to speak to her children one-on-one in order to heal any cracks, crevices, or crannies that existed.

Mostly, she needed to make sure she had done everything she could to heal herself, and her therapist had encouraged her to go through a similar program that alcoholics did. She needed to face herself and the things she'd done wrong, then try to make them right.

"Are we ready?" Cole asked after shaking Sean's hand. "It's pouring, and I'm freezing."

"You need to add some body fat to your frame," Janey said, grinning at him. She turned and laced her fingers through Sean's, glancing up at him. He wore a smile too, and he never seemed to get ruffled by anything.

The six of them headed for the van Janey had rented when she'd learned they'd be on the same ferry, and everyone loaded their luggage into the back of it.

Cole gave an audible sigh when he got in the back seat, and Janey flipped on the windshield wipers before pulling out of the parking lot and headed toward the Point.

"I hope the rain lets up," Rachel said. "I want to see all the things you've told me about."

"Let's see what the weather will be," Sean said, swiping on his phone.

"Looks like rain today and tomorrow," Cole said from behind her, and Janey glanced in the rearview mirror to see him checking his phone too.

Sean lowered his without saying anything, and the tension in the van skyrocketed, at least for Janey. It suddenly felt like Cole was going to compete with Sean for everything, and Janey wanted to diffuse the situation.

She didn't know how, and it wouldn't help anyway. Sean looked out his window, and Janey put a smile on her face. "Did you figure out the cake, Rach?"

"Did you not get the pictures I sent?"

"No," Janey said, meeting her eye in the mirror before focusing on the road again. Water sluiced off of it, and she too wished it wasn't raining quite so hard. There was so much to see from downtown Nantucket to the Point, and she wanted to show her kids the magic of this place.

She wanted them to have a fantastic experience here, the way she always had.

"I'll resend them," she said.

Janey wouldn't be able to see them right away, but it didn't matter. She'd gush over them at the cottage.

"Aunt Tessa made Gramma's clam chowder for your welcome meal," she said.

"Is Matt coming?" Cole asked.

Janey shook her head, a twinge of sadness pulling through her. "No," she said. "He's been dating this woman, and Aunt Tessa said it's gotten pretty serious. They're going to her parents' for Thanksgiving."

Cole nodded and looked out his window. Janey and Tessa had gotten their kids together as they grew up, but she hadn't anticipated Cole to ask about Matt. She'd be sure to tell Tessa, as it would probably make her happy.

Tessa had really been searching for a way to be happy, especially now that her divorce was final. She'd struggled with that more than she'd anticipated, and Janey had assured her that her emotions and reactions were normal. Expected. Worth feeling and experiencing and examining.

Janey swallowed, because these next few days should be filled with festivities and fun. They would be, if she knew Julia and Maddy, who were hosting dinner at The Lighthouse Inn. Tessa also had plenty of food planned, as did Helen, who would be catering brunch on Friday morning from the bakery she owned.

She hadn't told her children about her half-siblings. They didn't know that the man they'd called Grampa wasn't bound to them by blood.

At least Ryan wasn't coming for the holiday. She had pictures of her with him, and she'd tell her kids before they left on Sunday morning. They would have to decide what to do with the information, the same way she had. The same way Ryan Harper had.

She reminded herself that both Rachel and Cole were adults now, and they had to learn how to deal with adult situations.

She'd just pulled up to the bright blue cottage that bordered the beach when her phone rang. Cole opened his door to get out, and everyone followed him.

Janey reached for her phone and saw Julia's name on the screen. She hesitated, but her children had busied themselves with their luggage. Even Sean had gotten out to help the kids, and Janey swiped on the call.

"Hey," she said, keeping her voice low but hoping it came out bright enough too.

"Hey, hi," Julia said, which was Janey's first clue that something was amiss. Julia spoke in doubles whenever she was nervous. Janey hadn't known her long, but they had been spending more and more time together, getting to know one another. Julia had shared quite a few stories of her childhood, and Janey had too.

They'd both had good lives, and Janey hadn't felt like she'd missed out on something by not knowing that Ryan Harper was her biological father.

"Where are you?" Julia asked.

"I just picked up my kids," Janey said, watching

Rachel make a dash for the steps that would lead to shelter and safety. "We just got to the cottage."

"Okay, good. They made it okay?"

"Finally," Janey said. "Rachel and Travis's flight had some major delays. I had to rent a van since they all came in at the same time."

"A van is a good idea for the weekend," Julia said.

Surely she hadn't called to talk about this. "Yeah," Janey said. "What's up, Julia?"

She exhaled, another tell of her nerves. "Okay, I better just spit it out."

Yes, she better. Janey said nothing, because Julia could derail at any moment, for any reason.

"My mother and father are coming for dinner on Thursday," she said, her voice even and polished, like a newly laid hardwood floor. "It's one night. A few hours. I didn't know how to tell them no."

Janey's mind raced. She opened her mouth, but her brain didn't provide any words to her vocal cords.

"I'm sorry, Janey. You and your kids are still welcome, of course. I spoke to my mother, who *asked* to come. I couldn't tell her no. I've been texting Dad, and he said we should let you decide how you want it to be handled."

How she wanted it to be handled? She had no idea what that even meant.

"So..." Julia let the word hang there. "How do you want to handle it? Do you want to tell your kids? Just have me say they're my parents? I mean, they *are* my parents..."

Janey stared out the windshield, the scene in front of her blurry and warped because of the rain. She felt like everything wavered the way it did through the rivulets on the glass, and nothing in the world would ever be solid again.

"Janey?"

"I don't know," Janey said. "I've got a couple of days, right?" She flinched as Cole slammed the back of the van and hurried toward the cottage too. Janey was now alone, and she thought about what Helen had said about finding new strings to keep her tethered.

She'd really been trying to do that, but it suddenly felt fruitless, like a fight she'd have to endure every single day and she'd never be able to win.

"Sure, yeah," Julia said, using the doubles again. "Let me know."

"I will." Janey lowered the phone and let her half-sister hang up. She stayed in the silent van, two options in front of her.

She could start up the vehicle and drive away. Just go around the whole island and ignore her phone until she knew what to do.

Or, she could go inside and blow up everything by making a couple of announcements.

She took a deep breath, her mind flowing through several scenarios.

Then she got out of the van and headed for the door.

BOOKS IN THE NANTUCKET POINT SERIES

The Cottage on Nantucket: When two sisters arrive at the cottage on Nantucket after their mother's death, they begin down a road filled with the ghosts of their past. And when Tessa finds a final letter addressed only to her in a locked desk drawer, the two sisters will uncover secret after secret that exposes them to danger at their Nantucket cottage.

The Lighthouse Inn, Book 2: The Nantucket Historical Society pairs two women together to begin running a defunct inn, not knowing that they're bitter enemies. When they come face-to-face, Julia and Madelynne are horrified and dumbstruck—and bound together by their future commitment and their obstacles in their pasts...

BOOKS IN THE NANTUCKET POINT SERIES

The Seashell Promise, Book 3: When two sisters arrive at the cottage on Nantucket after their mother's death, they begin down a road filled with the ghosts of their past. And when Tessa finds a final letter addressed only to her in a locked desk drawer, the two sisters will uncover secret after secret that exposes them to danger at their Nantucket cottage.

The Glass Dolphin, Book 4: *Coming soon!*

BOOKS IN THE FIVE ISLAND COVE SERIES

The Lighthouse, Book 1: As these 5 best friends work together to find the truth, they learn to let go of what doesn't matter and cling to what does: faith, family, and most of all, friendship.

Secrets, safety, and sisterhood...it all happens at the lighthouse on Five Island Cove.

The Summer Sand Pact, Book 2: These five best friends made a Summer Sand Pact as teens and have only kept it once or twice—until they reunite decades later and renew their agreement to meet in Five Island Cove every summer.

BOOKS IN THE FIVE ISLAND COVE SERIES

The Cliffside Inn, Book 3: Spend another month in Five Island Cove and experience an amazing adventure between five best friends, the challenges they face, the secrets threatening to come between them, and their undying support of each other.

Christmas at the Cove, Book 4: Secrets are never discovered during the holidays, right? That's what these five best friends are banking on as they gather once again to Five Island Cove for what they hope will be a Christmas to remember.

BOOKS IN THE FIVE ISLAND COVE SERIES

The House on Seabreeze Shore, Book 5: Your next trip to Five Island Cove...this time to face a fresh future and leave all the secrets and fears in the past. Join best friends, old and new, as they learn about themselves, strengthen their bonds of friendship, and learn what it truly means to thrive.

Four Weddings and a Baby, Book 6: When disaster strikes, whose wedding will be postponed? Whose dreams will be underwater?

And there's a baby coming too... Best friends, old and new, must learn to work together to clean up after a natural disaster that leaves bouquets and altars, bassinets and baby blankets, in a soggy heap.

BOOKS IN THE FIVE ISLAND COVE SERIES

The Seafaring Girls, Book 7: Journey to Five Island Cove for a roaring good time with friends old and new, their sons and daughters, and all their new husbands as they navigate the heartaches and celebrations of life and love.

But when someone returns to the Cove that no one ever expected to see again, old wounds open just as they'd started to heal. This group of women will be tested again, both on land and at sea, just as they once were as teens.

Rebuilding Friendship Inn, Book 8: Coming soon!

ABOUT JESSIE

Jessie Newton is a saleswoman during the day and escapes into romance and women's fiction in the evening, usually with a cat and a cup of tea nearby. The Lighthouse is her first women's fiction novel, but she writes as Elana Johnson and Liz Isaacson as well, with over 175 books to all of her names. Find out more at www.authorjessienewton.com.

Made in the USA
Coppell, TX
11 September 2021